ONE LAST VIGIL

BY KEITH EDWARD ENGLISH

One Last Vigil

Cover art by: Larry Wilson
https://www.facebook.com/larrywilsonartwork/?fref=ts

Edited by: William Donahue

First printing: August 2016

ISBN-13: 978-0692768952

ISBN-10: 0692768955

Other works by Keith Edward English

Ravenswood Publishing:

-Thoughts of Steel (Book 1 of the Ruination Gods series)

Anthologies:

-Fragments of the Coil

Dargonzine.org:

-And Two Steps Back

-Sowing Seeds Parts 1-3

-Cursed Part 1-2

-Death Blooms Part 1-3

In memory of Ricardo Cota Jr.
My beloved god-brother
Who never stopped reaching for his stars.

You're performing for God now, Rick. See you on stage.

Letter from the Author

I wrote One Last Vigil in the four months that followed Ricky's death. It was the quickest I'd ever written anything. I'd return home after staying out at a local coffee shop working on the book, mentally exhausted, my emotions spent on the pages. It helped me get through one of the most trying parts of my life thus far. One Last Vigil was my therapy, and an integral element in what helped me move on after his death.

Ricky was twenty-three when he passed away, nearly a full year older than I was at the time. It was August 30th, 2014. I recall the phone call from my sister with crystal clear clarity. I recall collapsing on the sidewalk after walking out of my workplace so she could tell me what had happened. I recall walking back in to collect my belongings and leave for the day, tears streaming shamelessly from my eyes. I recall the pit that opened in my soul, that still has not, nor ever will, fully close.

However, the memories I cherish most are of the countless summer days I spent with him, our families blending into one while parents were away at work and we were on break from school. Ricky was outspoken, cursed like a sailor, sang like an angel, utilized his skills as an actor better than most people on TV currently, and was the absolute funniest person I knew. Life poured from him in everything he did. You may have even seen him in that Milky Way commercial where the three divers leap into a pool of caramel (he was the middle swimmer).

Everything in this novel is a metaphor for how I imagine Ricky's journey to be. Parts of it were even take directly from the eulogy written by me and Ricky's father. Giving that speech was by far the most difficult thing I've ever had to do, and I pray that you never have to bear a similar responsibility at a young age.

Although I knew of Ricky's struggle with cancer for the two years leading up to his passing, I never imagined that he could actually go. The thought never occurred to me, and I felt foolish for my ignorance after the fact. The one piece of knowledge I'd like to expressly share with you is to always love out loud. If you feel it, show it passionately. Time is not infinite, and the Fates cut cords far earlier than they should, and sometimes without warning a soul.

ONE LAST VIGIL

Prologue

A great and wonderful light encompassed me. I folded into it until I was as infinitesimal as a grain of sand at the ocean floor. In the same moment, I expanded and dissolved until I was unable to separate myself from the luminescence.

Warmth covered and filled me.

Serenity captured me.

But only for a brief instant.

The light changed from something that consumed me to something of shape, gently pushing me free of its embrace so I could exist on my own. It was a spirit in the form of a man, his face lost in the brightness. No longer was I ethereal and abstract, for I now saw through my eyes that the spirit gripped my pale arm in its golden, shimmering fingers. He pulled and we slid forward through this place of absolute darkness.

The comfort still held me, so I didn't resist. Nothing else mattered beyond this feeling of calm. We grew closer to something. I couldn't see it, but I felt it. It wanted us, asked that we come for it happily.

A disk of light exploded off in the darkness, motes and rays escaping the portal and swimming through the black. With its arrival there came a bolt of ice that struck through me then vanished. Despite the comfort the tunnel instilled in me, filling me with warmth once more, the surge of frost was enough to stall me. Part of me wanted to become lost in its embrace while something else within railed against its pull, vying that I turn and flee.

The spirit of light was no longer leading me for I was struggling against him with such intensity that we had come to a stop. I only wanted a moment of stillness to comprehend the beautiful terror that was the tunnel of light, but the spirit continued to resist me. My will bent as I tried to hold my ground and it was as though I was being ripped in half. I screamed out silently, urging my sense of self to remain together.

Panic set in me like claws of lightning shredding all down my body. He was pulling both of us toward the light now, and I realized it was a final escape of sorts, an exit I'd never be able to traverse again once I had passed through. I made another attempt to burst away while keeping him with me, keeping myself intact. I felt my grip falter and was torn in two, leaving me reeling in pain and confusion.

The light was suddenly gone. I was no longer there, but I was no longer anywhere. The warmth left, but it wasn't replaced by cold. The serenity left, but it wasn't replaced by chaos. Everything was just gone.

Chapter 1

I was falling through a black void. My body spun and twisted. I reached for a hold, but only found empty space. I wanted the blackness to leave, to see something, anything. I wanted to scream, but no noise would come from my mouth.

Where was I?

Who was I?

It all ended as colors blossomed before me.

I stood, surrounded by a forest, breathing terribly fast. My hands shook and my knees were so weak that I was certain I'd spill to the ground at any moment. My brief trip through the blackness and escape from the light was just as real as the air I sucked in. It had been something miraculous, but left me with a hole near my heart. I was hollow inside, an integral part of me lost.

Dancing lights drew my eyes upward. The spirit was there. I was connected to him and wished for our union once again only to find myself powerless. He floated upward until I lost him, feet sliding out of view behind branches thick with leaves. I reached out to the light streaming from between the gaps in the foliage but he continued to escape me until he disappeared altogether.

Once he was gone I felt healed of the ailment that had afflicted me as I'd watched him go. The ties that had connected us were severed and numbed. The hole in my being closed, if only to heal the exterior enough so that I'd no longer notice the absence of something obviously a part of me.

Something moved to my right. My eyes flicked that way and I saw long grass swaying back to a standing position. Nothing stalking along the forest floor revealed itself, however. All that was before and around me was an abundance of plant life.

Grass reached up to my waist, trees clad in bark ranging from deep brown to white crowded me, flowers of all colors and all shapes stretched to the sky, vines of varying thickness draped from the canopy. There was this and much more, making it so thick that I felt a sudden sense of claustrophobia.

Fragmented memories came to my mind and I winced as I tried to piece them together. Names were dredged up from deep within: Yosemite, Mendocino, Sequoia. Each one was accompanied by pictures although not a single one seemed more suited to a name than another. It was a scramble of shapes that just wouldn't create a whole picture regardless of how desperately I wanted them to.

This place seemed as though it had just too much in it. Like a hundred forests had been dumped on top of each other, then a hundred forests on top of that.

The branches of a tree suddenly jerked. Certainly there was a creature there, perched on the limb, ready to pounce. I stared long and hard, searching for another movement, a paw, an eye partially hidden behind leaves. Nothing.

Only scant holes in the canopy overhead provided glimpses of a clear blue sky, points of light blazing in the aqua-colored spread. Had I been here before? I couldn't recall how I ended up in this place. I could barely remember a thing that made sense. There were so many jumbled thoughts and pictures in my mind's eye that I couldn't trust a single one.

"My name," I suddenly whispered. "My name is..." My brow furrowed as I sorted through hundreds without a single one feeling as though it belonged to me. "What is my name? Who am I?"

Why was I this way? How did I possess pieces of a life lived before without a full picture of my past? It made such little sense. My heart began to thump against my chest and my hands grew clammy. Loneliness set in me and I whispered, "Hello? Someone."

Silence reigned in reply. I held my arms up and saw peach-colored limbs and hands I didn't recognize. Had they been mine, I wouldn't have been so perplexed by them. At least that's what I told myself. I felt my chest and stomach, found a frame emaciated and fragile. An odd shirt clung to my torso, seamed at an angle from the point of the V-neck and down to my right hip, a lively blue color, like the sky. The pants covering my legs were of a rough material, thick and black. A sash of braided, red rope spun through loops along my pants and cinched them tight to me. Boots of brown leather protected my feet. I still didn't recognize any of it.

All at once the forest swayed, but there hadn't been any wind. I had seen the grass near my feet leap to the side as if a gust had suddenly galloped by. I looked up and saw that the whole forest had lurched one way and was now relaxing. Had it been another creature moving through the brush that I just mistook as branches and grass being moved by wind?

All that was around me seemed to be leaning toward me, as if I was a magnet for foliage. What was this place?

The grass suddenly uprooted itself, green giving way to thin tendrils of white root, and I reeled back a step. Trees followed suit, ripping their long, thick roots from the ground, and vines dropped to the ground and writhed like snakes. I was stuck in place, dazzled by the animated forest.

Fear dulled to curiosity, compelling me to understand this place. I shuffled half a step forward and the world lurched after me. Grass tangled my feet. Vines wrapped up my legs to twist around my arms and neck. Trees crowded in and smothered me. A branch smashed into my forehead, causing a sunburst of white to cloud my vision. The light fled as quickly as it had blossomed and pain replaced it. I cried out in desperation as the forest began suffocating me.

I found a will to live, spun into the fabric of my soul, and began fighting back. I thrashed until my arms and legs ripped through vines and grass. The trees continued closing in, their trunks nearly touching, walling me into a deathly embrace. I ripped at my attackers, defying their onslaught with my own. Vines twisted up my neck and prodded my face, nearly shattering my teeth and gouging my eyes. Branches stretched for me but I tore my head to the side. I gripped the vines assaulting me in two hands then ripped them in half, thick tendrils going limp and falling to the ground, dead.

A branch hit me in the back and pressed me up against the rigid bark of a tree. I felt things crawling up my torso, taking away my freedom, seeking an end to my life. I pushed off the tree but found the branch still held me fast. I spun in a tight circle, ripping grass and vines as I did. I reached up and grabbed two separate branches of the tree I was against and pulled. The foliage resisted, trying to keep me in this place to kill me. With a final surge and cry of defiance, I broke free and lifted myself up into the tree.

Before I could find my footing on the branches, it moved as though the earth beneath it had begun to rip open. I slipped to the ground, expecting to find a net of suffocating foliage. But the earth there was barren, the soil loosened from the grass uprooting itself. I hit the earth and rolled to my feet, the ground shaking and vibrating as trees pounded behind me and other things slid or twisted after me. I ran and found myself coming upon more trees and foliage.

It was too late to stop or find another exit; every direction held the same thing as far as I could tell. I hollered as the trees before me ripped free of the ground, their branches swaying to meet me. A branch pulled back in anticipation of smashing into me. I ran toward it then leapt as it arced for me. It cut through the air just beneath my feet and I found myself coming down. Only, the ground was not flat. I was falling down onto a steep hillside populated by brush and other vegetation that seemed to reach up for me in anticipation of imprisoning me.

I crashed down onto grass that tried to keep me. I ripped free of it and began tumbling down the hill, bouncing and rolling. I slammed into a tree and my descent stopped for a brief moment. In that space of stillness, I felt a dozen bones in my back burst and dig their way into muscle and grind against one another. The mind-numbing pain consumed me and I forgot that I was spilling down the steep hill.

I suddenly realized that I had stopped rolling as something crawled over my face. Vegetation covered me as I lay still, immobile at the bottom of the hill. I couldn't turn my head. I could barely breathe. Nothing responded to my urges, not even a finger. The hill was too high for me to glimpse its top and I had fallen down the entire thing in what felt like just a few seconds.

No longer could I see, as grass had covered my head completely. Blackness began to settle in as I lost the ability to breathe. I couldn't feel much but knew that more and more weight was covering my body, engulfing me. I would die here then, not knowing who I was or why I was here or what I had done in life or what the hell here was.

A sound I understood came for me, broke through the blanket of vegetation. The grass wrapping around my body loosened its grip and fled. I began to breathe again, albeit as though a lump of cotton filled my throat. The blackness faded somewhat. I could see through the little vegetation still covering me and saw flickering shadows. An orange light blazed before my eyes, setting my scalp to tingling.

A man held a flame in his hand somehow. He spewed it at the foliage and it retreated, charred and smoking, leaving a wide swath of unpopulated dirt. I saw a face behind the fire, one with pink, purple, and red rings around two eyes that were perfect circles of black. I saw a nose with two wide nostrils that pointed straight out of the face, holes into the head. I saw a grin that undulated like a moving worm, several large, sharp teeth pointing either up or down. I saw large cheek bones, a wrinkled forehead, a round head.

Then, the pain in my back suddenly flared and everything turned black again.

***

Awakening this time was disorienting, much in the same way it had been previously. There was one significant difference to separate the two events, however. I pushed through the darkness and beheld color. I found a brown canvas over me, sticks that held it aloft, small windows to the sky above through little tears in the fabric.

But mostly, I found pain. A deplorably massive bounty of it.

I wanted to move, but knew that I wouldn't be able to. I had broken my back falling down that mountain, I recalled.

My legs responded though, knees bending and feet rotating. I immediately stopped because of the pain it brought, gasping aloud with spittle flying from between my lips with each pained exhale.

I lay there for a long while, tears streaming from my eyes, breathing raggedly, hoping that the pain would leave. Apparently my thoughts had some sort of power because the pain did in fact dull and then vanish. I ground my teeth together until I was sure they'd shatter, then rolled to my right side.

My back audibly popped as bones shifted. Terrible agony shredded down my spine and I nearly went into the black again. I couldn't stem my outburst this time and wailed, despite the waves of fresh pain each brought.

As before though, with enough time and enough wishing, the numbness set in and my screams turned to sobs. I could better handle those. Despite my limited mobility, my spine was certainly shattered. Perhaps I'd walk again if I didn't expire here beneath a ramshackle tent first.

The sound of someone approaching came from behind me, and a bit down on my lip hard to keep my mouth shut and feign sleep. I didn't dare move; I didn't need any more pain. The shuffling feet came close and I heard a voice.

"Should have tied you down. Rolling around like that, moving the bones around. I may be good, but damn... making my life that much harder. This will wake you up for sure."

Something stabbed me in the back and each individual vertebra exploded as though tiny grenades had been placed beneath each one then all simultaneously set off. I convulsed once, my back arching then locking into place. I suddenly couldn't move anymore but I was still able to scream, and scream I did, like a banshee in a microphone streaking out of the depths of hell.

I heard the voice again, this time only barely though, "Better that you're asleep."

The same thing that had rearranged my spine poked me in the head. Compared to the agony in my back, it felt like a butterfly's kiss but then it seemed to lance through my skull and into my brain. A loud zap sounded.

***

When I woke up next, I was momentarily afflicted by amnesia. I shook my head as though mixing up the stuff inside would put it back into a working order. The horrific event that had befallen me snapped back and I remembered the spirit of light, rolling down the hill, the bolt of lightning through my head that put me under. "Who the fuck did I piss off to deserve this?" I whispered.

I was now inside a house, or a hut, dried bamboo walls leaning toward me. It was hot inside, the source a small blaze burning in a cage of hardened clay or old metal a half dozen feet away.

Sweat leaked from my pores, spilling down my temples and pooling on the hard dirt floor beneath me. The discomfort prompted me to sit up and a small twinge of pain made me gasp and freeze. I reached back with one hand and ran my fingers gingerly across my back. I felt scars and even thought that my spine felt odd, like the vertebrae didn't match up exactly right.

I made to stand, and was halfway to my feet when a man appeared at the door, startling me back to the ground. I hissed as I hit the earth and he raised his hands as if to calm me. His face was so very odd, the same face I had seen when he had saved me from an early grave.

He spoke, although his wavering, fanged mouth didn't move. "Don't go and screw up that back again. I don't look forward to fixing it no more."

I didn't know when I had last spoken loudly. It must have been eons ago. My throat felt like it had been used as a furnace when I said, "You fixed my back? It was broken, wasn't it?" Oh yeah, that hurt. I swallowed what little spit I had to wet my throat.

"Shattered to pieces. That's the kind of shit that happens to people who roll down big hills."

"How did you fix it? And what is wrong with your face?"

I sat up and felt my back again. Those bones weren't right.

16

"Nothing is wrong with it. See." He grabbed his face and peeled it away. Only then did I realize that he had been wearing a decorative mask. "And I didn't do too much. I put the bones back where they should have been, then stitched you back up."

His skin was dark, long grey hair twisting from his scalp and brow. His eyes were set deep in his head and riddled with red veins, wizened pools that spoke of countless years of experience. A scraggly beard sprouted from his face adding to him an air of wildness.

"Are there others here who helped performed the surgery to fix me? I'm not sure how I ended up on top of that hill in the forest, or even where here is. Maybe they know, or you even? I just... something is wrong with me."

"Just me and I don't know nothing. You made one hell of a ruckus and I came to check it out. Found you floundering for air beneath the forest. Figured I'd help you out."

Thoughts, unbidden flooded my mind. I saw white halls lit by florescent lights, clear and sterile. My vision slid through them until I was tucked away in a room with a bed and little else that stood out beside some brightly colored cards on a stand and flowers on the sill of the window. There was a man lying in the bed in obvious disrepair, but then there were others coming and going. I wasn't sure which one I was, nor was I allowed the time to comprehend it all. The images flitted away and I was silent for a moment, staring at the strange dark man before me, frustrated at my inability to understand what my memories meant.

"Is this a hospital?" I raised my arms and inspected them. "I don't see any IVs or nurses. How did you keep me alive this whole time? I broke my back and it's healed now; that must have taken weeks. I've been asleep for that long!"

A blank stare greeted me. "What are you blathering about? Bunch of nonsense."

"I have these memories. Some of this feels familiar. I'm just trying to make connections. To make this make sense to me somehow. To figure who the hell I am and what I'm doing here."

The man waved his hand and said, "Come on. You're making me feel senile." He ducked out of the hut, dismissing my investigation. Apparently he knew that I hadn't started getting up yet since he yelled, "Come on!"

I scrambled up to my feet, using the rickety bamboo walls as support. I took a step and found that my back pinched, causing me to hitch the side, nearly tripping me. Certainly there'd be a surgeon to explain this all to me, and others to rehabilitate me further. Somehow I was sure I had dealt with a situation similar to this, and the next steps in the process I already knew. Broken memories lay at the edge of my mind, stuck in a brainfog that I couldn't pierce no matter how hard I tried, providing me with only enough information to get by. I stumbled from the hut and ended up outside in a terribly bright place.

I shielded my eyes and squinted at what I thought was the black man. His voice came from my side though and I realized I was staring at a tree. I shambled away from it in horror, sure that it was going to try taking my head off.

"Bright, bright, bright. All those stars out and the suns being so big. Can't see a damn thing sometimes. Here." Hands stopped me and he said, "Stop your dancing. It can't get you here."

A shawl covered me, draping from my head and blocking most of the light. The scratchy fabric smelled musty and old, as though it had been tossed into the corner of a closet and left to stand guard over the dust bunnies and mites that passed through for a century. I was able to make so many connections without recalling with clarity my experiences in life. Some malady certainly ailed me. I only hoped that something would provide me with a cure soon.

The light spearing into my eyes dimmed enough so that I could find the man who'd save me and asked, "So what is this place?"

The black man, now behind his mask, said, "Kid, I'm not sure what you're talking about. Again, I just saved you, that's it. How about you try to ask questions that make sense?"

"I don't know how to! I have these broken memories that don't tell me who I am. I was just in that forest all of a sudden. There was a light that I was going toward but then it left. The trees and grass attacked me. I rolled down the hill. Then you found me. I don't know my name, how old I am, where I was before, and I don't understand why! That's why I can't make any sense; none of this makes any sense to me."

He was silent for a while, the mask staring at me somehow making me feel as though I was insane. Finally, he said, "Well, crazier things have happened I guess. Maybe you aren't even from here. Your clothes look normal, though. To me at least. I've been here longer than I can remember."

How could he be so uninterested in my not having a memory? Or me just appearing in that terrible forest?

"What do I do?"

"How am I supposed to know that?"

I sure as hell didn't know. Someone should have known. Why not this man? Why not me?

"You fixed my back. How?"

"You really don't know anything about this place? You must have hit one of those trees a lot harder than I thought."

"No. I'm telling you, I remember all that. I was in the forest, no idea who I was or how I got there."

"This world used to be a little different. The trees and grass and bushes didn't attack everything like they do now. I was young then. Anyhow, there used to be something called night. We don't have that anymore. Night is when the skies get dark and -"

"I know what night is. The Earth spins and is half in the sun and the other half under the moon. I got it. Is this Earth?"

Again, he was silent, just staring at me, accusations in his thoughts, I think. "Stop interrupting with that nonsense. I don't know what Earth is."

Maps of a globe formed in my head, half complete. Text slithered across the green and blue flashes in my mind, nothing sticking or ringing any bells. I nearly screamed out in frustration.

He continued, "Anyway, one of the suns is always out. There's a bunch of stars up there too that shine real bright. And... Yeah." He popped his shoulders up, signifying that there was nothing more to say.

Earth I felt a connection with. That name had unlocked a fragment. It was obvious that I was not there but rather on a completely separate planet.

"Don't you have more to tell me? You still haven't explained how you healed me."

"Oh right. With this." He turned, marched toward the hut, then scooped a metal rod from the ground. Now that my eyes had adjusted and I could see a little farther without having to squint, I saw that we were on a flat of land without any vegetation. Dirt, red and sometimes in clumps, extended in all directions for at least fifty feet. Beyond that though, that living forest stood, crowding the edges of the empty patch, creating an almost impenetrable wall.

He pointed the rod to the sky and a blue jet came from its top. The blue stream was odd. It didn't look like fire, but what else could it be? There must be a fuel source inside that combusted and caused blue fire to come from it. Indifferently, he slid his hand through it and seemed fine. The blue stopped. Then he walked to edge of the clearing.

The trees and grass seemed to lean toward him, but they wouldn't cross over to the clearing. He pointed the rod at the trees and fire leapt from it. It wasn't the smooth, blue jet, but instead a wide gout of crackling, orange fire. The vegetation scurried away, a loud racket coming from the ripping and shuffling roots.

The flame was a cone only five feet wide, but the clearing it created was twenty feet around.

He turned back to me as if all my questions should now be answered. He held the rod out toward me to show it off.

"That fixed my back?"

"It restores the order of things."

"What does that mean?"

"Exactly what I said. That's all I know about it. It just does that. It fixed your back. It pushes the things that try to kill us away."

"Why won't the trees come after us? They make a perfect circle around here." The trees and grass had begun inching back to their place.

"This is sacred ground. That's why your back healed so quickly and the gash on your forehead isn't there any longer. The rod put everything back. You wouldn't be standing so soon, or maybe even at all, if not for this place. It isn't done quite yet, but even if you leave now it will continue to heal until your back is good as new."

"Sacred to who?"

"God."

I knew that word. Visions of crosses and men with comforting, albeit sad, smiles came to mind. Their images leapt through my muddled mind from my clouded past then vanished. I felt a connection with the being called God. I imagined someone all powerful and all knowing. I wrinkled my brow as I tried to flesh out more about Him. Nothing more came to my mind and I relinquished the thoughts from my mind with a prayer that he would see me through whatever journey I was on.

"If you were me, what would you do?" I felt lost and scared, partially because I feared the answer that would come from him.

"Sit around. Hope things got themselves figured out. Maybe your memories will come back. I can feed you for a while. Here, I'll give you this stick." I expected the rod, but he scooped a piece of bamboo from the ground and handed that to me. It was sturdy and I could lean on it. "And this." He fumbled with a pouch at his hip and came back with an orange flake.

The material was thin and papery. I took it gently for fear that even the slightest pinch would crumble it. "Thank you, I guess. So, what do I do with this?"

"Eat it only when you find yourself surrounded by the forest and I'm not around to help. It's a piece of a star."

I began to retort but stopped when I realized that I would probably be asking questions that would only irritate him.

"What does this do exactly?" I asked.

"To others, you'll feel warm to the touch. To the forest, it'll be like you lit yourself on fire. For whatever reason, the stardust tricks it into leaving us alone, but only for a time."

Remnants of what it meant to show gratitude for what one received was the only blockade between me nodding silently and begging him for more. Hell, had he been holding a chunk of this stuff I can't say I wouldn't have tried to take it by force. It wasn't just me in this mess though. Perhaps there would be others who would need his help and the stardust he offered. I simply dipped my head in acknowledgement and said, "Thank you..."

The black man removed his mask and said, "Morrissett. If you find yourself out there and that stardust runs out, you better find yourself some fire. And don't think that's the only thing you have to worry about. There's a lot of shit out there."

Rustling trees off in the distance caused a commotion that turned our heads. Morrissett's eyes grew wide and I could tell that he had an idea of what was coming.

He turned to me and yelled, "You need to go! Eat the stardust now!"

I didn't waste a second, just as my heart didn't wait to begin hammering against my chest in fear. I popped the flake into my mouth and it fizzled on my tongue. I swallowed it and a small explosion rocked my chest. The flake combusted within me causing a flash of heat to extend from my throat and to the tips of my limbs instantly. The heat disappeared and everything around me wavered as if the air before my eyes rippled as it might on a scorching day.

"Follow the path! A friend of mine waits at the end. She'll help you."

"What path?" I asked loudly over the din of the stampeding forest. I could now see leaves and branches a few dozen feet behind those circling the sacred ground swaying and shifting quickly to clear a path. I thought I caught glimpses of fire between the trunks.

Morrissett jabbed me in the side with his staff and I hopped away, stumbling a few steps. The bamboo cane kept me up and I eventually found my balance. I heard roots tearing right around me. I looked around and saw that I was standing amidst the forest, now receded to thirty feet from me. Below was a path of old stones, about as wide as my foot lengthwise. I imagined that they'd once been vibrantly colored, but were now dulled shades of orange, blue, red, and grey.

"He's coming for you. So soon this time! I'll hold him off for now. But you need to go! Good luck, kid. May God be with you." With that, Morrissett turned and sprinted toward the commotion coming from forest, slipping his mask back over his face and brandishing his rod as if he meant to use it as a weapon. He grunted as he stabbed the air and a wave of concussive energy blasted from the tip of the rod and ripped between the trees to strike the thing beyond.

Terror threatened to plant me to the ground and simply watch as that unseen horror converged on Morrissett. Something about his demeanor and willingness to place himself in harm's way for a complete stranger made me firmly believe that he would fare well, and that he'd done this before. He knew what came for me, and I wasn't going to waste the opportunity he allowed me.

Chapter 2

Exhaustion had quickly threatened to claim me as I hobbled along the path. I didn't have the energy or strength to keep up much of a hustle. The fear that had sunk into my bones at the arrival of whatever was coming for me forced me to move as fast as I could manage for the better half of an hour. Now, I felt as though I had earned the space between myself and whatever that thing was to slow to a walk.

As I walked along the path, my bamboo cane supporting my hitching gait, I chanced across several things that didn't scurry from me like the trees and grass did. A large reptile was once left in the wake of stampeding vegetation. It had been turned on its side and was quite fat. It struggled to get its feet beneath itself and I couldn't help but laugh at its dire situation.

I stopped and crouched down. "Why haven't the trees and grass gotten to you yet? You must not be all that tasty, huh?"

The reptile had since rolled over. It was roughly eight feet long from flickering tongue to jerking tail. It wore green along most of its body, red streaks that ran along its spine, ribs, and from the corners of its eyes breaking up the monotony of emerald. It hissed at me then charged. Well, marched really. Did I mention how fat it really was?

I danced to the side, the trees crashing into one another as they fled from the aura my stardust radiated. The reptile stomped by me and I laughed at it. If it hadn't been so overweight and clunky in its movements, its snapping jaws certainly would have caught me; I still moved awkwardly and relied on the bamboo staff heavily.

I took the shawl from my shoulders and waved it before the reptile, stabbing my staff at the air before its face in feigned attempts to skewer my foe. "The gladiator takes the stage with his fearsome enemy. He is rare in form though, and will certainly outwit this monster."

As if cued by my monologue, it charged again. I shuffled backward and it closed. I slammed my staff into the ground just feet from its snout and it stopped with a rumbling hiss, tongue flicking at the air. "That should do you in!"

But it didn't. The beast slowly walked at an angle, as if it meant to pass right by me, but then it lunged for me. I kept my distance, but only barely. "Ah, the beast is more cunning than the warrior believed. But can it deal with this!"

I whipped my shawl at it, snapping the fabric on its stuffed side. Before I could pull it back, the creature surprised me with a burst of agility as it struck out and snapped its maw closed on the shawl. We played tug of war for a moment but then the reptile wrenched its head to the side and ripped a corner of the fabric from the whole.

I stood there, immobilized for a moment. Finally, as the reptile stood there smugly, chewing on the fabric victoriously, I said, "You ass! Well, then." I bowed slightly then turned and continued on my path.

As I walked, I wondered why I had performed with that reptile. Immediately more memories flooded my mind. I saw stages flash by, some that seemed empty but for the props that created the illusion of the inside of a house, a busy street, a lush forest, and others that were packed with people. Lights beamed down at the stage and beyond those bright rays there sat dozens, sometimes hundreds of spectators. Peter Pan, Bugsy Malone, Oliver Twist. These names and others came to mind. All of it was a jumble that accosted me then disappeared without making much sense.

Despite the confusion that accompanied the fragmented memories, I was warded against the frustration that nearly claimed me. Performing with the reptile had felt natural and despite this place obviously not being comforting, I nearly felt what I thought home should be. A lightness of soul lifted me up, made me smile, and for a moment I forgot that the very trees were trying to kill me.

Later, the fun I had enjoyed with the reptile forgotten, I came across a lake. I was walking along the path, when the thick trees and grass to my left suddenly moved to reveal the pool of pristine water. In fact, I realized that I had been walking by the water for some time, the forest so dense that it had kept it hidden until now. I suddenly realized how thirsty I was. It was a miracle I hadn't been agonizing over my lack of water. Well, impending death could have played a role in my forgetting.

I heard a laughing girl and was drawn from the path. I came to the edge of the water, careful of where I put my feet. Morrissett had said that I'd run into worse things and there was no telling where those things would be. My feet firmly planted on a large rock that butted up against the raised forest floor, I looked across the water.

The small inlet was rimmed by the forest, vines dangling into the water and sinking down to its bottom. I could see straight through the clear blue, down to its sandy floor, which was not any deeper than I was tall it seemed. Rocks, big enough to lay down on and jutting from the water as well as those used to skip across a calm surface, were everywhere. Seaweed wavered and reached toward the sun overhead.

A plethora of sea life swam and hopped here and there: disk-shaped fish that reflected vibrant blues and purples, wide creatures that seemed as though they glided through the water on wings with tails wavering behind them, frogs in all the colors of the rainbow, birds with extremely long legs and lengthier necks plodded through the water. I saw this and more, dredging forth memories of these animals (blue gills, manta rays, poison dart frogs, cranes) sitting within the confines of their displays with signs proclaiming what they were and delivering facts about them.

I could better deal with the bright light, now that my eyes had adjusted. Or perhaps the brightness had dimmed slightly. I wasn't sure, nor did it matter, for I was staring at a mermaid lying across a large rock at the middle of the pool of water. She looked at me, smiling and my jaw nearly landed atop my toes as stories of these mythical creatures came to me.

From her human half, I believed her to be at least twenty years of age. Striking, green eyes peered at me from around a rim of wet, dark hair. Perky cheeks and a button nose caught my attention. Full lips smiled at me, causing a wave of weakness to spread through my legs, nearly spilling me onto the rock. Chestnut skin glistened in the sun. Her breasts were exposed and she showed no indication that she was discomfited by it, or even noticed.

I certainly noticed them, and turned my head away when I realized I had been staring. She dove into the water and I cast my eyes back toward her. She was cutting through the water, her blue, green, and purple fins propelling her right to me. I tried to look natural, but every stance I took felt forced and odd. Finally, I simply sat down on the rock beneath me to hide my trembling.

She came up, her eyes open and already staring at me. She rested her arms on the same rock as me, but fifteen feet away. "You're warm. Stardust, I take it?"

I merely nodded. What was one to say to a mythical creature?

"Are you okay?" she asked, staring at me as though I was a beast from a fairytale.

Again, I nodded and realized that I looked like an imbecile with my ogling eyes and malfunctioning voice. Finally, I blurted, "You're a mermaid."

"A what?"

"A mermaid. You know, half fish, half human."

"No. I am me. I'm Jacquelyn."

"From where I come from, we call you mermaids. And, you aren't even real."

"And where are you from?" she asked with an eyebrow quirked up and pursed lips.

"Actually, I don't really know. My memories all broken up and mixed around."

"You keep looking at my breasts."

A vice closed on my throat and I nearly fainted with embarrassment. She was right, of course. I mean they were there on the rock too, resting just like her arms. So enticing.

"Yes. Um. I don't mean to. Um…"

"It's okay. I'm just not used to it. We don't do that to each other and I rarely come across humans. You seem kind of odd. Why are you travelling through the forest? It must be important if you have stardust."

"I don't really know. And, I'm sorry. It isn't polite to stare."

"Then I'll help you out." Jacquelyn suddenly dove under the water and sped beneath its surface to the other side of the rectangular boulder I sat on. The rock sloped upward to where she rested, placing it at a higher point above the surface of the water, her breasts hidden behind it. Damn but did I want that rock to just melt away. "Better?"

"Yeah," I lied, dropping my eyes to hide my awkward smile. "So, how do you swim around so easy. I mean, doesn't the seaweed and whatnot try to pull you down?"

"I'm a bit too fast and slippery for it. So, what has you walking around in the forest? You surely aren't so fast and slippery. You are the only walking person I've seen around here besides Morrissett."

"You know him?" I looked back up to her, hopeful that she would be a guide of sorts like he had been.

"Plenty of people know him. He's a little odd, and too old for someone on land if you ask me."

"Huh. Small world, maybe. Anyway, I'm not sure what I'm doing. Morrissett had saved me, then something came after me from the forest. He distracted it, I guess, and sent me running off to escape it. It sounds ridiculous, I know."

"Part of it, maybe. But your journey doesn't sound all that different from others I've heard before. You know what they say lies at the end of this road?"

"What?"

"God."

"God? Really?"

"That's what most people say at least. He's there, in his kingdom surrounded by walls and towers."

"How do they know that?" I marveled.

"Well, they don't exactly. See, plenty of people have attempted to go see God. But to do so, one has to get past the Sentinel..."

"And?"

"They didn't do so well."

"How bad?"

"Most of them are dead."

"What!"

"Yeah. But maybe you'll be fine. I don't know. Oh, this is exciting. I've never met one of you so far from the Sentinel before. Well, besides Morrissett. Everyone has met him."

"How far away am I now?" I asked, fearful of the answer.

"Maybe a day and a half."

"That long!"

"Well, for me anyway. The rivers might be faster than land, or not. I can't say for certain."

"Hm. Are there others like you? Not you, you, as in other girls. Mermaids I mean?" I couldn't resist the urge to scratch my head and wince. I'd just met this woman – mermaid, really – and couldn't help but feel like an imbecile simply because of the chance that I'd made her think I was wondering about other women... Which I wasn't. Thank God these things stayed stuck in the confines of my head.

"Just a few dozen that I have seen."

"This place is starting to feel very small."

"You don't need a big world. You just need the important parts of the big world. Then, your small world is bigger than the biggest of them all."

"That actually makes a lot of sense."

She nodded and smiled innocently, proud of her little gem of wisdom. God it was hard to restrain myself from telling her pretty she was.

"What's your name?" she asked, moving the conversation along as I'd become dumbstruck by her beauty.

"I don't know," I stammered. "I can't remember much about myself. I mean, I certainly know what things are and can recall a few memories. It's like having a bunch of puzzles mixed up in the same box with still a bunch of missing pieces."

"Well that is odd."

Suddenly, I remembered that my stardust was running out.

"Um, I have to go."

"Oh, right. Stardust. Well, maybe I will see you at the Sentinel. Maybe I will see you before that. Take this. It's a kiss." Jacquelyn placed a pebble on the rock and smiled at me one last time before she dove beneath the waves again.

I watched her go until she was nearly gone from my sight. The pebble glistened with brilliant colors resembling those of her fins. I crawled over and picked it up, drying it on my shirt until the water evaporated completely. I inhaled sharply and my eyes grew to the size of dinner plates as the vibrant colors disappeared with the moisture and it became clear as a diamond. I marveled at it, and probably would have sat there for much longer had I not heard her giggle.

My head snapped in the direction of her intoxicatingly adorable outburst and I spotted her staring at me a stone's throw away, only her head poking free of the water. She laughed once more then dove beneath the water again. I watched her swim until she rounded a bend and was lost behind a wall of trees.

I found that the pebble fit nicely into the top of my bamboo stick. I jammed it down in there until I was sure it would stay lodged. I began to rise to my feet but stopped suddenly only a few inches off the ground.

Jacquelyn. Something about her stuck with me. Part of it, of course, was her lack of clothing and shame in front of me. But more than that, it was her spirit. I'd stay with her for hours if time permitted, whiling the time away just talking. A hundred pounds of stardust would be an acceptable price to hear that luring giggle again.

I shook my head to clear her from my thoughts. Failed. Then rose and began my trek back to the path, colored fins and honey-colored skin commandeering my mind.

***

Tremors ran through me as I attempted to stand stock still. Death was closing in, ever so slowly, like sitting at the top of a volcano as it began to tremble, preparing to release a massive blast of magma to swallow and eradicate everything for miles. Shimmering waves exuded from me, evidence that the stardust was remaining effective. However, the flora was creeping toward me, and in the minute I had stayed inert to observe the terror, it had wriggled nearly an inch closer.

Five, maybe six strides separated me from the bravest vine, snaking back and forth as it vied to reach me. My nerves began to fray, threatening to shatter altogether and plunge me into a mad sprint for the inlet where I'd met Jacquelyn. With every passing moment, death was worming closer. Would the stardust suddenly cease to work altogether, or would the flora continue its slow convergence to murder me? I wasn't sure which was worse.

The end of this path seemed like it was much too far away to reach on this failing piece of stardust. I'd need fire. But how would I find that out here? So many terrifying thoughts hindered me, and I knew I needed to get moving. Focusing on progress would stem the fear rising in me, at least I told myself as much.

"Go," I whispered to my feet, seeing as how my brain didn't have the gall to make them move. "Go goddammit. Go!" With that last forceful edict, I took a step forward and the forest staggered away, rekindling my hope enough to break me of my paralysis.

The dull roar of trees and grass uprooting themselves as I walked had become normal to me, so had the sight of the narrow path the stones afforded me widening at my approach. Still, something about what was transpiring before me felt abnormal. I hid from my fear by focusing, intensely, on what laid ahead and I noticed the cacophony of shifting flora increase in volume. Trees too far beyond the reach of my stardust quivered as they shifted for something I couldn't yet see.

I stopped and waited, sure that Morrissett was going to appear. After a moment of thought, I realized that the only way for that to be possible would be if I had turned around at some point. I hadn't turned around ever. I was immediately certain that this was the thing he'd stalled earlier, and it was obviously not all that friendly if Morrissett had sent me running from it.

Black, bulky armor seething with an aura of malice and a great, flaming sword appeared before me as the vegetation cleared a path.

Horns sprouted from the helm the knight wore, two curving backward from either side of his head resembling bat wings and two others pointing to the sky. A full face of dark metal reflected the firelight but still I couldn't make out a single orb or sliver of flesh in the voids where his eyes should have been. Thin spikes reached out from points all along his body, seeming like fangs hungry for the life of others by their wicked design. A cape the color of blood billowed behind him, sliding over the upturned soil with the grace of a ghostly ballet dancer.

Fifty feet separated us but the knight did not slow at all, not when he saw me, and not when I put my hands up and screamed, "Stop!"

Twenty feet separated us now. Instantly, my mouth became as arid as a barren desert and tears began to swim at the edges of my vision. I prepared myself although I was near collapsing from fear. I told myself to move when I needed to, not to let the terror paralyze me.

Vertigo crept in, but I maintained my focus as the knight pulled back his sword for the killing stroke. Crackling flames leapt for my head, trailing the massive length of sharpened steel. Instinct and fear drove me to my belly, hard enough to nearly crack my ribs. I twisted my head to the side and up painfully to see the imposing tower of black steel looming over me. He reversed his grip on the blade and lifted it above me. I rolled and felt the heat of the flames as it plunged into the soil near my side. The blade rose from the ground and I right alongside it, sprinting awkwardly and painfully away as my back protested. Smoke from the sword clouded my vision for a moment but the roar of it announced its cutting through the air for my head once more. I put my head down and trudged on, hoping it was enough to keep my skull in one, unburned piece.

I was suddenly falling. I had expected a murderous chase to ensue, but the ground was simply gone from beneath me. Wind whipped past me, filling my ears with a roar that almost beat out the sound of my scream. My eyes shut tight and I was absolutely incapable of opening them as I plummeted.

Cold liquid enraptured me and I sucked in a breath only to find myself choking on water. I hit a sandy bottom and pumped my feet into it to rocket up and burst through the surface. Before I could steal another breath, I vomited a torrent of water and my eyes snapped open. A waterfall behind me pounded the pool I stood waist-deep in, coming off of a ledge that had just enough space beneath it to hide me. I scurried behind the thin veil of water and waited, trembling and fighting the urge to flee from my hiding spot like a bat out of hell. I watched, inert, as the shawl Morrissett had given me slid across the surface of the water and floated away to be swallowed by a cascading waterfall a few dozen feet away.

Swallowing the fact that a knight in dark armor wielding a flaming sword was certainly stalking after me on this path was a damn difficult feat to accomplish. I leaned against the rocky wall and ran my hand through my hair only to grip a handful and squeeze in frustration. "Why?" I seethed. "What the fuck did I do?"

Tears came quickly after I admonished the universe for the hand it had dealt me in this venomous world. I sobbed for several minutes with just the sound of the falling water to accompany me. After there wasn't a sign of the knight coming to cut my head from my shoulders, my emotions calmed and I thought of family.

I wondered about brothers and sisters, my parents. A slideshow of people flipped before my mind's eye. I saw dozens of people, hundreds maybe, their features somehow shifting, never concrete and perfect. Puzzles with missing pieces. Still, I felt a connection to them that made me sure they were all dear to me. I wanted desperately to know who they were, to call upon them now and hold them.

Sunlight filtered through the waterfall in a brief, intense flash and I was reminded of the spirit of light that had left me. I was sure that he was a part of me and must have been something integral. I imagined that if I moved quick enough, I could catch him on my journey. Or, perhaps he was waiting at the end of the path of stones.

God could have existed as the being of light. It could very well be that reaching him in his kingdom would provide me with the answers as to why I was here, what my life had been before, why my past was fragmented and parts missing. I pushed down the fear and frustration as I reaffirmed my resolve to reach him.

"This place won't take me," I proclaimed in a shaky, yet determined voice.

Something about that statement rang true in me and I felt a section of that brainfog disperse. This was not the first time I had been surrounded by wolves. And then, just like now, I had held hope tightly to my breast and fought with vigor borne of a deep will to live. I latched onto that will now and the tears dried from my eyes, replaced by a steely gaze that looked much further than my current predicament and to the victory lying at my road's end.

Confident in my steps, I crept from the water. The seaweed I waded by pulled its roots from the sandy bottom and swam away. I found the edge of the pool, this one even smaller than the inlet before and leading to another fall that dropped at least thirty feet. I climbed out and looked around, up the cliff I had dropped from. I wasn't any more hurt besides a throbbing in my back from evading the knight's infernal blade.

No flaming swords or black armor came through the forest. I was absolutely terrified of that demonic thing, of the idea that he would be stomping along the path as I went along. I wondered if it would be better to stay off the path, but then I realized that the trees were just a foot closer than they had been before.

I needed to find fire... or my own massive flaming sword.

Fear kept me in place for a long while though. So much so that I watched as the trees closed another few inches. I just couldn't come to grips with the idea of the knight chasing me through the forest without my knowledge of it happening. A deep terror grew in me as I knew with certainty that he would continue coming for me and I'd have no idea where or when he'd appear again.

Finally, I returned to my journey, the encroaching sense that death was closing on me in several forms spurring me onward and forcing me to cast worried glances over my shoulders often. I climbed the hillside for several minutes until I found the path again. The trees had closed in once more and I wasn't certain which direction would lead me forward and which would result in me tracing the steps I'd already made. With the knowledge that my stardust was depleting, however, I didn't have the time to arrive at a sure answer. I scrutinized each direction once more, then chose the one that felt right. After several steps, regret and worry built in me, but I trudged on nonetheless.

Chapter 3

My chest constricted, squeezing my lungs shut, as though the vines reaching for me had snagged me once more. Flora was all around me, encroaching on my space, allowing me only a single large stride between us. The anathema my stardust exuded was nearly depleted, and taking each step forward took every bit of confidence I could muster, which wasn't much. In the past few minutes, I'd barely resisted the urge to run forward into the clutches of the forest or simply lay down and wait for it to cover me.

Something brushed my ankle and my eyes darted to it. A low creeping vine had ventured close enough to touch me, prompting a shiver to run through me as though it had been a slick, cold tentacle that had molested my leg. It recoiled immediately though and writhed on the ground like a worm would do when it was cut in half. It reared up then slapped the ground several times as though it was wreathed in flame and trying to extinguish them as it fled.

"Little fucker," I whispered. "The stardust is almost out. Shit."

If it had been so brave as to whip out at me, what would everything else do?

It was time to run.

I burst into a sprint but nearly stopped when the green death before me stayed in place. At the very last moment, right before leaves and vines would have started coming for my neck, a path cleared before me. If not for the stones beneath me, void of vegetation, I would have certainly been wrapped up.

My charge along the stone path was short-lived though. Reaching branches had me ducking and weaving, slowing me. A vine suddenly fell on me and looped once around my neck before I pulled it off with one hand. The tendril of forest wriggled like a snake might do and I dropped it as if it had fangs that had pierced my skin.

I put a hand out as I ran, hoping that the faint power still coming from my body would buy me more breathing room. It did, but not anything substantial. The forest seemed to know that the stardust was nearly exhausted and risked injury to find out for sure.

I had a moment of reprieve as I ran along the path, free of obstructions. If I kept to the path, I'd never get out of the forest. I needed to find something away from all of it. Maybe I could find Jacquelyn in a lake. I needed help.

I made a split-second decision. I turned and sprinted completely away from the path, hoping I could find something near and remember my way back. Immediately, the forest tore at me, but I swept my hands at it and pulled things from my body and neck.

I leapt over roots that were too slow to move. The cane in my hand I now used more like a weapon than a tool to aid me in walking. Vines leapt for my throat and I smacked them with the dried staff of bamboo.

The forest kept closing though, ignoring the little power left in my stardust. It wrapped around me for a few moments before writhing in what seemed like pain then retreating. Soon, I was stumbling slowly along, tearing and beating at the vines and branches. I was certain that I would soon be stopped and engulfed.

I screamed as I thrashed. I spun and fought. It wasn't going to be enough though. I leaned completely forward, the forest a wall that kept me up and pulled me back. Things twisted around my legs and up my back, coming to kill me. If I died, I'd do so with broken vines and snapped branches in my hands. I jerked to the side and found a moment of freedom to push forward.

Resistance gave way like I had ran and smashed through a wall. I staggered across a wide flat rock and fell to my knees, then rolled onto my back immediately and brought my legs in, ready to kick at anything that reached for me.

But nothing did. The forest only slowly crept toward me, across the large rock I lay on, hesitant to leave the soil. Persistence had prevailed, and it always would as long as I fought hard enough and with enough heart. I got up as quickly as I could, ignoring my labored breathing and trembling limbs.

I whirled around and found a thin valley that ran between two hills reaching up to the sky on either side of me, forest all around the area. From atop the rock, I could just barely see down to a small stream that ran through the ravine.

The stream drew me forward as my eyes sought some sign of Jacquelyn. My toes inched out over the edge of the rock until I was thoroughly afraid that I'd tip forward. Glittering fins and the chestnut colored girl they belonged to was nowhere to be found and my heart sank. I looked down and discovered that I was actually standing atop a cave. Inside seemed barren and deep enough to house me away from the vegetation. My mind immediately drew a comparison between this place and Morrissett's sacred ground and I wanted nothing more than to crawl inside and rest for a week. I went down to my stomach and pushed my legs over the ledge.

A vine snapped out from the forest and caught my ankle. I felt it attempt to dislodge me from my perch and drag me into the rest below. I pulled and twisted my leg and the vine ripped, the short length around my ankle becoming limp and falling to the rock below.

"That's right," I growled at the forest. "I'm getting real sick of your shit."

I continued my descent until my feet touched down on the rock beneath me. I hustled toward the back of the cave to put some more distance between myself and the forest. Roughly ten feet separated the wall of the cave from the vegetation surrounding it and I was crouching as I moved.

Against the back was a small palm tree on its side. I froze, a lightning bolt of fear nearly prompting me to turn and sprint out into the forest. However, its dry, yellow complexion announced that it was dead. I wondered how it had gotten there for a moment, but then, I simply thanked my lucky stars, and went after it like it was a feast.

I knelt next to it and cracked its dry, broad leaves from the trunk. Silently and still, I mulled over it for a moment, not sure of what I should do now to actually make a fire. After a minute, I walked to the edge of the cave and put my hand out near some grass. Maybe I could go down to the stream and keep looking for Jacquelyn. Those bolds little blades of green leaned toward me until they were just inches away. Then, they uprooted themselves and I pulled my hand back and fled back into the cave.

The absurdity of feeling afraid of a few blades of grass hit me like a hammer blow. However, it wasn't just the individual pieces of this massive problem that terrified me; it was the entirety of it. With the grass came so many other obstacles and hindrances. When all of it hit me at once, it was overwhelming and all-consuming. I could deal with the easy stuff, but everything else made even that so much more difficult.

I wracked my brain for a way to create fire, and memories slid into view of my mind's eye. Square images flowed and in them I saw people I didn't know sitting amongst trees, brush, or surrounded by

35

rocks. Sticks twisted between their palms, smoke issuing from its contact point. Rocks raked against one another and sparks flew from them to land atop patches of kindling.

If I could find a rock, I could maybe create sparks to start a fire. I found one on the ground and threw it against the cave wall. It hit hard, causing me to yelp in surprise and curl into myself as it ricocheted back right next to my hip, but not a single spark leapt from the wall.

"Damn."

Exhaustion was taking me.

I just wanted a moment of reprieve, but to give in now would mean death. At least this one issue had to be resolved or placated before I could even consider rest, but even finding the energy to throw a rock was becoming as difficult as scaling a mountain.

I sat down and crossed my legs. The rock beneath me was terribly uncomfortable. I realized that this wasn't a normal cave. It was just two large rocks on top of one another.

I began to feel myself falling into sleep. I fought it though. I still needed fire.

I pushed myself up to my feet and paced around, crouching awkwardly. I was using my cane when I heard it scratch on the rock beneath me. The sound was odd though, and so I looked at the cane and found that pebble in there.

The kiss was a pattern of red and orange. I walked over to the dead leaves and pressed it against them. Nothing happened, despite my wildest wishes. I put my hand on the pebble and found there was no heat exuding from it, as it should be.

I slashed the wall with the cane, the pebble striking across the rock. A shower of sparks would be an understatement. A geyser might be close. Red, angry, hot sparks erupted from the wall and coated the dead leaves. They lit immediately.

I laughed aloud and found the energy to raise my fists in triumph. My knuckles struck the rock directly above my head and I cried out in surprise and pain. Immediately, I took turns sucking on my fingers as though that would somehow abate the pain, stomping my feet as I did so. The back of my head hit the rock as a result of my childish antics and I went still, begging the pain to recede. I nearly went and kicked the flaming leaves in my anger.

Instead, I rubbed my skull for a moment and thanked God that no one was around to watch me act a fool then snatched the leaves by their unlit ends and dragged them toward the cave opening. I then lugged that dead tree to the fire and tossed it on. The flames hungrily consumed the fuel.

The whole thing burned large and hot. Remaining in such close proximity to the heat was difficult but I surmised it better to be hot then suffocated by vines.

I lay down near the fire and immediately despaired in the idea that there'd be no way I could fall asleep. Not with this horrible rock beneath me. God, how did people find sleep at all in this place? No night. Everything trying to kill you. Rocks for beds.

As I complained in my head, the sight of the fire began to blur. My eyes shut. I wondered, briefly, about myself, hoping the smudged and missing memories would clear and unlock something more. Alas, my efforts were in vain. At least the rock was mostly smooth. Then, I fell asleep.

***

Wind blew past me, roughly pulling and pushing, making it difficult to maintain my position. The figure of light cut through the otherwise absolute blackness off in the distance. My arms and legs didn't respond when I asked them to carry me forward.

He was far from me already, arcing through the blackness with grace. His eyes were aimed at me, I swear it. I tried waving, failed, and then he waved at me. The connection that bound us obviously played a part in that.

I tried to call out to him but nothing happened and I resigned myself to inaction, finding solace in becoming nothing more than a viewer. Something in the distance, beyond the being of light even, suddenly shined with a dim luminescence.

Lines and arcs pressed out from the darkness ever so subtly here and there and I traced the shapes with my eyes. Had my sight not already been drawn to that general area, I never would have noticed what I was now sure was a building of some kind.

From the direction the being of light glided it was plain that his target was the building, whatever it was. I longed for that part of me to return, but realized that, just like me, he had a mission.

I wished him well on his journey.

***

The quiet stillness of my slumber was rent by a screech and I was thrust into consciousness. My heart was trying to crush the bones in my chest and goddamn was it close to succeeding. An orange ape was hanging from the rock above me with one hand and ripping at several vines with his other hand and feet. He killed the vines then looked at me with intense eyes. I witnessed an animal fury within his orbs that terrified me to my very bones.

But then, the intensity left, and he was merely analyzing me. Long orange hair covered the creature's body, sheathed his lanky arms, and rimmed his black face. His eyes were so human that I was sure I could see his soul reflected.

He let go of the rock and plopped down to the side of my fire. Well, fire isn't the right word. I had a few red chunks of wood protecting me now. And they weren't doing a good job.

Vines had snaked their way into the cave. They were just feet from me even now.

Two more suddenly swung down to land next to the first. I discerned that they were female by the obvious difference of their genitalia from the first, the younger of the two carrying a stick beneath one arm. They looked upon me with care. I could see a smile in their eyes.

The male looked to the younger female and nodded toward me. She plodded forward and laid the branch on the ground. I found one end of the thick, lively stick was coated thickly in an obviously sticky, golden brown substance. This, I realized as a puff of fog slid away, was a torch made of pine resin and a freshly removed branch.

I looked up to the three orangutans and found compassion staring back. A feeling welled in me, a ball forming in my chest that threatened to escape as tears. The gratitude I felt was such that I wanted to rush forward and embrace these guardian creatures. The male simply nodded at me and I returned the gesture. He spoke to the others in their own language then they all left, running through the grass without being attacked by it.

How could they have known I needed help? Why would they even help me at all?

I wished they would come back so I could be with them. I wanted to be one of them.

The vines continued closing on me, so I took the torch, which was deceptively heavy, and thrust it into the dying embers. The globule of sap crackled against the red-hot hunks of wood. I shuffled away from the encroaching vines on my knees, keeping the end of the torch in contact with the embers. "Come on," I prompted.

Flames slid along the top of my torch as if cued by my command. I rapped the slithering vines with the flaming end and they sped from the cave and were gone in a second.

I suddenly realized how hungry and thirsty I was. Now that I had slept, the need to find sustenance was most important.

I rose to my feet and hissed from the throbbing pain in my back and the soreness all along my body. Sleeping on that damn rock did me absolutely no favors. I held the torch out before me as I ventured out of the cave and into the forest. Grass, shrubs, and trees all fled before the small blaze. They gave me a wide berth and I was glad they decided to remain placid rather than risk damage to get past my flame and consume me.

Not a thing about my life since awakening in the forest felt as though it was how the world should have worked. For a brief moment, walking across the disturbed soil without having to worry about imminent death, I found beauty in my surroundings. The air tasted sweet enough to simply stand here beneath the sun and revel in the relative calm. "This is how life should be," I murmured to myself.

Fire didn't last forever, this much I knew, so I stemmed the urge to bask in the environment and made my way to the stream I had seen earlier. I kept the torch in one hand in case it was needed to fend off a leafy attacker then used my other one to scoop water into my mouth. Cold rejuvenation slid down my throat. I gulped and kept gulping. Finally, I plunged my whole head in the water and let it sit for a moment.

I felt as though I had won something. I had overcome some part of this journey. If I died now, at least I'd be able to commend myself on getting this far.

I pulled my head from the stream and sucked in a deep breath, rubbing the water from my eyes. I needed to find out who I was, and why I was here. Bathing in a stream wouldn't bring me that revelation.

I stood and looked around, hoping to find fruit somewhere amongst the trees. To my surprise, I found it everywhere. "The shit you notice when stuff isn't trying to kill you," I mumbled as I shook my head.

Shining apples the color of blood nearly broke from their perches, as fat and ripe as they were. Oranges reminiscent of the sun burned brightly against the green backdrop. Pears, bulging enough that I was sure their succulent bottoms were even now about to burst with juice, strained against the branches holding them aloft.

The closest to me was a pear tree. I set my torch down so the tree wouldn't up and flee from me as I came closer, leaning it on a rock, and approached slowly. I was within reach of a pear and the tree inched toward me. I snatched the fruit then skipped back and grabbed my torch. The tree just stayed in its place, seeming somehow saddened that I'd managed to pilfer one of its fruits without it causing me any harm.

I repeated this process several times, figuring out how close a tree would come to my flame then reaching out and taking a low-hanging fruit. I sauntered back to my cave with two pears and three oranges. I sat next to my torch and rolled the hard pears across the rock with ample pressure to soften them up.

I then enjoyed my feast, finishing all but one orange. A boulder had certainly taken up residence in my stomach; nothing else would explain the pain that came with being as full as I was. I imagined I was the lizard I'd preformed with earlier and felt remorse for poking fun at his terrible ailment. My body suddenly rumbled and I grabbed my stomach in the hopes that applying pressure would keep it from exploding. The pressure grew then suddenly escaped from my throat in a massive burp that shook the very air before me.

Had there been others around to hear it, they would have stared at me incredulously. Hell, I was surprised that I hadn't caused a tree to snap and fall to the earth from the volume of the sound. The pain and pressure immediately fled and I smiled in absolute relief.

I wasn't sure how long I had slept but I felt rested enough to continue. Besides, my torch would eventually consume the pine resin and begin burning the wood I used as a handle. Already it was damn hot and I firmly believed I didn't need blisters to add to my list of terrible occurrences to befall me as the imminent future would be arduous enough.

Before I could stand and set out, I saw a small patch of loose earth at the lip of the rock I sat on. It was empty, and I hadn't seen much of that. Perhaps my flame inside the cave reached further than I thought. I crept toward it, just wanting to feel the dirt.

Grass less than a foot from my fingers leaned toward me as I prodded and traced lines in the soil. It was cold and gritty, but familiar. I understood what normal earth felt like. I still didn't understand this world but I had some of the pieces to make one that felt normal to me.

I began to move my fingers in a pattern. I didn't know what I was doing, what shape I was creating, or why. Despite my confusion, I continued to allow my hand to move of its own accord, tracing lines through the soil. The fog hiding my past seemed to vibrate as though it longed to move on, and I prayed it would.

After a time, there in the soil, were figures of people. I saw six, two of them short, with four limbs and oblong heads. I stared at the picture for a moment, recognizing the human ones, but the others confused me.

They weren't letters. I understood those. I told myself this and decided to prove it. I made an 'R' in the soil, then a 'C'. I knew all that. I could have done more, but decided against it.

I wondered if others would cross this way after me. People in my own situation. Would they see this and understand it better? Would they feel confidence and inspiration for knowing that someone under the same circumstances had made it this far? Perhaps they would believe that I had made it to the end of this road and survived, somehow, and was happy.

Despite the reprieve I felt while relaxing and pondering what was happening to me, sitting still was not going to get me any closer to the end of the path. I collected my belongings, my cane and torch in the same hand although pointed in different directions to prevent the former from catching flame. I tried to keep the remaining orange in my pants somehow. It slipped from my waistband and down to me ankle. I kicked it away, cursing. Why the hell didn't my pants have pockets? Why didn't I have a bag? Morrissett should have given me one.

Trees and other greenery cleared a path beneath the scorching gaze of my torch, parting as though I were a king among his subjects.

Keep myself alive. God. Staying alive shouldn't be so hard. Staying alive should be a thing as simple as breathing.

I turned once I cleared the edge of my cave and began scaling the steep hill. The stone path was just beyond the trees, and I made my way back to it, the flame from my torch leading the way.

Chapter 4

Finding new branches was, of course, important. They wouldn't keep like the torch did, I knew, but I could use them in a pinch if necessary. Perhaps I would stumble across a hunk of stardust. The burning torch in my hand had been going for nearly twenty minutes and I feared it would soon begin travelling down the branch.

I moved along the path warily, anticipating the return of the black knight and his flaming sword. Instead, a new, unanticipated enemy entered the game as the ground suddenly gave way beneath my feet. The path of stone became no more solid and supportive than a pile of dead leaves.

I slid down a tunnel through the earth, hugging the torch to me tightly despite the flame that nearly melted the skin from my face. I splashed down in a shallow pool of water, my bamboo cane, which I only now realized had slipped from my grasp, crashing down next to me shortly after. I pulled it from the water and inspected each end to find the kiss from Jacquelyn still lodged in it. By some miracle, I had kept my torch from the water and stood up with it held out and blazing.

The plunge had felt so very brief. A bounce here. A free fall there. Now I was suddenly in some other place. It was all different. It was some kind of madness.

I imagined that I had been standing before a massive and terrible monster that had suddenly devoured me. I had been outside in the normal world. Things still made sense. Then, suddenly, it swallowed me whole. I remained intact and went down fine and easy. But when I hit the bottom, I stood up and was in a whole new place. I found myself in the belly of the beast. That's what must have happened. This world had a stomach, and I'd been thrust into it.

The sun and the intense burning light it emitted were gone. Instead, an odd gloom replaced it, like night. Extremely dim lights weaved here and there amidst hanging vines, all wrapped around each other, seemingly dead. The lights moved and swayed until I discovered that they were bugs, their backsides aglow with florescent blue. The water was murky, only up to my knees, but I couldn't see my feet. Odd trees were here and there, gnarled and smooth, made up of a hundred vines fused close together. They reached up to a ceiling of earth just ten feet above me. A few bushes made up of thick bladed grass with yellow spots sprung from the muddy bank a few strides to my right.

I was beneath the surface of the world.

Above, I could see the horrors that came for me. Down here, in the darkness, I was limited to the light my torch cast and the dim glow of the bugs. A vine, or even the claws of a monster, could snake around my ankle without me being any the wiser until it was far too late.

This place was dark and cold, the opposite of the mad world I had grown accustomed to. I was terrified of moving. I stood still and simply listened, trying to pick up on something, but it was so terribly silent here.

I was also horrified of staying in the water. Not knowing what was down there was figuratively – although it certainly could be literally - killing me. Indecision wracked me. I was torn.

A drop of water fell in the distance, twisting my head in its direction. The soft sound was enough to get me going. Either it had come from the ceiling, or something had splashed down ever so lightly.

I plodded through muddy water, regretting each noise my feet made as I slowly moved. I was inviting so many things my way with each splash. Fear made father time slow his rhythmic steps to a near full stop, each step feeling as though it took torturous hours.

The bank was soft, the mud sliding beneath my boots in waves. I came to the crest of the bank and stopped before a shrub of thick yellow leaves. I was now on watch duty, listening to make sure that I hadn't alerted anything. All was quiet.

If anything could dispel my fear, it'd be ample light. I put my torch to the shrub and waited. The thick leaves were stubborn and likely full of moisture. They smoked. Crackled a bit too. I gave up after a while and pulled my torch away, disappointed, to find that one broad leaf was putting out a small lick of flame.

I went back to helping it along and soon had a slow burning fire. I sat down in the mud before the fire and looked around. Light only shined a few dozen feet in all directions and danced with the shadows.

Brown water and mud was all around, a few twisting trees spiraling upward sparingly, giving this land the qualities of a swamp. The flying bugs didn't illuminate anything else out there. I couldn't help but imagine that things were lurking through the mud and water beyond my field of vision.

My smoldering fire suddenly became a bane as I realized that I sat in a spotlight that certainly drew the eyes of anything out there. I wanted to relax, but my heart hammered in my chest and my eyes shot back and forth. I was left to sit and wait as paralyzing fear began to seep into my bones. It weighed me down until I was sure that I wouldn't ever get up. The fear overwhelmed me so much that I covered my head as much as I could with one arm and shut my eyes, concentrating only on the noise of the small fire before me, not caring if a demon was lurking just inches from me. Fear had me ready to die like a coward.

***

My pants had soaked through from the wet mud by the time I convinced myself to get up and move. The fire from the plant hadn't yet burned out. It continued its slow smolder, thick flame wavering in a lazy, controlled manner. Remaining inert was the hardest thing I had done thus far, but I realized that finding the strength to get up and continue onward into the unknown would be exponentially more difficult. Despite the horrors that moved out there in the darkness and the fear that tore at my soul, I needed to understand this, to reach the end of my journey.

"Come on. I don't want to die. Someone owes me answers. I can't get anywhere unless I get up." I was whispering so low that I barely heard myself. I didn't want anything else to hear me. "Get up. I need to get up. Goddamn this place."

Memories slipped over the wall that barred me from the majority of them and I shut my eyes tight, enraptured by it. A blurry woman stood before me. I was sitting, quietly crying. Something buzzed and then my skull vibrated as the contraption she held slid over my head. Brown locks of hair fell before my eyes, then the memory left.

Emotions were attached to the memory and they mirrored my own at this very moment. Whatever had happened then, there had been a terribly hard journey ahead of me. One that didn't allow me a choice, but I still wanted to run and hide from. Then, I had swallowed the inevitable and got on with what I needed to do, and I would do the same now.

I stood up and swiped the mud off my backside. I was afraid of making any kind of noise now. I felt like little traps and snares had been set up in every direction of me within inches of my feet. Making even the slightest noise would trigger them, snapping me up and ending this journey I was on.

My steps were big and slow as I plodded across the muddy bank. I stayed away from the water to avoid making sound and continued on the bank to God knows where. The ghostly lights above me didn't even reflect in the surface of the water. It was like black ink that sucked up light.

Something was behind me, and so very close. Its presence suddenly thickened the air around me, giving me no room for doubt that it was there. The change in my surroundings was drastic, as if I'd been walking through a valley flooded with sunlight then night had suddenly snapped me up. I felt and heard breath spewing across the back of my neck. I waited for the death stroke. It didn't come. I tried to make myself turn around, but I couldn't even breathe. I couldn't even blink when I tried.

There was a stink on the breath that flowed past my shoulders and into my nostrils despite my not breathing. I should have stayed by the burning bush. It wouldn't have found me had I stayed.

Did I face death, or did I instead stand idle and with my back to it so I wouldn't know when my time was up? Neither.

Struggling with my inner self, warring with my thoughts, I began to move. I took a short step forward and the thing behind me inhaled sharply, a sort of click coming from it. Then it held its own breath for a moment.

I needed to breathe. I had been holding it for so long that inhaling would be a loud motion. My vision was starting to blur and the blackness all around me was closing in. My heart was pounding terribly hard before, and now, I could hear it thumping as if it had travelled into my skull. It shook me.

Either I was going to take a breath, or pass out. Both felt like they were going to end in my death. I inhaled. It was a noise that drowned out the sound of my frantic heart, broken by a quiver and labored by the lump in my throat. The thing behind me keened softly and I felt it get closer. Tears began to fill my eyes as I stood still, just breathing ever so slowly.

Molten lead was filling my being, weighing me down and burning my insides. What was this demon behind me?

I was going to die. But I would do it now, and without living in such suffering another moment. I whirled around.

The keen became a quick and short screech. My eyes shut tightly but not before I caught a glimpse of something. It was smoky. Or maybe cloudy. It wasn't made of flesh, I think. Deep, wide eyes of jet black. A cavernous, fang-filled mouth opened as large as an abyss.

Wind flashed by me momentarily. I kept my eyes shut, expecting death. Somehow, it didn't come.

I opened my eyes after a time and found nothing before me. I was alone yet again. Had that thing ever truly been there, whatever it was?

Another memory fell from its perch amidst the fog. This one was even more shrouded than the last, however. I only understood the emotions involved. I'd come face to face with death before only to narrowly evade its clutches. Once free of it, I had felt a sort of accomplishment, a drive to continue onward, knowing that my time was finite, wherever it was I had been before.

I would start on my path again. First though, I would take my time to breathe the fear from my body; it weighed me down so much that lifting my feet was impossible. If I came across another one of those, I would stick my head beneath the murky water and drown myself. That terror was too much to live with a second time, especially now that I knew what it looked like.

The blood rushing through my body slowed to a normal rate. I continued on.

Time passed oddly. I felt as though I wasn't making any progress, I moved so slowly and cautiously. My eyes bounced in my head, shifting this way and that, trying to track the source of the sounds out in the darkness. However, I turned to look back at the fire I had left behind, the burning bush, and there was nothing.

Had I moved around a bend in a wall that I hadn't seen and now the fire was behind that? Had I really gone so far that the light of the fire was lost? Or had something extinguished it?

My foot splashed down in the water as I stupidly deviated from the bank. I slipped and nearly fell down into the water. I regained my footing and quickly shuffled back to my muddy path. The racket I made was loud enough to stop even my heart from beating.

Water must have been dripping from me. As the drops hit the mud, they made little splashes. The sound was even growing. I cast my eyes

46

down thinking that I would see a torrent of water spilling from my pants, but instead there was barely a drop.

But then, the noise became far too loud. That was the sound of something splashing through the water as it converged on me. It didn't sound like just two feet. It sounded like hundreds.

This thing wasn't going to be the same phantom from before. This would be something that could touch me, something that could tear me apart and it would if it caught me.

I ran, using my cane to help me as I struggled. I wasn't going fast enough, I already knew.

I avoided puddles and the water along the banks at first. Fear made me clumsy, however, and I splashed down in a few of them before I gave up on keeping quiet. I sprinted across the bank, splashing through water without a care as to how loud I was. Flames from my torch blew past me several times, singeing my arm and face.

The terror coming after me was close. I looked over my shoulder for a brief moment and caught a glimpse of it. A squat but long body wrapped in olive-green scales sped for me on six legs. Spikes of bone jutted from its back, thicker along its spine. Its thick tail whipped back and forth behind it as it closed on me. It opened its mouth, full of fangs meant to shred, and screeched. Small, beady eyes a more vibrant green than its body stared hungrily at the back of my thighs.

Perhaps now was the time for me to stick my head into the water and end this. It surely would be better than what that thing was going to do to me. I railed against the hopelessness, turned my head and kept running. Maybe there would be a cave I could duck into. Or maybe Morrissett would come to save me. The family of orangutans perhaps.

But there was nothing. No hideaway. Nothing appeared to save me. I was alone.

I spun around and faced it, standing in the middle of a wide part of the bank. The ground beneath me was hard, albeit still damp, but not the mud that made up most of the bank. This would be as good a place as any to make my final stand.

The flame in my hand was my sword, my cane my support, and even my shield if I needed it to be.

I felt the horror in my being. I knew that I wasn't a fighter. I also didn't want to die. A fighter would feel the weapons in his hands and courage would flood through him. All I cared about was the fear, and it made me fight. I'd lost my choice at flight.

The creature slithered side to side as it closed. Then, it vaulted at my legs, its maw open terribly wide. I let instinct guide me and swung my torch down and smacked it between its eyes. The creature slid past me, shaking its head against the flames. Its tail smashed into my leg as it passed though. Goddamn luck.

I ended up on one damaged knee. That thick tail packed a punch and it hurt like hell.

It shook its head around as it turned and oriented on me again. It took a moment though, and had actually overcompensated when it turned around. The flames landing atop its head had obviously impaired its sight.

The pain in my knee tried to keep me down, but I wasn't going to be low enough for that thing to rip my face apart. I used my cane to get back to my feet as it came after me again.

Before it could get too close, I thrust my fire toward it, stopping it. It screeched and shook its head.

I had found a weakness in this thing and drew a comparison between it and myself. Thus far I'd been the prey, everything else hunting me, picking out my frailties.

Now, it was my turn to be the victor. Some of the fear left.

The creature scrambled to the side, getting past my flame, then hurtled at my legs. I sidestepped the poorly aimed attack then stabbed at its side with the torch. I felt the wood crack on its hard side. That wasn't a good idea.

It turned away from me abruptly and the tip of its tail cut across my shin. I felt the sharp end tear into my skin and open my flesh, sending me staggering away to avoid further damage. Each labored step sent a fresh knife stab of pain through my leg but I hid from it, lest I allow it to slow me enough and result in my death.

Beating this thing wasn't going to be so easy. It wasn't as dumb as I hoped it was.

When it completed spinning around, I was already swiping at its face. The torch and its flames caught it in the side of the head. It tried to scurry away but I kept on it, swatting at its eyes. It screeched at me. I got overzealous though. It suddenly turned and snapped at me.

Dozens of fangs would have clamped down on my shin and torn me apart. However, I interposed my cane and it clamped down on that. The bamboo shattered. I noticed, with horrific clarity, that the end housing the kiss was the side nearest the creature's mouth. I couldn't lose that.

I pulled the cane and it broke completely. The creature held on to its short end. It ripped its head side to side and I was terrified that the kiss would go flying off into the black water.

"Hey! Come on, you ugly shit!" I kicked it in the side and suffered a shock of pain through my toes. It still tore at the bamboo. The fire must have blinded it and it must think it had my leg. I then stomped on its head and that was enough to make it stop.

Teeth smashed together and its jaw cracked against the damp earth. Its mouth hung open, slack for a moment and I shoved flames in there. The fire scorched its mouth and it screeched. It scurried away, thrashing its head and rolling over its side.

The creature didn't wait there long. It rolled into the water and submerged its head for a moment. It then came back up and took off into the blackness. I had won.

"Yeah! You don't screw with me! Prick!" I wanted to keep on yelling into the darkness. As the splashes grew distant, I realized how loud I was being in this quiet place. "I should really shut up."

My victory was short-lived, however, as I suddenly remembered that the kiss had been torn from my cane. I staggered to the edge of the water and sifted through the remains of the bamboo. Nothing. Shit!

I fell to my knees and immediately regretted it. Pain shot through my legs from where that creature's tail had slashed and smashed me. I hissed, shutting my eyes tight. Once the pain abated enough, I went back to searching. I dug through the mud, ran my hand along the bank.

I found it! My hand came across something hard and I pulled it from the water. The kiss was there. I put it to my lips and felt its cold, hard surface on my skin. I smiled.

***

Getting out of the stomach of this planet and back to its surface was my only concern. I'd beaten one of those things, but didn't think myself capable of doing it again, not with my injuries. I crept along the winding bank quietly, limping at the pain in my legs now that my cane had been smashed and rendered useless.

Splashes of water echoed from far off in the blackness. A short screech cut through the relative quiet and I imagined a weak creature being snapped up by a predator of this place and devoured. Still, I maintained my cautious pace.

A dome-like shape loomed in the darkness before me, pressing out from shadows as though reaching for me. Water circled around the sides of it, the lights from the insects allowing me to see that the cave was an opening to a larger cavern. Standing before it, I felt as though I was at the base of a mountain, gawking at its size, trying to pinpoint the top of it, hoping that it was an exit to the outside world.

Flames licked along the end of my torch weakly now; the fuel source was running out. Soon the flames would begin consuming the wood to stay alive, and I'd be forced to discard it. Even if this was a way out, without fire I'd be defenseless. I stuffed my thoughts down deep, swallowed, then entered the cave. Crystals embedded in the rock reflected the light of my fire with magnificent intensity throwing slashes and points of light across the walls of the cave.

I walked warily, ducking stalactites, looking over my shoulder often. Several times I was sure I had heard something scuttling on the ground behind me. Each time I looked, however, there was nothing. The gash in my knee flared with fresh pain each time I imagined that something might be coming for me. It was like the very thought forced another stream of blood from the wound.

The tunnel fell away behind me. I entered into a large chamber, the ceiling so high that the light of my flame didn't reach up there. Something cried out.

I stopped moving immediately, my eyes flicking back and forth. What was that? I'd kill it. Beating that creature had given me the confidence I needed.

It cried out again, and sounded so small. Weak even. Perhaps it wasn't a predator set on killing me. No longer did I want to run from or attack it. I wanted to find it.

I began walking along the wall. It whimpered, whined. Slumped shapes came into the range of my torch. Something moved beyond them. It was a tiger cub.

The cub was on its stomach behind two other tigers. The latter were both dead. A mommy and a sibling. The living cub stared at me intensely. Black stripes covered its white body. It wasn't any longer than my forearm.

A little pit opened in my heart for that poor orphan. I couldn't think of my own mother, but knew that I'd been taken from her to wind up here at some point. Sadness welled in me for the tiger cub and its dead family.

Despite the cub's size I recognized that it was still dangerous. I carefully leaned my torch against the wall. Its eyes never left mine.

If this took me out, I'd be really pissed. I'd already gone through hell. One swipe of those sharp claws in the right spot and I'd be breathing blood.

Slowly, I began walking around the big momma tiger. Maybe the cub wouldn't want to leave. Maybe it wanted to sit here and die with the rest of its family. How could it though? Nothing so young would want that.

Crimson stained the fur of the two dead ones. Something had torn into both of them. I thought of the creature I had fought earlier. I saw that one of the momma's legs was bent awkwardly.

The whole family had fallen just as I had then. She must have gotten hurt and made too much noise. With no fire to protect them, I wonder how many of those creatures came after them. She had saved one of her babies, but couldn't protect the other. She must have gotten them both here right before she passed.

The cub scrambled forward and laid across its mother, guarding her body. My heart ached.

I continued for the cub, moving around its sibling first, freezing as it let loose a low growl.

"Hey, little one. You're okay. I'm here to help you. It's okay. Everything is going to be okay."

I sat down within arm's length of the cub and found that it was a boy and was hurt as well. Those creatures must have gotten their teeth on him at some point. A small amount of red stained his fur right where one back leg met the rest of his body.

I reached out and set a hand on his momma. His eyes were open wide and he was breathing hard now, staring intently at my hand. She was cold and stiff. I slowly stroked her. "You don't want to leave your momma, huh? I know. I'm sorry. It's okay though. I'll help you."

I carefully ran my hand along the tiger's body until I was just a foot from the cub's front paw. He growled a high-pitched noise. We spent a few minutes talking then. I told him that he would be okay, that I was sorry. He breathed hard and showed me his sadness with his eyes, growling here and there.

"Okay, I'm going to pick you up now. Please don't tear my hand off..." Slowly, I moved my hand to the cub's back, making sure to keep away from his injury. "You can't stay here, buddy. Come on."

Gingerly, I picked him up. He hissed and wriggled against me a bit. "Just no biting and scratching." He went on like that for a moment, me holding him out with extended arms. It wasn't long before he quieted. I held him beneath his two front legs and we just stared at one another for a moment.

He was tired. He had given up his fight.

Simply leaving didn't feel right. I turned him so his injured side wouldn't touch me then I pulled him close. "We need to go now. You can say goodbye."

I lowered him toward his mother's face. He put both paws on her then licked her. He stopped then put his nose to hers. I moved him to his sibling. He placed one paw and his forehead on its side. It was time to go.

I scooped up my torch, making sure to keep it well away from the cub and as I stood, something had clacked on the floor near the cave entrance into the cavern. I aimed the fire that way in the hopes that it would brighten the cave more.

Dozens of shining eyes gleamed at me ravenously. There was a horde of those things. The same things that had killed the cub's family.

I walked backward, moved around the tigers, and into the cave on the other side of the cavern. The creatures crept along with me. They didn't like the fire; I knew that much. Still, I was only one man with a small flame. Why weren't they coming after me like the other one had?

I didn't realize how much time had passed. The mouth of the cavern came into view, circling around me. I was still beneath the surface of the world, though, a few steps outside of the cavern and within the larger cave. The creatures had stopped a while ago, refusing to continue following me. I could barely even see just one of them.

Fetid breath whispered across stirring winds behind me. The cub squirmed and whined, but it wiggled closer to me, flexing its claws against my stomach, seeking protection.

I whirled around and saw dozens of those phantoms arcing through the air. They moved slowly, most of their body shrouded in inky smoke. I was certainly between a rock and a hard place. The biggest goddamn rock ever and the hardest fucking place imaginable.

Light shone so brightly from an opening behind the mass of phantoms that it may as well been a star that had crashed down inside the cave and continued to burn. I just needed to make it past them, then I'd be free from this hellish underworld.

I wasn't going to double back; the gash in my leg made those things very real. I wasn't going to stay still; I'd told this cub that we were getting out of here. The phantom had scared me half to death earlier, but it hadn't hurt. They were terrifying, but nothing more, I hoped.

"Come on. We move fast. Nothing will happen to us. Nothing at all."

The cub began to shake. That didn't help to reassure my statement. I had no idea what these things were, but I would run right past them before they could touch either of us.

I spared one last glance at the darkness behind me, saw a few eyes fixed to me. Then, I took off along the winding, muddy path that cut through the black water. The portal of light shook and bounced in my vision as I vaulted toward it.

The phantoms surged through the air, excited by my arrival. They screeched and keened, darted this way and that, plunged toward me. I shut them out as best as I could and just ran.

Wind blew past me as I moved, each new gust colder than the last. The first phantom dove toward me and I screamed out in terror as its face slid past mine within inches of touching. Then, its claws raked through me, passing into my chest, seizing my heart for a moment, then exiting my body. The torch tumbled from my hand and splashed into the water, sizzling as the flames died.

Cold shocked me to a halt and another phantom struck through me, again putting a stop to the beating of my heart for a moment. The cub screeched in fear and I looked down to see him digging his nose and claws into my stomach. The cold running through me begged me to lie down and die, but I had to keep fighting.

I would just keep running. I would just keep running.

The fear won though, and began to shut me down.

I realized that my eyes had closed. I was ankle deep in water, slowing down. I needed to open my eyes. I needed to stop moving and readjust my path. Doing so meant accepting that I was in the midst of these things. If I kept going on blindly, I'd be able to keep them from my mind, but I'd never reach the exit that way. Stumbling into a rock, a hole, or the claws of those reptilian creatures put a different fear in me.

I stopped. I opened my eyes. I saw the bank, and beheld so many terrifying forms before me and out there in the darkness. The water was so very dark, something vile must be down there, hungry for my body.

I staggered back on to the mud, but I was moving so slow. My bones seized up, my muscles locked, my brain shut down. I felt the passing phantoms, their ghostly touch gently caressing my soul away. I heard their tormented screams, a sound that made me want to beat my head against stone.

I couldn't move. I couldn't think. All I could focus on was the fear.

God, what were they?

I finally shut my eyes against them again. It was no use; I was already on my knees. Their presence pressed me to the ground completely. I cradled the cub against my chest. If not for him, I would have died right then. He provided at least a little comfort. He was alive, real, normal.

I was prepared to lie there and fade away. My journey had been so terribly hard already. Giving up required nothing but submission. Continuing on, getting to my feet, that asked too much of me. I didn't have that in me. It was better that I finish this now.

I wished that I could have seen a family in my mind's eye, but there was only the fear.

Tears were streaming from my eyes. My body trembled. Blood rushed through my body, the sound of many crashing waves pulsing in my head.

I opened my eyes. A congregation of phantoms dove upon me from up above. Their cold, smoky bodies passed into mine. A shock lanced through me and I screamed, soundless amidst the torrent.

Nothingness.

Chapter 5

Large white squares of rock extended out before me in a straight line, creating a wide avenue through the rampant forest. It was fifteen feet wide at least. Trees and vegetation sprang up to either side, branches leaning out over it, but did not come onto the road.

How did I get here? I'd just been in the cave, dying beneath an onslaught of those phantoms. Perhaps I was dead.

My arms were empty, no sign of the cub but for the tears in my shirt and skin beneath. I could still feel the kiss inside my boot as I wiggled my foot. My legs burned fiercely and quaked so much that I suddenly fell. Sharp pain surged through my knee and I looked down to see a rent in my pants and crimson beneath.

I simply stared at the road, relishing in the quiet calm on my knees. Wind blew through the trees, setting their leaves to rustling, creating a soothing sound. I almost wanted to walk right up to one and lie down beneath its shade. They would kill me, I knew. Unless my memories from before were wrong.

I looked over my shoulder. A wide cave mouth was there. I saw soft, floating lights within. I had come from the cave with the phantoms and the other creatures. But how had I gotten out?

Something brushed against my thigh. The cub was there, leaning its head into my side, looking up at me.

"Did you get us out of there? How did any of this happen?"

I noticed the blood on his side again. He couldn't have gotten us out. He was far too small to drag me and injured even. I doubt he could have even gotten himself out.

So what then?

Had I blacked out only to get up and run from the cave? That fear was overwhelming. It had rendered me useless. How could it had been me?

As much as I wanted to understand what had happened, I put it all away for now. I figured that there would be plenty of odd encounters like that one. Besides, I was awestruck when I looked down the path of white stone to behold a city bustling with people.

Orange and pink walls ran along the perimeter of the whole city, their tops wavy and sporting dragon heads with wide nostrils and flowing whiskers. My vantage point put me above the city's walls, albeit half a mile away, and I could just make out huts and other squat dwellings among tall buildings of stone and bamboo.

"Other people. And so many of them. How could they survive here?"

I didn't see a shred of green inside the village. It was all grey and yellow, void of any living vegetation. Atop the walls, every few yards, were large fire pits blazing with great intensity.

The cub reared up and placed his paws on my stomach. Claws poked at me playfully.

"I know. I'm ready to go too. It's just... Should this be so odd a feeling? It's just a city. It feels like God though. Maybe He's here."

I began walking, the cub tracing my steps. I was glad that I had saved him. I felt a connection with him. We were both lost now. Two stragglers in life that had gotten caught up in something far bigger than either of us.

Would the people there even speak my language? Would they attack me on sight?

The path of large, white stone began to narrow as I walked. The trees at its edges leaned toward me. I was so caught up with worrying about a vine or branch snaking out and gripping my throat that I didn't realize I was about to pass into the city.

Muffled shouts, the clang of metal, the continuous shuffle of thousands of feet and a cacophony of other sounds turned my attention forward to find that I was a few feet from the entrance. I looked upon a stone archway with iron double doors tall enough to fit three of me stacked atop one another and wide enough that I could lay down and roll through sideways and still have a few feet of clearance on each side. Etched into the top of the arch were the words "Haven Sprawl".

To either side of the open doors stood two odd people. From the breasts beneath their jackets of a rough, scratchy material, I could tell they were women. From their faces, I wasn't sure they were even human. Full helms of smooth metal covered their heads, similar to the black knight's although void of any menacing spikes. Gloves with small plates of iron over their knuckles hid their hands. Pants made up of the same material as their jackets ran down to boots tipped with iron. Not a single inch of flesh showed, and they seemed imposing figures in their armor.

Scorch marks marred their helms in several places. One of them stepped forward and stopped me with a raised hand. I looked for eyes within the helm and discovered that a dark glassy shield covered those even.

Her voice came at me slightly muffled beneath the helm, "You can't have that just walking around. And why would you anyway? Someone will take it. Hell, I might take it."

I followed her finger to the cub.

"That? Him?" I asked. "Why would anyone take him?"

She held a large rod with a canister attached to it. There were hoses here and there that ran along it. Some switches too. A trigger. Then a larger hose led to something strapped to her back. It was all black metal.

She suddenly lifted the rod, placed her cheek along its side as she aimed it, then pulled the trigger. A spear of flame shot from the tip, crackling as it shot into the forest. Licks of fire arced back at her, caressing her helm and fingers before dissipating. A gaggle of vines coiling from a tree had begun moving over the wall. The flames hit the side of them and they writhed back into the forest.

Without acknowledging my wonderstruck face, she continued, "Why the fuck won't they? Listen, I don't get paid for telling dipshits not to be dipshits. But I am at least somewhat nice. Just shut up and go in or turn back around. But pick that up before someone takes it."

For a brief moment I wondered about how others could think they had some kind of right to things that didn't belong to them in the least. Then, I was overcome with the sheer power that flamethrower contained. I wanted one desperately.

"How did you get that?" I pleaded.

She was silent for a while. She looked me up and down. "From the guard, obviously. You aren't acting right." She turned to her fellow guard and said, "Wanna take him in? Might be he was sent here by the Ochari."

Ignorant to what those things were, I waved my hands and said, "I'll go in. I'm sorry for wasting your time. I just went through a lot out there." Although I couldn't see the expression beneath the mask of metal, I was sure she was giving me a caustic look. "To get him." I pointed at the cub.

"Just go," she demanded. "I'm done dealing with idiots for right now." I heard a giggle come from the other one standing at the gate.

I shook my head, confused. Discomfited, I turned and picked the cub up, held him tight to my chest, then went inside the city.

***

What I had seen from above didn't do this place any actual justice. The buildings in Haven Sprawl were tightly packed together and shut up well, the opposite I expected from their name. Instead of windows, there were metal plates with small holes that allowed nothing but air and perhaps a dozen pinpoints of light to enter. The buildings nearest the wall were so close as to make up a second wall. Poured cement and brick comprised most of the structures, colors varying from grey to a reddish-brown, while wood was used exclusively for trim and molding, mostly along doorframes.

The lack of greenery was terrible obvious, the light from the sun and stars above skipping off the dull grey cement ground. Likely, the ground had at one time been smooth. Now, it sported hundreds of crisscrossing lines and dozens of blotches of varying shades of grey, obviously hasty repairs made after a crack in the foundation formed.

The aura exuding from the city reminded me of an arid desert, dry, lifeless, and unforgiving.

Perhaps when it had first been built this city had been more open, a bastion of freedom from the suffocating forest. Now, though, there must be far too many people living within the walls for it to remain anything but a massive container with far too much stuff inside it.

People constantly glared at me and the cub on my chest as if they'd soon attempt to eat him while he was still in my arms. I held him tighter and wished I had a weapon. Guards in similar uniform to those at the gates patrolled the streets, their flamethrowers held at the ready. Maybe they would protect me if I needed it.

I spent a long time just walking around Haven Sprawl. I found more open space in the middle of it in the form of a large square packed with stands. I saw dead animals hanging by hooks at some, fruits at others, barrels of odd pastes at a few. There were plenty of brutish individuals standing around those barrels, toting bare swords, axes, and spears.

After perusing the city for several minutes, I realized that I wasn't fending for my life this very moment. I was simply walking, keeping the squirming animal in my arms when he decided to become restless.

Immediately, I felt at ease. The prying eyes of the people around me and their comments whispered about the cub didn't faze me any longer at all. I was so very comfortable. I kept on my tour of the city, aware, but relaxed.

Eventually, I came to a stream of water that ran through a crosshatched grate in the wall of the city. It flowed between two angled slabs of concrete, creating a moat that split the city in half. The other end wound beneath a bridge and was lost behind a building.

I sat down at its edge, another person sitting across the ten-foot stream.

"Hi," I said.

"Are you selling that?"

"This? You mean him? No."

"I'll get you some fruit if you just let me have a little. Some akkies even."

"What? No. I'm not interested, and I'm going."

"Wait. I'll even get all the seeds out of them. I'll get you four for a leg."

I ignored the odd man and stood up. I walked to the grate in the wall and sat down there. I could still see him, but he didn't move to follow me. He did, however focus back on the stream. I realized that he had a net in the water there.

I lay back and looked up at the sky. The bright sun was hidden, dropped down behind the wall to my left. The stars were still there, hundreds of orbs burning in the sky. The sun seemed roughly the size of my palm and the stars ranged in magnitude from that of my fingertip to a near invisible speck. The polka dot sky was interesting to look at, but a little much for my eyes. I squinted hard and focused on the wall to my left.

The cub rolled off me and lay down, snuggling against my side. I thought of him, of the people's odd response toward him so far. They wanted to *eat* him. Tigers weren't hunted for food... At least I told myself they weren't, unsure if that was completely true or not.

They wouldn't get this one. Not the one that I had saved.

And what was an akkie? He said it had seeds. It must be a fruit. Did the seeds try to kill people too?

I lay there for a while. Thinking. Staring. It was so nice to feel like I was somewhere at least semi-normal for the first time in so long.

I was falling asleep. I only realized it when the cub screamed and hissed. A teenage boy leapt away from him and me, his hand recoiling back so very fast.

I scrambled to my feet. "Hey! You get out of here!" I was yelling at his back. The boy was already running away. He had tried snatching the cub. Bastard almost got him too.

There were a few people strolling here and there, others sitting along the stream with nets. They all looked at me blankly. There was even a guard staring at me. I walked over to him.

"You're a guard, aren't you?"

"Yes. What of it?"

"Didn't you see what that kid tried doing? He was going to steal from me."

"Then keep that close to you. I don't even know why you're just walking around with it. Sell it or eat it would be my advice to you. Besides, if it ain't green and from the earth, I don't spray fire at it."

The guard turned and walked away. I felt very alone in Haven Sprawl.

Without a safe place for me here and a foolproof way to keep the cub from being snatched, I felt as though I needed to leave the city. I had only just arrived here, and leaving meant going back out into the wild. At the very least that was somewhat worse than this city. If I just got rid of the cub I wouldn't have much to worry about.

But I cared about the little hairball.

Something occurred to me then. Right before I had gotten up, a moment before I had fallen asleep, I had seen something. The light from the sky had all arranged itself into shapes. The dots had swam to meet at a single point and had become a figure. At least I think. Perhaps my mind was just playing tricks on me, making me believe that even though nothing of the sort had happened.

I went back to the stream, this time sitting across from the man who had spoken to me earlier. We locked eyes. He said, "Better get rid of him before someone else takes him without paying."

"People are going to eat him, huh? That's what you all want?"

The man looked at me oddly. His skin was peach, like mine. A large, but tame beard of brown and grey covered the bottom half of his face. His eyes were dark. The hair atop his head was short and brown, like his beard but without the grey.

He said, "Of course. Did you just come from some place where animals are people's friends? Bet they have meat there that they just hand out too, huh? Boy, that must be nice."

"Ya know, I wish I knew where I came from."

"What are you talking about?"

"Nothing. What's your name?"

"Kanute. Yours?"

"I actually don't know. I have a memory problem."

"Oh." He held the sound for a long moment. "That explains you. You're like a babe in a man's body. Well, good luck with the whole memory thing."

"What are you doing?"

I stroked the side of the cub, now calm and lying down near me again.

Kanute was looking in the stream and moving his net this way and that. He didn't speak for a while. I thought about asking him again. Instead, I just looked in the water and tried to see what he was up to. There was such intensity on his face that I grew extremely interested in what he was looking for.

His arm suddenly jerked to the side then he pulled the net up and out of the water. I saw within the mesh, a squirming creature that I realized to be a shrimp. I recalled seeing those small creatures on skewers sitting across metal bars, fire licking between the bars to caress the shrimp. There was a man standing before the grill cooking the meats upon it, and a wooden deck beneath them both. To the right of them was a short expanse of grass with a walkway that led to a pool of water. Kids were swimming and leaping into the water, some from the small, man-made waterfall coming from the rocks piled into a mound on the right edge of the pool.

I lost the rest of the flashback and found that Kanute was only mildly interested in me. He was now standing, staring at his prize with admiration. He did cast a glance at me after he gripped the shrimp in a fist. It was big. I could still see it wriggling between his fingers. "See you around."

He turned to go. I watched him leave, as did the others around the stream, albeit the latter with obvious envy of his catch. They seemed forlorn for a moment, but then looked back at the stream with renewed ambition. Kanute was nearly lost behind a building when I decided to chase after him.

I leapt up to my feet and began jogging with the cub, definitely not able to ignore the pain in my knee but just not letting it slow me. The cub growled at me as he bounced against my chest.

"Sorry. Just stay put." By the time I had crossed the short bridge, Kanute had slipped away behind a building. "Hey, Kanute! Hold up!"

I rounded the corner and he was still on the move. He wasn't far though and I pulled up next to him quickly.

He barely acknowledged me. Like he was expecting me to follow him. "You rethink my offer about the cub there?"

"No. It's just... We don't know what we're doing here in this city. I could use some guidance. What do you say?"

"Hell no."

Well, I wasn't prepared for such a blunt reaction. "Come on, Kanute. Just a little help."

"A dozen other people there at the stream and he picks me." He was mumbling. I am not sure he knew I could hear him. "Listen, I'll make this real easy for you. Fuck off! And in case that memory thing kicks in real soon, I'll say it again to help it sink in." He stopped and turned to look at me. "Fuck off! Bye, now."

Kanute turned and continued on with a skip in his step. I stood there, a solid wall of grey to my right and an expanse of large white rock to my left. I didn't realize how dull life seemed without the colors of the wild around until now. Everything was white, grey, black.

I watched Kanute go until he rounded another corner. I wasn't sure what my actual goal was, but I decided to follow him. I would keep my distance, but it seemed a good way to figure out a bit more about this city. At the very least it would give me a way to pass the time and keep from falling asleep outside.

***

After a few hours of following Kanute, I began to get a better feel for the city. I also ended up getting caught.

But, before that, I found that people ate that paste stuff I saw in the barrels at some of the booths. They were given a bowl of it in exchange for something. Fruit, nuts, weapons, small animals, plenty of other things. They drank the paste down right there, licking the bowl until it was clean. Then, a guard would take the bowl back and shoo them away.

The guards weren't the same as the metal-faced ones. Rather, those that stood vigilantly around merchant booths didn't seem too nice. They had a blade in at least one hand, and the promise of violence on their scowling faces.

Several times, I jumped at the roar emitted from a flamethrower toting guard as they sprayed fire against a wall or the white stone floor. Plant life had sprouted through a crack and paid dearly for its invasion into the city. That green was taken care of immediately then filled with some kind of grey mix.

At one point, while crossing a wide intersection with what seemed like a billion people, I thought I had seen something walking amongst the others that wasn't human. Whatever it was, it was lost too quickly within the crowd. The creature, if it was that, had blue or green skin. I dismissed the wild idea as being nothing more than a colorful mask or clothing.

Shortly after traversing the crowded thoroughfare, Kanute had come to a large pit with a blazing fire within. Others stood around it too, cooking animals. Sweat poured from most of those around the flame, their backs glistening as they spent a few minutes roasting their meals. Even from the hundred or so feet that separated myself and the fire, I could feel its heat. I poked my head around a building and was wiping my brow soon after.

Kanute put the bag slung across his shoulder on the ground then pulled a long metal rod from it. He took the shrimp and placed it on the ground. It feebly flopped here and there. He cut its head off with a knife. Then he stabbed it onto the sharpened, forked end of the rod. He left the head on the ground and thrust the shrimp into the fire.

He spent a single minute there, wiping his face often and even shielding it a few times. When he pulled it out, the shrimp was nearly as black as the rod. It certainly didn't look edible. He used a cloth to pull the shrimp off then wrapped it up and walked off after putting the rod away.

As he walked, he blew on the shrimp. He came to a stop against one of the walls, his back leaning against it. I hid behind a building and watched him. He looked out over the city and adjusted his position ever so slightly this way and that. I wondered what he was doing. Then, he settled on a place just minutely different from his original spot.

Kanute pinched the charred shrimp between two fingers and held it out before him. He used his other hand to peel the shell off and beneath that, the meat was still burnt, although not as badly as the shell. Perhaps it was edible... to a starving man who had a real hankering for blackened seafood. He tore it in half with his teeth and chewed it slowly. He closed his eyes. I like to imagine that he was so satisfied with the meal that he moaned.

He finished it then just stood there against the wall, staring forward. The sun was just barely hidden behind the building I used as cover. The other stars still bathed Kanute in light but he wasn't blinded. I realized then that he was actually looking up over the tops of buildings.

I tried to follow his gaze with my own, but I was much too close to the building. I only got a close up of grey brick. Whatever Kanute was fixated on, I wanted to see it.

I scampered to the back of the building, hoping to find a glimpse of something in the sky while getting dangerously close to revealing myself to Kanute. The surrounding buildings crowded in on me far too much. I couldn't even see any of the fires burning atop the wall on the other side of the city.

Something slapped against my forehead and pulled me back. I dropped the cub who tried to keep hold of me but instead just scratched my stomach with his sharp claws. Something cold pressed against my neck. I wanted to say something, to curse at the burning pain across my stomach. I was sure, however, that uttering a single word would end up with me sprouting a second smile.

"I'm starting to think that memory loss thing was a lie. What did I tell you earlier?"

Kanute removed the knife from my neck enough to let me speak. "To fuck off." The blade returned.

"That's right. But you didn't. Why are you following me?"

"Because I don't know what else to do." There were a thousand things I wanted to say. Because Morrissett had told me go on this journey and I needed a break from it. Because everyone else wanted to take the cub. Because I didn't know who I was. Because I was scared and didn't want to feel alone.

But I didn't say anything else. I just let Kanute make his choice.

The blade left and I sighed in relief. I began to thank Kanute and apologize. I was cut short as something hard smashed into the back of my head. I yelped then found myself on the ground. Did my teeth crack against the stone?

Through the haze, I could just barely hear the cub hissing and screaming. I thought I was pushing myself up, at least that's what I was trying to do. A dizzying moment slipped by until I realized I was actually just lying flat on the stone, as if I was stuck to it. My arms moved a little, I didn't feel it. But I saw them slide up. I put my palms down and my arms began shaking like thin branches in a maelstrom.

The small amount of strength remaining fled and I fell into the darkness of sleep.

***

It wasn't all black this time. There was now more to the realm where the being of light resided. He rose up and out of Haven Sprawl. The dim lines of light that made up the city perimeter guttered out.

I watched the light, that piece of me that had gotten away somehow, float up. The black sky he arced through was suddenly marred by a purple imperfection. It swirled ever so slowly in every which way, each movement an independent thing.

The being of light seemed to take interest in the purple blotch. He spun in the air to face it for a moment, staring at it hard. Still, he continued to glide away from the purple swirling mass. He must have been deciding whether to leave or to investigate it.

The purple mar grew in brightness, becoming saturated with thin lines of orange. The neon color intensified until it was all blazing orange having snuffed out the purple. The spinning vortex of orange shades took on a definite shape and I realized what was coming.

The being of light must have realized it too. He picked up his speed before turning and cutting through the black sky. "Wait!" I tried to say. "Don't leave me behind." But nothing actually came from my mouth. There was no noise.

The orange light was an inferno burning a hole in the black sky. It was also right above me. The fire spewed from the hole, then came down. It lit the lines of the city before covering it all in flame.

I didn't feel the heat, but I felt anxiety and terror as the city exploded. I saw writhing figures in the streets and falling from the tops of buildings. It all rushed toward me as if I was a magnet for the suffering. Flames, people, the city, it all came for me in a wave. I tried to scream.

Chapter 6

The first thing I did was vomit. I woke up to such terrible pain and pressure in the back of my head that I just couldn't stop it. Fruit paste and juice spewed from my mouth.

Then, after I stopped hacking, I listened for the cub. Nothing. Shit.

He was gone. I looked all around. I couldn't see anything. The sun was far too bright right now. I felt around for my fluffy comrade but didn't find him. Kanute had taken him.

"Hey. Can't you hear me? Are you alright?"

"What?" Was that Kanute? What kind of madman knocked someone out then sat around and waited for them to wake up just to ask if they were okay? "Kanute?"

Goddamn I had a terrible headache.

"Who? Are you okay? Taking a nap out in the hot sun didn't work out too well for you, did it?"

It wasn't Kanute. I could now see at least a little. I saw legs and followed those up to a person. He wore a helm of metal and was looking down on me.

"I didn't fall asleep. Someone hit me." I felt the back of my head and found a large knot there. It was tender as hell.

"Well, good thing you aren't dead." He turned to leave.

"That's it?" I called after him. "You aren't going to go after him?"

The guard responded while walking away, "We never do. Good luck."

So these guards worried about the plants coming into their city and nothing else then? Certainly they could turn those flamethrowers on the criminals and psychos of this city, like Kanute.

I needed to find him, and hope he still had the cub. My better judgement screamed that he had either cooked the cub or sold him. I would gouge his eyes from his head. It's not like anyone here would stop me.

The import of the ominous vision that had come to me stopped me dead, though. The being of light had fled the city just in time. Was I already too late? Or was there still time? I wasn't even completely sure that it was a message. The urge to flee Haven Sprawl was near impossible to deny, but I told myself that my dream was nothing more than a concoction of my mind. It couldn't hold any actual meaning...

Fire from the sky... that seemed far too unrealistic to actually come to pass, despite the other madness I'd endured thus far.

Preparing to stand, I brought my feet up and found them bare, my toes scraping across the hard ground. My boots were next to me, but the kiss wasn't anywhere to be found. Kanute had taken that too. Bastard.

I fought through the soreness, standing up and wincing. A cold shiver blasted my senses as a gust of wind caressed my sweat-soaked body. Then, scorching pain seared the back of my arms and neck. I looked upon my forearms to see red, sunburned flesh. I felt like I might vomit again. I swallowed it then looked up, trying to find the inferno burning a hole through the sky. There was nothing but bright stars.

My first destination, the fire pit. I found it quickly. No Kanute.

Next, the stream. Again, my target wasn't there.

Now, I was out of ideas. I simply walked along, zigzagging through the city, slinking along its walls. I rubbed the bump on my head often, glad that it hadn't split open. I couldn't be too elated though. That headache hurt worse than anything I'd felt before. It throbbed and the beating sunrays did nothing to help.

I continued on, keeping to the rare shade as often as I could until my legs grew stiff. My mind was blank. The sliver of hope I clung to threatened to shatter and drop me into a pit of despair. I stumbled across a pallet of wood nestled between the corner of two buildings pressed terribly close together and plopped down on it, hidden from the worst of the sun. I wondered how anyone here found relief from the light that came from the sun and the stars up there as I sat on the pallet. How did they keep their skin from baking and peeling from them in large, torturous swaths?

Natives must spend most of their time inside, away from the light. Kanute was likely lounging inside one of these buildings somewhere. Did I run around and kick in every door to find him?

It was tough, but after some time, I realized that I had no options. I had nothing of value. I was at the mercy of fate.

Fate could have been trying to urge me on, telling me to get the hell out of there while I could. Sure, I'd already been burned by Kanute pretty bad. It was completely likely that it would only get worse from here. I couldn't fathom the idea of heading out into the forest again though. Not after going through what I had so far. I wanted some comfort, and more than the few minutes of reprieve I'd been allowed so far.

If that fire was going to come down from the sky, it would have to wait until I decided to leave.

I scooted into a corner, leaned my back against the wall of one of the buildings and began to fall into sleep immediately.

My head tilted and the knot back there rolled against brick. That woke me up like a shockwave to my spine. I found a good position for my head, one that I didn't think I would deviate from. The pain subsided and I quickly fell asleep.

***

The fire was gone. I stood in desolation. Dim lines made up the ruined city. Light from far away slowly descended. It went behind what looked like the tops of a tree-filled forest.

Ghosts rose up from the ground, their translucent forms twisting as they ascended. One flew up from the earth beneath me and stopped before my face. Clawed fingers reached out. They touched my forehead.

Skeletal features looked at me. I saw past the hand before my eyes and into the face of the ghost. Shrouded in darkness was bone and teeth. Pale blue light flashed inside the hollow pits of its head, giving the appearance of eyes.

"Die," it whispered, the noise riding a gust of wind past my ears and then off to forever ring on the air.

Chapter 7

Waking up felt right this time. There was some pain in my head, but not too much. I didn't feel an encroaching sense that something was bearing down on me. My eyes fluttered open and I was calm. I must have slept for hours. I felt quite rested.

I left myself in that same position for a time, collecting my thoughts, scrutinizing my journey so far. By now, Kanute had certainly gotten rid of the cub and the kiss. He'd traded them for something better or consumed the former himself. I was without anything again, except for the pit of anger smoldering in my gut.

My current predicament was so very similar to how waking in the forest alone had been. Had I even made any real progress at all? I still didn't know much about myself and had that terrible journey to resume, praying that I would discover who I was. I had nothing, barely even hope.

Even if I did find Kanute, how would I beat him? He seemed much more skilled than me. I was weak and terribly hungry. He'd figured out and survived in this horrid place for decades. He also had a knife, this much I was intimately aware of.

Would I simply get back on my journey? Should I stay in this city of thieves and ruthlessness?

I decided I would worry about my next move after I got some food in me. As I wiggled my way off the pallet, a portly man turned the corner of one of the buildings near me and was jogging right toward me. He was breathing heavily and sweating profusely.

"Hey!" He had to stop and lean against the wall. "Hey. Who? What are..." He must be passing out right now. His eyes had shut. Could I catch the fat man as he went crashing to the ground? Did I care to be so nice to try? Not really. If he did pass out, I could raid his person for something. I could find something to trade for some food.

Alas, he opened his eyes. Damn.

"Are you taking that? I didn't... You aren't supposed to be there. Where is Olef?"

"I don't know who you're talking about. I wasn't taking anything."

"Well." The fat man put up one finger and closed his eyes again. "You move. I need to sit."

He shambled over to the pallet and plopped down on it as I got up. Breath flooded into his wide open mouth and spewed back out in short bursts. He exhaled a great sigh and cursed, "Shit goddamn!"

I thought about leaving as the fat man huffed and puffed. "Should I just go?"

"What were you doing on my pallet?"

"Sleeping. It was just there so I slept on it."

"Why? Where is Olef? He was supposed to take this to a client of mine. I was almost screwed!"

"I don't know who that is. I just saw it and thought it would be a bit more comfortable than the ground."

"Why would Olef just leave this out here? Anyone could have taken it in a moment." He was silent but for a few massive breaths. Then he looked at me as if I wasn't built right and said, "Why didn't you take it?"

I shrugged. "I just didn't think about it. I could have traded this for something good, huh?"

"A month of food. Maybe more if you haggled right."

"Boy, I missed out."

"Damn straight you did."

"Maybe Olef found a better opportunity and couldn't bring the pallet with him."

"Maybe. And I bet with you sleeping on it people kept away as if you were guarding it."

"So... Do I get something for guarding it?"

"You did. You got a bed for a few hours."

"You still have to get this somewhere right?"

"Yes I do, and I see where you're going. Name a price."

"I don't know. What will get me a meal?"

"Moving the pallet. Deal. You help me, I'll get you a meal. I pick the food though."

"Done."

"Just give me some time here. I need to catch my breath a bit more. I'm not too great a runner."

"You don't say."

"That kind of smart ass talking won't help you when it's time to pick out your food. I'm thinking a handful of dead bugs at this point."

"I'll shut up. You take your time."

We both sat silently for a while. I imagined this was the first bit of luck I'd chanced across. Then reevaluated my thinking. Although I felt overworked and as though the world was against me, I'd been fortunate on several occasions. Morrissett had been near enough to hear me fall down the hill, save me, then heal my wounds. Jacqueline, if anything, was a sight of beauty in an otherwise terrifying land. The cub had helped me go on, even when I'd blacked out, and it felt damn good to have been a help to something.

The fat man sighed loudly, then said, "Alright. Let's get this done before I'm so late that I miss this deal."

"How far are we taking it?" I asked as I stood up.

He smacked his hands against his knees then pushed himself up, shaking as he did so. "Not too much farther. Olef got it most of the way there. He's a big son of a bitch. Easy job for that one. For you and I though, not so easy. I may be out of shape but you're under shape."

"Well let's see how good a team we make." I said as I pulled the pallet away from the walls. It was heavy. The crossing slats of wood were sturdy, thick, and far from perfectly rectangular in shape. The nails holding it together were quite large.

"What would someone want this whole thing for anyway?" I asked as I got behind it and gave it one last shove away from the walls.

"Protection. You feel that thin coat of sap?" I did, sticking to my hands and leaving behind a film. "One lick of flame and - Oof!" We both lifted the pallet. I thought my arms would snap. I pitched forward, sending fat man reeling back. He stumbled, I tripped, but we both kept ourselves upright. We wobbled back and forth for a moment until we found our balance.

I looked at him with an innocent smile. He glared at me seemingly in the hope that his stare would wilt the flesh from my body. "Sorry," I offered.

"You really need that meal. Come on, and shut up from now on. Just carry it. Don't do nothing else."

I nodded and we continued on. The pallet bit into my forearms, tried to pull my arms off my body. I felt as though this wood was still alive and fighting to take my life too.

We had to start and stop several times. Fat man would scream and holler at people who walked in our path.

Eventually, we found ourselves in front of a tent beneath which sat another tubby man. How could anyone get so overweight in a society where just the basic things seemed so difficult to come by?

We slowly put it down, both of us quaking. Sweat dripped from my forehead and I thought I was going to pass out. Actually, I did.

I stumbled and was about to go down when I ran into a man standing beneath the tent. He caught me and the feeling was akin to running into a brick wall. He shoved me away though and I kept myself from falling as I caught my balance.

All three men around me looked at me oddly. The man I had fallen on looked quite offended. So insulted was he, in fact, that he pulled a long knife from behind his back and twisted it around in his hand, staring at me with malice.

"Sorry. I'm not feeling well."

My fat employer said, "He hasn't eaten anything in a long time."

The other fat man seethed, "This is very late. And why are you doing your own scut work?"

"Olef ran off. This man took his place."

"I hope you don't plan to use him often."

"No. Just in a pinch. He was a little handy. But he's not worth much else."

The fat man sitting beneath the tent looked to me then said, "You can leave now."

I said, "But -"

"I told him I would feed him for his help."

"Then, here." The fat man snapped and the guard walked to a store of crates behind him. "Not too much. And nothing too good either. It looks like he'd eat maggots if they were on a plate for him."

The guard chuckled and threw me a contemptuous look, looking down on me and my weakness. He came back with two pears and a thin brown thing about as big as my palm. He showed them to the fat man who then nodded. The guard shoved the food into my chest and the brown thing snapped. It broke into three pieces, two of those hitting the floor and breaking a little further.

I bent down and scooped them up then immediately left. I quickly moved out of eyesight of the men and stuffed my face. The brown thing was some kind of biscuit. It was nearly tasteless besides a scant earthy flavor. The pears were hard, as if they had just been picked this morning and days before they were ready. I devoured all of it though.

My stomach craved more to fill it, but I was still content. Now, then, what to do?

Without a good decision, I went to the stream. And it seemed as though my luck was holding. Kanute was there. The cub was on a short leash tied to Kanute's belt. His back was to me as he fished. I walked up slowly, not sure what I was going to do.

The cub saw me and got up. It came toward me and was yanked back by the leash. It moved Kanute enough to cause him to turn his head. We locked eyes and I thought about rushing him.

"Oh, hey. How's that memory thing coming? Do you remember me? You must if you're sneaking up like that. What were you planning?"

"I don't know. But I want my stuff back. The rock and the cub. They're mine."

"The cub is mine. In fact, people are bidding for it even now. It'll fetch a very, very nice price. The rock though, I already sold that. So that belongs to someone else. Long story short, none of this stuff is yours."

Kanute turned back to the stream as if I didn't exist. I rushed forward and managed to wrap an arm around his neck. Next thing I knew, however, I was splashing down in the stream on my back. The water had cushioned my fall. Kanute stood over me. I attempted to ready myself for the death blow and realized how unprepared I was to die.

"I just want what's mine," I blurted.

"When you're weak, nothing is yours."

Kanute turned to leave. I got up and ran after him. I must have really wanted to die.

"Just tell me who you sold the rock to," I pleaded.

He stopped in his tracks. "Why?"

"Because I'm going to get it back."

"How?" He turned to face me.

"I'm going to steal it."

A smile pulled one corner of his lips up. "You're going to steal it? How?"

I marshalled the small bit of confidence from within and proclaimed, "Doesn't matter how. I'll do it though. I want it more than you know."

"You'll never get it done on your own."

"Then help me. I might not look like much, but I did spend most of a day out there in the wild. I fought my way here, and the things I encountered... Worse than anything even you can imagine." I was bluffing, but felt confident in my delivery. Hopefully, he wouldn't see through it.

Kanute was silent for a moment, actually considering my offer, although even I felt I didn't have a chance in hell at delivering on it. "Fine. We'll work together. Only, we're going to steal a lot more than just a rock."

***

"Here," Kanute snapped as he untied the length of rope from the cub's neck. He scampered over to me as soon as he slid from the leash, letting out a whimper.

"And the rock? I'll get that back too, right?"

"Maybe. We'll look for it. I can't promise you anything though."

How could I ever trust Kanute? I couldn't. Ever.

Regardless of my mistrust, I'd hold hands with damn near anyone in order to get back the little things I believed I could call mine. I'd call the devil himself my closest friend if he'd assist me in the least.

Kanute had taken us back to his home, which turned out to be a small one-room cell in a large building made of brick. There was a cot in the corner, two animal skins that covered it, a short table that one was meant to sit before by crossing their legs on the floor, and a window covered by crosshatched bars that barely let any light in from the outside. The cub had marked its spot, a corner empty of everything but its feces and urine.

Being inside, away from the sun was a welcome feeling. I didn't fret about my skin cooking off of me for the first time in a long while.

I sat on the floor, the cub insistent on using me as a big chew toy. He excitedly nipped at my fingers as I waved my hands before him. I suffered a few scratches that reminded me how dangerous he still was despite his size.

"How difficult is this going to be?" I asked as played with the cub.

"Either way you slice it, fucking hard. Aaliyah is beyond wealthy. Big fuckers for guards. She's got this... this, comet of stardust. It's a boulder in comparison to the stuff we normally see. We get even half of it and we'll have enough to last us a lifetime each. We'll be immortal, living in the forest without a care in the world really. We could travel all over the world!"

I didn't share Kanute's obvious thirst for travel. I couldn't, however, repress the thrill of hope that shot through me as I imagined that much stardust. Enough to allow me and the cub to dance through the forest without so much as another hiccup.

"You follow every order I give," he continued, "and this goes as smooth as possible. You don't, I chop that fur ball of yours up and sell his pieces."

I fixed my deadliest gaze on Kanute, the threat awakening a red fury within that begged him to try so I could tear his throat out.

He looked away as though I was nothing more than an angry insect and said, "She has a massive store of everything you can imagine in a warehouse smack in the middle of Haven. I'll make history, hunting these lands until I have a map that's a complete picture of the world."

"Hunting? You want to do all this just so you can go out and kill animals?"

"Memory problem again, huh? Hunters don't just kill animals, though that's important and well-paying work. Hunters exist in the forest for days, weeks even, and make it back to show their mettle. Shit's worth something, if you ask me."

I didn't care in the least to ask him. I just wanted back what was mine and to be on my way. Hell, if I felt like I could survive in the process, I'd up and leave the city now. But I didn't have a source of heat to keep the forest from consuming me, and I was certain that Kanute's knife would have a few sharp words with me if I tried that.

Kanute said, "We need to get a better look at her warehouse. It's not a palace, but it's big and I want to know what we're heading in to."

I continued focusing on the cub, partly because I missed him but mostly because I was afraid he would bite a finger clean off it I didn't, as I said, "So are there windows we can look through?"

"Nothing that will give us a good look. The windows have more metalwork than mine. Guards rotate between the warehouse and her home. Sometimes it's just the big ones. Other times there are more. The three giants have been with her for as long as I can remember. Once saw a guy ripped in half and his torso used to beat the living shit out of his buddy."

"Are you trying to scare me so much that I change my mind?"

"Just letting you know what we're up against. We'll be smart about it though. We'll get in there and map out the place before we make our attempt."

"Why don't the guards just steal the stardust? It seems like that's something people in this city do regularly."

"We steal when there is a good opportunity to do so. Those three giants aren't like normal men. They're content in her service. And they keep the others in check."

"So how do we get in?"

"By trading something. Aaliyah lives to barter and sell. We bring something of value and we'll have plenty of reason to take a look inside the warehouse. Once we know how it all looks, we'll know how to hit it."

I pulled the cub close to me. "You said he wasn't going to be sold. I'm not letting that happen."

Kanute rolled his eyes. "Oh, shut it. You sound like a child. We'll get something even better."

"Where? Are we going to steal something else?"

"We want one big score then we need to both disappear. We fuck up stealing one thing just so we can try stealing the thing we really want, then we'll be out there without a candle to save us. Even with that memory thing, you're quite the idiot."

"You're a real saint, Kanute."

"I know. Now, we are going to head out into the forest. We'll hunt for something that's worth a look in her warehouse."

"Have you spent much time out there?" I realized that asking such a question of someone born to this world was not too bright. Thankfully, Kanute let me know how much of a dipshit I was.

"I've spent enough. You think you can do better than I can out there? Only reason I don't hunt all day is lack of resources. Don't ask stupid questions. Now, I traded that rock of yours for this."

Kanute fished his hand behind the cot and came back with a net weighted at its ends with metal spheres. "This and a few other things. That was a real special rock you had."

"I could strike it on another and it'd make a shower of sparks. A mermaid gave it to me. Did I thank you for taking it from me yet?"

"A mermaid? And no, you didn't. Nor did you thank me for the knot on your head."

"At least I wasn't bleeding." I remembered that not even the mermaid knew she was a mermaid. "Never mind. When are we leaving?"

"Now sounds as good a time as ever." Kanute reached behind his cot again and this time pulled a sword off the floor. It was wrapped in leather. He revealed a thick, one-sided blade.

"For the forest?"

Kanute admired the sharp blade then said, "And anything else we run into out there."

***

It wasn't so easy to just get going like Kanute wanted. Or maybe he knew it was going to be as tough as it ended up being. We needed fire to go out there. All the stardust would have been behind walls, he said. Getting our hands on that was out of the question. We'd have to rely on torches.

There were stores of wood that weren't behind walls. We found several, each one watched over by a few weapon-wielding brutes. Workers dipped the ends in sap, some of them wrapped by a thick, rough material that reminded me of burlap. If only I had simply taken that pallet from earlier, we'd have all the wood we could ask for.

We were walking past a third pile of wood, several guards standing near it all, when I asked, "You don't have any at all?"

"Not enough at least. Shut up for a moment."

I rubbed the cub's side as we walked. Of course everyone stared at me greedily. I could have left him in Kanute's home but I didn't trust him not to have set it up so that someone would come and take the cub while we were gone. As far as I was concerned, I could only keep something in this city if I had it with me at all times.

Finally, after coming across one last hill of wood, Kanute said, "Okay. We will go back and hit the smallest we saw earlier. All the others have too many eyes."

I didn't know which one that was exactly. I wasn't counting muscle watching over the stores of wood like Kanute must have been. "Hit it how? We're just going to steal it all?"

"No. We can't take all of it. We'd need plenty more hands for that. You'll distract them, then I'll take what I can."

"Distract them how?"

"With one of the guards. You'll get tangled up into him and then you'll *accidentally* grab his thrower. Pull that trigger like your life depends on it. I want flames jumping all over the place. While all that is going on, I'll take a few torches."

I let the plan sink in and waited, mostly because I thought Kanute was screwing with me and was going to give me the real plan in a moment. Instead, he just nodded his head sharply once and looked at me as if I was an idiot. "Kanute, you can't actually think that will work. There's too much left to chance. Wouldn't the sentinel just light me up? How could I do it with the cub? Do you really think no one will notice you stealing an armful of wood?"

77

Kanute shrugged then said, "Much of my plan hinges on good luck. Why not start it by testing that?"

"Because we won't even make it out of the city. Nope. Find a new plan."

"Wasn't the deal that you do what I say?"

"Not when it involves something so insane." I had an idea. I didn't want to suggest it. It felt wrong. I knew I had to do something. Otherwise, Kanute would go through with something destined to fail. Helping him right now was just a means to help myself. "Animal skins."

"What?"

"I can't believe I'm doing this. The cub, he had a family. They were dead and inside the cave I found him in. They might still be there."

"Perfect! We'll use that to grab ourselves some torches. Hell, Aaliyah might even think them so valuable that we won't even need to go hunt for something bigger. Do we need to go through any forest?"

"No. But I won't go back in there without fire. There are things in the cave."

"Cave? You're talking about the basilisks, then?"

"Six-legged things covered in spikes?"

"Yup. That's their home. You made it out of there?"

"I wouldn't have if not for the fire. And the shadowy things seemed to repel them."

"Shadowy things? What do you mean?"

"The things that fly. You probably have some name for it. They're dark. Phantoms."

Kanute didn't snap back with an odd name. How could he not know what I was talking about? "Haven't you been inside the caves?"

"Yes, but I've never heard of or seen those. You sure you know what you saw in there?"

"I'm certain... I think. You sure you've actually been inside the caves?"

"Of course!" The intensity with which Kanute barked back had me thinking he'd only stuck a toe into the cave then called it a day.

I thought of how I had passed out then suddenly found myself outside of the cave. Had I been hallucinating? No. The cub was real. I was holding him even now.

"I'll keep an eye out for them," he continued, steering the conversation away from his apparent lie. "We'll do things your way this time. Come on, I have one torch at my place. Not enough to get us far in the forest, perhaps an hour of time. Is that all we'll need?"

"Less than that even."

"Good."

Despite the knowledge that this likely wouldn't end well, I still couldn't stem the excitement building in me. I didn't need to jump a man with a rod that shot fire, but now I needed to go back into the cave. I wondered which was worse, but still followed Kanute to his home.

Chapter 8

Someone must have wanted me to look like a real nutcase. We entered the cave, me sticking close to Kanute and his torch. No phantoms. And it seemed as though the light from the torch reached much further than mine had.

"Memory problems, right?" Kanute asked. He smirked at me over his shoulder.

I was sure they had been here. I decided to stifle any reply, kept an eye and ear out for proof and continued on. The sooner we got out of here, the better.

"We almost there?" he asked after we'd walked along the winding path of mud and hard dirt surrounded by black water for a few minutes. The massive cavern was too big for our light to reach its end. I kept thinking that I saw the mouth to the enclosure where I'd come across the tigers but it never emerged from the deep darkness.

"I think so. I'm not sure exactly."

"How could you forget something that soon?"

"Well, I didn't really get out of here by just walking out. I passed out. I just woke up outside."

"You blacked out then. If you had really passed out, you would've either drowned or been eaten. We keep on for five more minutes. If we don't find them, we go back and do it my way."

"We'll make it there before the torch runs out. Besides, there's no guarantee that we'll run into any trouble here. Your method, though, and we'll be neck deep in angry, weapon-wielding guards."

"We'll run into something. You can be certain of that."

It was unfortunate that I held a cub instead of a weapon. I hoped Kanute was good with that blade. The cub squirmed against my stomach, his eyes shifting back and forth, peering into the dark, searching for the bastards that had killed his family.

We plodded along until I finally spotted the tunnel that lead to where I had found him. I pointed it out and Kanute nodded grimly.

"That'll be a good place for them to wait. Bet we find a few of the basilisks in there. More than a few even."

"When I came through it, they seemed to be hesitant to go in. The first one I fought came after me hard and fast. Not the others."

"You fought one?"

"Well I didn't kill it. I burned it and blinded it. It turned and ran off at some point."

"How big was it?"

"Um... I guess the cub's mom was close to its size."

Kanute nodded his head then said, "Maybe we'll be that lucky this time."

I nodded despite my inability to understand exactly what would be so lucky about running into one of those creatures again.

As we closed the distance to the tunnel, I thought of the phantoms. How could I have seen them and Kanute not ever have even heard of them? Was all of that in my head? That couldn't be right; I had blacked out because of them. They had to be real.

We got to the mouth of the cave and Kanute raised a hand, stopping me dead. I thought I heard something clicking on the ground. The sound, if it were real at all, vanished as quickly as it came. Was that a flash of movement in the cave? The stalactites suddenly looked menacing, like razor sharp, thin fangs that were even now descending on us. The darkness grew thick yet again, eating the light of the torch before it could reach far. I imagined Kanute and I walking into the cave to find that it was actually an abyss where we would never escape from.

He waved his hand forward and we continued. The absence of sound made me imagine that something was lying in wait within the shadows to ambush us. Even the cub was mute. I wanted to howl, to break the silence. I was afraid to even breathe. I felt like thousands of horrors, their lithe bodies covered in limbs that could shred and pulverize flesh with ease, were converging on me, masking their sounds with stealth. Hearing the ominous splashing of a predator descending on me would have been comforting when compared to this space of time void of noise.

We crept into the chamber. The firelight reached as far as the walls and nearly to the other side of the tunnel. Blood stained the ground. Fur was strewn about, ripped from the bodies of the cub's family by the basilisks. Crimson trails were all around the cavern, painting the floor in a demonic, chaotic scene. The beasts had fought over the bodies, flinging and dragging them about as they tore the meat from their bones.

I wondered first if the cub understood. How did I fail to imagine this to be a possibility? Looking at it now, it made more sense than any other option, especially finding the animals intact and waiting retrieval.

"Goddammit!" Kanute hissed. "There's nothing left to take. Back up slowly."

I listened, afraid even to move my eyes too quickly for fear that even that would attract the attention of the basilisks surely lurking in the shadows. My toes came down on the ground as if it were made up of bear traps. There was that clicking noise again, which turned my skin to gooseflesh as though hundreds of bugs with sharp legs had just travelled down my body from head to feet. I shivered and wanted to tear my skin off to rid myself of the feeling. My body twitched and I took a quick step back. My heel hit something. A rock. It clattered off along the ground and struck the wall. Something hissed nearby, sounding so very close but still hidden from my sight somehow.

Two shimmering lights suddenly twinkled on the other end of the cavern. Then, they multiplied by too many to count. I continued on, shuffling back slowly. I only managed a half step when Kanute suddenly turned and bolted past me. Something hit me in the back, knocking me toward the horde. An earth-shaking chorus of hisses, screeches, and roars permeated the air as basiliks leapt from the shadows and bounded toward me.

I turned and sprinted after Kanute. I felt the cub writhe against me. I screamed incoherently as I ran. Fear didn't just affect me, it became me. I couldn't think of anything else. I even let go of the cub. He sank his claws deep into my chest and stomach, shocking me back to reality, destroying at least a little of the fear with pain. I gripped him yet again and continued on.

The creatures at my back screamed, their chorus of mixed, demented songs ringing as though from a single demon from the depths of Hell. My legs moved of their own accord, covering bounds of distance twice that of my normal step. I may have even been flying.

The stampeding creatures grew closer and I could feel their feet pounding the earth. The bite was soon to come. Teeth would sink into my calf, pulling the muscle clean from my leg. Then, I'd be devoured in a moment. My body, my blood would be spread out over this cave just like the tigers had been.

I barely recognized the moment when I exited the enclosure and was darting across the muddy bank in the wide open cavern. A loud thud came from behind me followed by a deathly roar. I spared a look over my shoulder and saw a commotion ensuing in the cave mouth. The basilisks had stopped somehow, wedged against one another in their attempt to consume me.

But the roaring and screeching was too much to allow me any relief. I fled faster, toward the circle of light at the exit. Although it was in sight, it was still several hundred feet away, and my heart sank at the distance that separated me from it. Something slammed down on the bank behind me, slapping the mud heavily. I chanced another look and saw what would surely kill me.

A basilisk, the point where its leg met its body as tall as I was, covered in hundreds of bones of spike as sharp as swords, was bounding after me. Another one similar in stature trailed it, competing with each other for my body. Dozens of others much smaller but up to half their size followed. The one I had faced was just a babe. These were the ones that had torn the tigers apart.

I turned my head back and put my eyes down as I ran. Kanute was still a good distance ahead of me. He was closing on the exit faster than I was also. Even so, I didn't believe he would make it out.

It wasn't long before the pounding steps of the beast behind me began to shake me so much that I didn't think I could run any longer. The exit was still at least a hundred feet from me. Kanute might actually make it out as long as they all feasted on me, and I was sure he relied on that possibility to survive.

I veered toward the water then dove. I heard snapping jaws, a thunderous clack splitting the air inches from my heels. I lost my grip on the cub and he wasn't quick enough to sink a hold on me. He careened through the air to my side. We both splashed down and my head sank beneath the water.

I rolled and swam away, then popped up facing the horde. Towering and riddled with muscle, the closest one fixed its terrible gaze on me. The cub's head bobbed at the surface of the water as he swam back to shore, meowing loudly. Then, the great basilisk pounced on him. I lost him beneath the fountains of water that shot up, beneath claws and muscle, and screamed out in despair.

Other beasts were coming down on the cub, although there was likely nothing left for them. I wouldn't waste what opportunity I had been given. I turned and sprinted from the water. Kanute was just exiting the cave. I slipped several times but kept my feet beneath me and never stopped. I needed to go as hard and fast as I could, anything less and I was dead.

The ground beneath me began to harden as I came to the exit. I heard the wet slaps of the basilisks turn into clicks and scratches and knew that at least some had given up on getting a piece of the cub and were coming for me. Kanute stood at the exit, a black silhouette against the brightness. His machete was as dark as his body, sticking up from his hand, poised to strike.

I was nearly out when a claw sliced into my calf. I didn't slow at all, but neither did my pursuer. Kanute suddenly swung his blade toward my stomach. He was going to cut me in half! I leapt and pulled my legs up, hoping that would be enough to save me from death. The blade cut the air a hair beneath me and I was sailing through the open air, bathed in sunlight that was blinding.

I heard a weak screech then Kanute grunted. I hit the hard stone ground and was rolling across it. The world spun so rapidly that I felt sick. It pummeled me with stone fists all along my body. I came to a stop and wanted to lie still while I assessed myself. To do so, however, would be to invite the widow maker to a brief and painful meeting.

I clambered to my feet then immediately went down on one knee. The world seemed to be pitching back and forth, the sunlight only aiding my vertigo, and the pain in my calf did me no favors.

"Where's the cub?" That was Kanute's voice.

I cracked an eye. I could see his waist. I couldn't look up any higher. He was rocking side to side, but so was the ground. In his hand was the bloody machete.

"I couldn't keep him."

Kanute's knuckles clamped down harder on the hilt then they flexed open and closed one at a time. Was he going to kill me now?

I remembered what he had done earlier. I was beginning to feel better as I got breath back into my lungs. "Are they still after us?"

"No. They won't come out into the light."

"What about the one that chased me? It came out after me."

"It thought it could get to you before it left the cave. You really screwed us. I'm not too keen on what you put me through either."

"You shoved me. You threw me to the beasts." I felt well enough to stand. I didn't think Kanute knew my eye had been cracked open the entire time. I waited for him to raise the machete. I was going to tackle him, run him back into the cavern.

"Better you distract them instead of me. Besides, what's that matter? We both made it."

"You would have lost the cub anyway then."

"Not if I would have had him. I should have sold him when I had the chance."

Squinting, I looked upon Kanute. Blood spattered his arm and cheek. Over his shoulder, slumped at the cave entrance, was a basilisk bleeding a pool of red onto the white stone. The contrast of color was breathtaking at first. It made both the stone and blood look pure, like they were two perfect substances blending.

"That is why you aren't dead," Kanute barked. "The basilisk will get me much more than the cub would have."

Screeches and yelps came from the cave. The cub was bounding up the ramp and near the exit, a basilisk scrambling in pursuit. It snapped its jaws on the air right behind the cub and then tripped over its dead kin. It stumbled across the stone, slipping in the blood. Its eyes were shut against the sun.

Kanute darted for it, despite its being twice the size of the one he killed earlier. The cub ran toward me but failed to stop and instead continued on as though I didn't exist. I wanted to turn and grab him but was fixated on Kanute. He closed on the disoriented basilisk quickly and chopped down at its head. He hit flesh and the bone atop its head. One eye was gashed and ruined and even I could see the bone beneath the cut. Somehow, the basilisk wasn't dead.

The beast whirled and caught Kanute's leg with one of its own. Kanute stumbled to the side then fell down hard. The basilisk whirled toward him and charged. I watched in anticipation of it leaping atop him and mauling him to death. It was at least as big as him if not bigger. I would be free of Kanute.

But he sat up, opened his legs, and brought the blade down with two hands. This time, the blade sank down through flesh and shattered skull. It was dead instantly.

I turned to find the cub. He stood at the edge of the stone path, one paw in the grass, eyes on me. I took a step to move and grab him but something stopped me. I whispered, "Go! Get!" while flicking my hand at him. He wouldn't budge though.

He stood a better chance away from Kanute.

I continued on until the machete slid across my shoulder. Kanute was breathing heavily behind me. "What are you doing?"

I didn't say anything. He knew what I was doing, telling him wouldn't accomplish anything.

"Go pick him up. He's mine until we finish our job."

85

I did as I was told. I walked halfway to the cub then bent down and rubbed my fingers together. He heeded my invitation. He ran to me and then put his head against my hand. I looked down at him and felt a pang of sadness for us both. We were both in a place we shouldn't be without a thing to lean on and with plenty of enemies we didn't ask for pitted against us.

"Good," said Kanute. "Now come help me. This is all we'll need to get inside that warehouse."

I grabbed the cub and held him against my chest, now bloody in several spots from his claws. "Will it be enough to trade for the stardust and the rock?"

Kanute continued walking to the basilisks and said, "Every basilisk in this cave wouldn't be enough to buy all that stardust. Maybe a week's worth. And I couldn't care less about that rock."

I ambled over to the corpses. I wondered how we would get them back to the city. It was a long walk and they were both heavy. If we worked together we could get one, and probably just the smaller of the two.

I was looking down at the basilisks when Kanute said, "Hey. You're right, I tried to kill you in there. Don't think I won't put you in front of me just like that every time death is coming my way. But we made it out, and you have nothing to worry about right now. This ended up working out. Still, you know what I'm capable of. Don't fuck up again."

What a heartwarming thing to say. Then and there I vowed that the next time I fucked up, I'd include Kanute's death in it.

***

A sea of wonderstruck faces on still bodies with dinner plate eyes greeted us. That is how one describes the majority of the people in the city when one comes strolling in with two dead basilisks on a cart. Kanute had given me his machete, taken the cub, then went into Haven Sprawl to acquire the cart. It was difficult to part with the cub, but I didn't think Kanute would risk pissing me off when I had his favorite weapon, even if I wasn't any good at using it.

Even with the wheels, getting the basilisks into the city was nearly an impossible feat. The cart kept wanting to take off down the steadily descending trail of stone. I stood at the back of it, holding the handles and pulling with all my might most of the time. Kanute was at the front, keeping his hands on the basilisks and pushing with what looked like only some effort most of the time. I wondered if I just let go... Would it roll over him and maybe a wheel crush his head?

But I didn't. I wanted the rock back, and needed a few torches. Maybe I could even get my hands on some stardust.

Merchants swarmed us the moment we walked into Haven and Kanute told them all to screw off. None listened as they tried ever harder to make the best offer. They even begged me to make a deal, several times including the cub I held. We were slowing rapidly and I began to think that they would just take everything from us in a moment anyway. We were in the middle of a mob that desperately wanted what we had.

I felt them inching closer, touching their noses to mine, shaking my shoulders. I took my hand from the handles and just stood there, gripping the cub tightly, on the verge of curling into a ball to keep him close to me. He flexed his claws against me and my eyes began to water due to the little holes he put in my skin. He lashed out once and caught a man across the forearm. The man yelped and leapt back but immediately resumed screaming about what he could trade for our bounty.

Kanute noticed that I had stopped and I saw through the throng of people that he had stood tall and was eyeing me with death written on his face. He turned to the people then unhooked his machete from his belt. He suddenly shouted then swung it above the heads of several of the vultures crowding him. They threw themselves to the ground and shut up.

Kanute then leapt atop the cart and stood on the ribcage of the largest basilisk. He pointed his blade at the crowd and swept it back and forth slowly. He hollered, "Listen up! Another one of you idiots gets within my range and I cut your stupid head off. This is not mine to deal with. This is Aaliyah's property. The cub is too. Last and only warning. Move!"

He suddenly leapt down with the machete raised above his head. People dove and pushed backward, forcing the whole crowd back. Kanute brought his blade down and nearly cut through the skull of one fat woman, her hair a mess and partly pasted to her brow from profuse sweating.

To her good fortune, the blade cut through nothing but air and the people scurried away. Kanute smiled at me wickedly as he stood up. I wondered if he would have even felt remorse had his blade caught her. I felt like I could suddenly breathe after being trapped under water.

Kanute took up his place again and I took mine. We began to move the cart. A brave few still hawked deals at us but kept their distance. Soon, we were in front of a building with a massive canopy stretched above its entrance. A large door of wood with bands of metal nailed into it stood shut, walling us off from a peek inside the warehouse. Beneath the canopy stood two giants.

They must have been at least two heads taller than me. I wondered if they were even human. Their eyes seemed distant and they didn't react to the basilisks, to me, or to Kanute. They were both bald and reddish of skin. One had a beard and the other was missing half an ear. It seemed as though he hadn't even cared to salvage what he could after such an injury; the remainder was gnarled, even tattered at one point.

Armor of grey metal covered their chests, groin, and thighs. Those massive arms were left bare and wrapped by thick muscle.

Kanute grunted as he pulled the cart a few inches closer. I had stopped pushing the cart in my awe of the two giants.

"Can I see Aaliyah?" Kanute asked.

One-Ear asked, "For the cub?" His voice wasn't as deep as I expected from such a large man.

"I've decided to keep that. For the basilisks."

Both of the giants kept their lifeless eyes on the cart for a moment. They then looked at one another. Were they communicating somehow? They both sheathed their swords, longer than my arm and as thick as their biceps. Beard pulled the curtain back from the door and One-Ear gripped a handle on it and pulled. The door slid up above the giant's head until it locked in place at the sound of a click.

One-Ear disappeared inside and Beard turned to face us, clearing his weapon and putting its tip in the ground before him. That thing could cut both Kanute and I in half, and the man holding it would have no problem doing so, as strong as he was.

A thin woman with a black braid twisting around her shoulder and hanging across her breasts came strolling out. She wore a green, gaudy dress with gold trim. Baubles galore clung to and dangled from her. One-Ear followed and I could see several other figures, albeit much closer to my size standing within the warehouse. The dimly lit building didn't provide us with a good look from out here. We'd need to get inside to survey it the way we needed.

"What a catch!" Aaliyah said as she glided past Kanute and to the side of the cart. She ran her gold and jewel covered hand across the larger basilisk, stroked its horned head, then stuck two fingers into its skull. I watched in horror as she twisted around brain and blood. "Still warm even."

The wet, sticky noise that came from her playing in brain matter made vomit rise in my throat. I was sure I was going to puke when she smiled at me. Cold surged through me, whether from fear or excitement, I didn't know.

She kept looking at me and I felt small. I looked away but she said, "Who are you?" turning my head back around.

"Me?" Shit, I didn't even know that. Did I just make up a name on the spot? I almost said Kanute. "Um... I helped Kanute with this."

"That's who you are? That's not the most informative answer. Do you live here?"

She kept playing in the basilisk's skull. Chips of bone and strands of brain covered her fingers. How could she just carry a conversation like this?

"He's kind of an idiot." Kanute said, capturing my attention from Aaliyah's sick behavior.

"And yet he has the cub you were going to sell me. No, there's more to him that he doesn't want to tell me. I can see his mind working behind his eyes. What are you not telling me?"

"He doesn't know. He has memory issues."

"Like what? And shut up, Kanute. I'm talking to the man with the tiger, not you."

I thought myself to have a pretty good understanding of Kanute's character by now. His shoulders popped up as he dismissed the insult as if it was no more than a gust of wind caressing his cheek. He turned his attention on me, waiting an answer as much as Aaliyah was. Had this been anyone else, I would have expected fire to spew from his ears. As it was, even I both respected and feared Aaliyah enough to know that she could insult me anyway she wanted and I wouldn't so much as frown at her.

I stared back at Aaliyah's fingers and nearly forgot that I was supposed to speak. She cleared her throat and I looked back to her, my eyes blinking several times. "I don't know who I am. I just came to a few days ago. No memory."

"So you hooked up with Kanute? Anyone with half a brain would've stayed away from him. Then again, looks like you both make one goddamn lucky pair." She slid her gore covered fingers from the basilisk's skull and advanced on me. She gripped my shoulder with those bloody fingers and rubbed the cub's head with her other hand.

I wanted to rip her hand from my body. She let go then began cleaning her hands on the front of my shirt.

"Kanute," she said casually, "how the hell did you kill these two basilisks? We both know you aren't a hunter."

There was that character I knew. Kanute lost his slight smile and adopted a frown. "Well I took both of these out on my own."

"But why?"

"You ask a lot of questions for a merchant."

She was apparently satisfied with her fingers, despite their still being blood-stained. "Whoops, missed some." She plucked a bit of brain from a ring and held it over the cub's head, right before my eyes. The cub looked up and pawed for it. She let it fall and he snapped it out of the air and swallowed the gray, mushy string.

"I'm more than just a merchant, you know that." She walked back to stand before the giants. "Besides, if you want to deal with me, you should answer all my questions."

"We went looking for something. Catching shrimp in the stream isn't doing it for me and this idiot said he knew where we could find the cub's family. Well, the basilisks found them first. We got lucky that we even got out alive. Two of them followed us out into the light. You know how they do in the sun."

"See. Not a hunter. That's the equivalent of killing a sleeping man."

I recalled the cowardly way he had hit me in the back of the head so that I'd be a distraction for the basilisks. I hadn't really seen him actually fight something or someone face to face that wasn't disoriented or surprised. Maybe he wasn't the hunter he claimed to be.

"Then sell me something that will help me out. I want two throwers. And a bit of stardust."

"Not a chance. I wouldn't even give you one thrower, let alone two and some stardust, for both of these."

"Weapons and armor then," Kanute demanded, crossing his arms.

"One blade and one set of armor."

"Deal. But I want to see what weapons and armor you have."

"Then I'll bring out a few things for you to choose from."

"No. I want to see it all. I know you have a lot in that building. This is a catch worth a look at all of it."

A pit of cold nervousness opened in my stomach. I was fearful of things getting too heated and Aaliyah suspecting something. Or, she could just outright hurt us. I wouldn't put it past her to have Beard and One-Ear twist our limbs into unhealthy, painful positions then send us off.

"Fine. Bring those inside with you." She nodded to the basilisks and I nearly sighed loud enough for her to hear me. Kanute fixed me in place with a deadly glare and I held my breath, fearful that she'd whirl on me. She continued on as though she hadn't heard me and the tension melted away from me, my shoulders slumping in relief.

Kanute and I resumed our positions at the cart, the cub sitting on it next to the basilisks. He began to paw at the brain matter spilling from the open wound in the corpse's skull and I swatted his backside to no effect. He spun on me and took a playful swipe at me then went back to the basilisk's brain.

The giants stood to either side of the doorway, towering pillars that loomed over us and promised violence at the slightest transgression. I shrank beneath their gaze, hoping they'd pay more attention to Kanute than me. We passed from the blistering sunlight and into the cool shade within the warehouse. Shadows clung to everything, the ceiling only barely visible by the pinpoints of light above that let in shafts of sun.

Playing inconspicuous was damn hard to do. Kanute didn't fair too well either. A maze of shelves, chests, and armoires wound through the middle of the compound, some of them so tall as to resemble mountain peaks. Hunks of ore sat in piles atop the shelving, red, gold, and blue in color. Weapons leaned against and hung within the armoires. Armor gleamed when the pinhole shafts of light struck their metal surface. Dozens of other items were strewn about the maze, some of it in an orderly fashion, most of it piled wherever there was room.

"Leave those there," Aaliyah commanded as she strolled around a cabinet and disappeared into the maze. Several other guards followed her in, two others taking a position behind Kanute and I.

We plodded forward uncertainly, our eyes turning often to the naked steel held in hands of the guards. Tarps covered several rectangular shapes placed near the concrete walls of the warehouse, the nearest inventory another ten feet away from them. The corner of a wooden pallet stuck out from under one tarp and I realized that they were placed as a defensive barrier in the event that the forest somehow breached the city walls and came for the people. I scooped up the cub and then we slipped away into the maze.

Beard and One-Ear stomped to the corners of the maze, their massive heads poking above the shelving and peering down on us. We were getting a damn good look at the inside of the warehouse, and it was terrifying. How did Kanute expect us to take this place with the half dozen guards and two, or even three, giants that kept watch over it?

I shrank into the background as Aaliyah and Kanute made their deal.

"You learn how to use a bow yet?" she asked Kanute.

"I'd actually need a bow in the first place to learn, wouldn't I?"

"Yeah. So how about one now?"

"I'll stick with a sword. I've had this one for years. It's done me good, but I can't go wrong with a new one. You got anything sharper and shinier than this?" He patted the sword hanging from a loop in his belt at his side.

"Everything I have is of better quality than that piece of shit. Here, pick one." She threw open an armoire and within there was a rack with a dozen blades hung by their hilts from it.

Kanute selected a few, testing their weight and feel in his hand, slicing the air. He finally decided on one after balancing it on the back of his hand and holding it steadily for a few moments. It resembled his current machete in shape and size, but seemed a shinier, more reflective metal. "Armor?" he asked.

We moved along to another rack with a suits of armor hanging from it, helms and gloves piled on a shelf above, boots and greaves sitting below. Kanute rifled through them, pulled a suit of dark brown leather studded with brass and sporting a few plates of steel to cover his chest and stomach from the rack and threw it on. It slid into place well and he zipped up the middle of the suit then stretched in it. It looked quite impressive, and it was obvious to see that he was instantly sold.

"How about torches to go with it?"

Aaliyah smiled innocently, the fear she'd instilled in me melting away and giving way to a hot stirring in my loins. I grew intensely interested in her, the curve of her lips, the soft skin of her breasts visible above the low cut of her dress, the sway of her hips. Then, she spoke, and the fear returned. "How about you get the fuck out of my warehouse now, Kanute?"

We barely had time to nod before we were being pushed back out of the maze and into the sunlight. A guard shoved the pants that matched the jacket Kanute had traded for into his arms then disappeared back into the warehouse, hidden behind the giants standing at the entrance.

Aaliyah strode out and said, "You sure you don't want to trade that cub. I'll give you enough stardust to last you a few days."

Before Kanute could blurt a response, I hollered, "No! He's not for sale!" as I hugged him close.

She shrugged and said, "Don't bring the girl next time, Kanute."

He was too busy admiring his new swag to look at her, but mumbled, "Trust me, I won't."

Chapter 9

Kanute's plan was idiotic and full of holes. It was going to fail and we would die.

I didn't try to talk him out of it though. I didn't offer up any great alternatives. I wasn't past antagonizing him though. After dealing with him and his disdain for me as long as I had, I was growing tired of him and that meant the fear had less control over me than it probably should have.

"You're an idiot, Kanute," I mumbled as I stroked the side of the sleeping cub, sitting on the floor of Kanute's home, my back leaning against the wall.

He sliced the air with his new blade again. "It's so much lighter than my other one. Come again?"

"I have just realized that you're really an idiot." It felt good to say that.

"Because you think my plan is shit. What then?"

"I don't have anything else."

"Then we're both idiots."

"I just don't care. To hell with you and everything else. You're a shit hunter too. Shouldn't a hunter have brains?"

"And they should be daring. They should realize when they don't have anything to lose. I've spent my whole life getting shrimp out of a fucking stream. If doing this gets me killed, then so what. But if it gets me that stardust, then I'll have something to actually live for. So I don't give a shit if it's a bad idea or not."

The reason for his existence, for his brutal attitude and willingness to take advantage of people finally came out. I was livid that I had no control over anything that had happened to me since I'd awoken in the forest. At the moment, it was Kanute who held the reins, so I hated him most of all. I wanted to take the cub, take a torch, and disappear into the forest. As it was, he was demanding that I leave the cub locked up here as we go commit a suicidal mission.

Fury bubbled in me, and I couldn't hold it in. "Goddammit, Kanute, you don't need me for any of this! Let me leave with the cub."

He waved the idea from the air as if shooing a fly and said, "I'd likely be better off with anyone else, but you'll have to suffice. I need two sets of hands and two sets of eyes for this to work. Besides, you leave now and I'm keeping the cub, which means you won't."

"You don't know what I've been through. It isn't just you. This whole fucking world has treated me like this, Kanute! I'm sick of it! I deserve a break. I deserve to get what I want!"

Kanute turned his cold gaze on me, icy spears piercing me. "You don't *deserve* anything. You earn it. And so far, you haven't earned shit."

"Bullshit! I've earned something. If not for me, you wouldn't have any of that. I'm the reason you got the basilisks. You won't let me go, I get that. But I want something." I thought of the ruthlessness of this world and realized the importance of fighting to survive. "I want your old blade."

"Nope," he said plainly.

"You give me that blade or I'm done. I'll get up and leave this moment. I mean it. With or without the cub." I stood for effect, hoping he wouldn't call my bluff.

Kanute was silent for a moment, inspecting his new blade and mulling over what I said. "Fine," he relented. "You can borrow it for today. We do well, and you can keep it."

***

Sharp, heavy metal hanging at my waist was not something I was used to and I couldn't deny how good it felt. I liked the power that came with that machete hooked to a belt around my pants. I don't think I'd felt anything like it before.

I wanted to take it to Kanute's neck. Images of the steel slicing through flesh and muscle, a geyser of blood spraying back at my face as the machete opened his trachea and snapped his spine, flooded my mind. He'd turn his eyes on me, opened wide in terror and surprise. Then, I'd watch the life drain from them as he pitched to the side and slumped to the ground dead. I wondered if he knew how I felt.

We walked together, quiet and determined. Sunlight beat down on us, exposing us. I quelled the urge to rub my already seared neck and nose, knowing that the pain that would follow would be far worse than the discomfort I endured now. I felt like every prying eye that fell on us knew what we were doing. I also felt like they didn't care.

We were only in the first stage of the plan. It'd been a difficult thing to leave the cub locked up in that tiny room Kanute called a home. I'd been curious about certain things, those that lead Kanute to this idea, but I kept my mouth shut until now.

"So the flamethrowers are just sitting in a bunker in the middle of the city? Anyone can get to them?"

"Yes and no. They are certainly sitting there. But not everyone can get them. A hunter has to be able to coerce. Let's see how good I really am."

"So you're going to lie our way in?"

"We'll be going on a special hunt for a family of bison that we saw earlier while coming back from another hunt. They'll send a few others with us. I'll be a liaison of Aaliyah's. You'll be a guide that knows the forest and caverns."

"But I don't. And won't I have to act like I know stuff?"

"Not really. You'll just have to keep saying that the forest has been moving, shifting as the bison trampled through. But someone might see that there aren't any tracks. Well, who am I kidding, they're all going to see that. The shifting forest will give us a bit of credibility at first. But there would be tracks at some point. And they'll know that."

"So what do we do then?"

"I don't know. That's the part about being a hunter that I'll have to prove."

"What is this obsession about? Why does it matter if you're a hunter or not?"

"I've been nothing my whole life. I've always wanted to head out into the forest and survive for months. I just want to know what's out there. Hunters can do that kind of thing, easy. They can stay out in the forest for as long as they want. They're smart enough and ballsy enough to make it. Everyone else isn't. There are things out there that I want to see."

For Kanute being the person he was, I was surprised by his answer. It hinted that he had another side to himself that actually thought deeply about things and sought a purpose in life. I wouldn't dare tell him that though. It would seem too much like a compliment.

I pondered for a moment what one really needed in order to hold the title of "hunter". My experiences thus far had taught me that nothing but random fate chose what someone was and the events that befell them. I hadn't chosen this journey, just as Kanute hadn't chosen the life of fishing for tiny morsels in a stream. We both wanted to change our predicaments, and recognizing that we shared something in common was sickening.

I remained quiet and Kanute just continued on walking. After several blocks had fallen away behind us, he said, "What will you do once this is over? You'll have to leave immediately."

"Go to God, I guess."

"What? That's it. No, you have to explain it better than that. And, in case you haven't heard yet, no one ever makes it past the Sentinel."

"I don't know who I am. Someone said I should travel the path of stones and someone else told me that God waits inside a kingdom at its end. So that's what I'm doing."

"So all that memory bull was real? Hm. Well, what have you been doing staying here then? Shouldn't you be on your way?"

"I wanted a break. I dealt with a lot of new and terrible things before getting here. Being able to sit down without a tree trying to smash me to death was nice."

"Yeah, that always feels good after being out there for any amount of time. You know, they've gotten inside here before."

I didn't care too much but I felt as though talking to him would at least keep my mind from drifting to the cub. I wouldn't get the urge to make use of his machete so soon then run on back to the small tiger. "How?" I asked, my tone flat.

"You seen the Ochari? The things that look like reptiles but walk around like us?"

I was suddenly interested. "I thought I had seen one. What did you call them?"

"Oh-car-ee. Yeah, well we haven't always been on great terms. We aren't now even. I want to leave before they come back with all the green shit with them."

"They bring the forest? How?"

"That stream used to be a bit bigger. It also wasn't so well sealed up. They broke it open and kept sending stuff down. It was all wet so fire didn't work all that great. They have other ways. Weapons too. See, the forest doesn't attack them, and they want the things we have. When we don't come to good compromises, a fight happens. They attack and try to put us back in line. It never works but then we all agree to stop fighting and they get a little something. Then, we keep making deals. They can hunt a lot better than we can. They get to see the whole world and walk around without fear. I should have been one of them."

So there were several reasons why he was so desperate to get out. No wonder his plans seemed half-baked and rushed. "That why the guards are always walking around with the flamethrowers?"

"Partly. They are there always. Just a bit more now. We all become guards if the Ochari come over the walls though. Fire in every persons' hand and a fight to survive. I've been in one when I was younger. We're here."

From his hard tone, I knew that meant it was time to shut up.

A squat, rectangular building of grey stone was before us. We approached a door with two guards standing outside of it. Each had a flamethrower, a metal helm, and also a curved blade hanging from their hips.

Kanute hailed them by raising a hand then said, "Would there happen to be an officer I can speak with?"

One of them said, "Concerning what?"

"My guide and I were coming back from a hunt when we spotted a family of bison. It hasn't been long since we saw them. We hoped to get a team together to hunt them down."

"Bison? I haven't had bison since I was a boy! I'll get someone for you."

"Thank you. We'll wait out here."

The guard who had been speaking pulled an oddly shaped stone key from a pouch on his lower back beneath his pack and used it to unlock the thick stone door. He pushed it open and went inside the dimly lit station.

The other guard said, "How many were in the family?"

"From what we saw, at least ten. Maybe there were more."

"You're a hunter, right? You didn't try capturing any of them?"

"We were already full. We had two basilisks with us."

"That was you two? Wow. Yeah, I heard about that. How'd you manage to get them?"

"They chased us out of their cave. Usually, they stop well before they get into the light. Seems like two of them must have been extra hungry. They came right out and were blind immediately."

"That's the luckiest hunt if ever I heard of one. What would compel people to go inside the basilisk caves?"

"My guide has been through them before. He's masterful when it comes to hiding and moving quietly. He thought we could get in and take out one then get back out quickly. We ended up attracting far more attention than we wanted and had to book it. Worked out in the end though."

"I'd say. Well, if we get authorized to go on this hunt then I want to see the both of you in action."

Just as Kanute was going to respond, the door opened. All I could think about was how I was now supposed to play the role of someone who was a master at stealth. I didn't think I could pull that off. With my luck I'd end up tripping over every fallen leaf and upturned grain of soil right in front of the people I was supposed to be deceiving.

A middle-aged woman came out, her brown hair short and straight, hiding the crow's feet branching out from her right eye while leaving bare her left. She smiled when she saw us then said, "A family of bison? It's certainly interesting. But you came back with the basilisks a while ago. How can you be sure that they haven't moved on by now?"

"We can't. But they would have stopped at the stream to rest. They could take quite a while there. When my guide saw them, he watched them for a moment and saw that they were moving toward it."

"Alright. You're not a new face to me. He is. But I've seen you before, at the stream fishing mostly. You aren't a hunter as far as I'm aware."

"I wasn't until Aaliyah conscripted me. When we brought her the basilisks, she was so grateful that she employed me for future hunts. The only condition in this hunt is that forty percent of the catch goes to her."

I was no expert in this field, but forty sounded pretty damn low in this kind of deal. Of course that made it that much more enticing an offer.

"Done. You and your friend come in and we'll get everyone ready to go. You know, I wouldn't do a thing for you if not for the basilisks you brought back and Aaliyah supporting you. Come on."

She turned and went inside. We followed, one of the two guards following behind us. We walked a dark corridor with iron doors along the wall. This seemed like a prison. The short trek spit us out into a larger room with a plain brown rug dominating most of the floor. A table sat on the rug but without chairs to accompany it. Atop the table was several documents with writing on them, a map of the area, several blades, a bow with a quiver empty of arrows, canisters both small and large, and a host of other small items. A few dozen wide iron bars were set in the wall, separating us from an armory.

Everyone continued past the table and to the iron bars besides me. I stopped at the table and looked at the map. There were several dry pens on the map and little figurines. I moved those. The map was drawn on thick parchment in black ink. There weren't any trees on the map to delineate a forest but I could make out dozens of streams, lakes, the caves, mountain ranges, and two cities. So anything that was blank on the map was forest, and the vast majority of it was free of ink. And people went out there to hunt. We were going out there.

"Before we leave, you two need some equipment." I turned at the sound of the officer's voice. Her eyes were fixated on me. Should I not have acted so interested in the map? I was, after all, an expert guide. Thankfully, she didn't call any attention to it. "You won't get what my guys have. But it'll work nonetheless."

She slid a key into a thick bar and twisted it. Two doors slowly swung free of their position, leaving an opening into a room lined with flamethrowers, weapons, and armor.

***

I'd been given a thick leather vest that was a bit too big for my lithe frame. It was stitched together by thin straps of the same material that comprised it. There were several patches on it that didn't quite fit the color of the original armor. As I donned it, stitches stretched and a few burst at the slightest pressure. I knew that this would be the last time this armor was used, if not close to it. I took it begrudgingly, and only because the officer said it would turn an Ochari spear... a little. Then Kanute added, "If a child threw it, maybe." I didn't have too much confidence in it.

There were four other guards with us, all with full flamethrowers. Kanute and I each had one as well, only ours was about a fourth the size of the others. A small canister was strapped to each of our thighs, a hose running from that to the short rod in our hands. Three of the guards had blazing torches, pushing the trees and grass and bushes back. Those of us without the torches stood in the middle of them.

The foliage remained closer than I felt comfortable with though. Some of it stayed beneath our feet even, gripping our boots and ankles. We stomped it off every once in a while, cursing.

We stayed near the stream but not so close that if the bison were there we would disturb them. That was my genius bit of advice for this hunt so far. Everyone seemed to accept it as a smart move and I blew a big sigh of relief.

The others did my job for me half the time.

"That looks like a track, there," one man said behind his metal helm. I could barely see the others' eyes within the dark eye slits but they all nodded and mumbled agreement.

"Anyone else's mouth watering? Bison; thick, meaty animals. Mmm. We could even cook up a leg out here on our way back."

Kanute said, "Well, you certainly could. But whichever bison you cut open would go bad around that big hole you make. We still need to send someone back to get a team and enough carts to bring them back. That bison wouldn't belong to Aaliyah though. That'd be part of the city's cut."

"Oh, he's just thinking out loud 'bout shit that he won't do," another said. "We all got food to hold us over. But, yeah, a big bite of a fat steak of bison. Goddamn!"

"Guide, how far do you think they would have gotten? You brought the basilisks into town a while back. Also, what's your name? Calling you 'guide' is going to get old fast."

Giving the guards my memory spiel would ruin our plan. I couldn't think of anything. I only knew a few names. I nearly blurted that my name was also Kanute. "Tiger!" I settled on.

I barked that much too loud. In fact, the guards all stopped moving and their heads snapped back and forth as they scoured the forest around us. One of them asked, "Where? Shit, I don't want one of those chewing my leg off."

Kanute tried to wilt me with his gaze. I had to continue it though. "No, my name is Tiger."

They shared a look then turned to me, standing still. One finally asked, "Tiger? What the hell. Why?"

"Well, I changed my name. I lived out here for a while. I found a tiger and took care of it. It was just a cub. That's why." I felt like big, heavy, lie-induced beads of sweat were running down my forehead and across my cheeks.

"With a name like that you better be damn good at what you do."

"Yup. And we should stay quiet now."

They all nodded, but then one grumbled, "You're the one screaming your name."

Thankfully, they turned around and continued on after that.

Plenty of time had passed and I hadn't said a thing as to our hunt. A vine fell down from the trees and didn't scurry away, but it did writhe around. One of the guards torched it. They did that because it wasn't a vine; it was a snake. And now it was a dying, or at least very hurt, one. Kanute stepped forward and sliced its head off with a flick of his wrist.

"This was well worth it," he said as he held his blade up and scrutinized it. Worth what? Coercing me? The near-death experience in the caves?

"Tiger, it's been a while. What's going on? Are we on the right path?"

"Well the moving trees have been shifting the earth around. I can't get a good read on any tracks."

"Don't give me shit I could have said. I'm not an expert on stuff out here like you are. Tell me something about bison that is useful. Would they stay at the stream for as long as it has been since you've seen them?"

"They would." That cold feeling struck through me. I was lying through my teeth and I didn't think I was any good at it. Everything coming from my mouth felt fake. A big tattoo was on my forehead that read 'liar'. "We should just keep on."

Another guard asked, "Why did you even wait so long to come back out? It's been hours since you both came back with basilisks. You saw them when you were coming back. What held you up?"

They all seemed suspicious of me. My throat was swelling shut, dry and cracking. As one, they stopped and spun around to face us, their fingers sliding to the triggers on their throwers.

Kanute said, "We were tired. We had just killed two basilisks. Wouldn't you like something to eat and a soft place to put your head after all that?"

"That's all good and well. But why didn't you just tell us so we could have come out at that point. You would have gotten your finder's fee. Tiger is walking around here without a fucking clue. Seriously, I haven't seen him do much tracking at all. And, you know what I haven't seen around here? Shit! Guess what a family of bison do a lot of? Shit! I'm about ready to take you both back for making this whole thing up."

Kanute had been ambling in a slow circle as the guard berated us, kicking small stones in the loose soil, innocently putting the three of them between him and I. There was a strategy behind his movements that I could plainly see, and my palms immediately grew clammy. Was I supposed to take some kind of hint and blast these guys with fire? I didn't think I had that in me.

"Why would we stage this? That's idiotic," Kanute fired back.

"You tell me!" one of the guards seethed.

The only sound now was the slightly shifting forest around us and a light breeze. I tried to think of something to say, but couldn't. I hoped that Kanute would try to defuse the situation instead of having the arrogance to test his new armor and weapon against these three guards. My whole body was numb now besides a tingling in my legs. I didn't reach for my weapon like the guards were doing. I felt useless.

Motion from above them all stole my attention. A tree branch sagged slightly. Brown and green all blended together but there were streaks of blue and white here and there that didn't belong. I squinted and tried to understand the slightly moving thing behind the veil of leaves and vines. Two orbs, rimmed by white with diamond-shaped irises the color of the leaves, glimmered within the foliage. Then, I got it.

I thrust my finger toward it and screamed, "Look out!"

Kanute threw himself to the ground and the guards lunged in all directions. I stood still and a spear slammed into the ground near my feet. The Ochari that had thrown it was beginning to scramble away but one of the guards aimed his flamethrower at it and a jet of flame leapt from the tip. The tree shuddered and ambled away from the blast.

Flames licked at the Ochari but didn't engulf it. The creature wobbled atop the tree then lost its balance and plummeted. It came down hard on the loose soil. It was tall and lanky with lithe arms and legs. A harness wrapped its shoulders and a pack was on its back. A belt with several weapons in it circled its thin waist. It was fast and agile as hell too.

It hit the ground then rolled and came up to all fours. Kanute was coming after it with his machete. The lizard-like creature spun on its hands and lashed out with its legs. One foot slapped across Kanute's face, knocking him to the side. Then, it was on its feet.

Orange and red flames swallowed it as it spun toward the guards, a knife in its hand. The Ochari was lost as fire from two flamethrowers roasted it. Immediately I tasted and smelled the rancid scent of melting flesh. The Ochari came dancing from the flames, swinging around and screaming wildly. Another guard planted an arrow in the thing somewhere and it fell to the earth, a blazing heap.

Before any of us could speak. Before the dying Ochari could even stop squirming, a spear sliced through the throat of the guard holding the bow. He went down, blood pooling around him. I didn't see where the spear had come from, nor did I care. Kanute was running toward me. He wasn't going to use me as bait again. I turned and ran before he got to me and found myself in the midst of the forest.

I didn't have a torch. The guards were the ones who did. I was tangled up in tearing vines and grass. Like I was accustomed to, I tried getting away. I pulled and flung myself away as hard as I could but the vegetation held fast.

"Use your fucking thrower!" Kanute yelled. His voice was immediately replaced by the roar of flame. Heat suddenly blasted me, freeing me from my bonds. A sharp stinging pain sliced across the back of my neck. I slapped at it but it abated along with the silencing of Kanute's flamethrower.

Kanute sped around me, a small lick of flame coming from the tip of his flamethrower. The putrid stench of charred hair and fuel swept by me. I broke into a sprint to catch up with Kanute, the man now spitting flames out before him every so often to clear his path.

I made it to his side quickly. I then realized that I also had a flamethrower. It was damn near impossible to force myself to focus on getting mine working while I ran, as terrified and scrambled as I was. I didn't want to look away from the forest before me for even the briefest of moments. I was sick of simply hoping events would unfold in my favor, especially given that they normally didn't. I actually took initiative this time as I attempted to turn my flamethrower into more than just a useless piece of metal in my hands.

Glances down showed the switch I needed to toggle to activate the weapon. Then I found the trigger by feeling around the rod. I ignited the flamethrower with a loud crack and a gout of flame shot from it to spear the ground at my side. "Whoa, shit!"

"Aim it forward! We switch off spraying!"

"We take care of each other!" The words came from me without having to think on them first. I didn't realize how much my distrust for Kanute had become a part of me. I didn't believe that he would do his part for anyone but himself.

He nodded as he ran then shot a stream of fire that cut through the air in a horizontal arc, clearing a wide area in front of us. After several steps, I took my shot.

Screams of the dying guards came after me. They called accusations at my back as I ran through the forest, saving myself and a bastard that deserved to be in their places well before they did. I had no way of knowing if they deserved to die. I certainly wasn't what should be the cause of their death. I had no right to that.

They were fighting with all they had, but the Ochari must have been all over the forest, casting spears at them as they struggled to keep the trees, grass, and vines from engulfing them. The noises began to fall away and I only hoped that the Ochari weren't pursuing us yet. I wondered what God would think of what I had done though. I know what I thought of myself. I should have tackled Kanute to the ground and held him there as the world ate us. But I didn't. I was too busy wanting to live.

Chapter 10

It was like nothing had happened. Or that's how it was supposed to be. I still had that blade at my hip though. And I wanted to use it now far more than ever before, whether on Kanute or myself I couldn't tell.

Life had been extremely difficult for me thus far, but how much did I deserve as recompense for that? Sending those guards to their death was a means for me to simply maintain my hold on a place that offered a small bit of respite from what I'd endured so far, and so that I could keep one little life close to me. I was being selfish. At first, I thought I had deserved to be. Now, I was sure that I was placed in this predicament for a reason, and that did not include causing others around me to suffer so greatly.

My knuckles grew white around the hilt of the machete at my hip as I resisted the urge to cut down Kanute then place the blade against my throat and fall on it.

The screams had been lost long ago. Nothing had come after us though. We'd made it back far quicker than when we had set out and now Kanute and I walked around the outside wall of the city.

He spoke for the first time since abandoning the guards, "Don't say anything at all. I'll talk if we need to. We're going straight to Aaliyah's and getting that stardust. Then, we leave the city. Simple, right?"

"Almost too simple. But sure. So, I just start spraying fire all around when we get inside?"

"Something like that. Throw the tarps from the pallets and hit those too when you have the chance. Once we get a fire started, it'll all take off. That place will get smoky real quick. Her men will come after us with everything they have. Stop hitting the pallets if they get too close and light them up. We find the stardust and get our asses out of there as soon as we can."

"How do I get the cub?"

"Soon as we get the stardust and make it out of Aaliyah's warehouse, you can have my key to the place. If I could trust you not to turn that thrower on me then book it, I'd give it to you now. Even then, don't think I'm not watching you, because I am. You make a turn the wrong way, and I will light you up."

I grunted to show that I understood the plan, disturbed by his ability to apparently read my mind so well. Hell, his answer to my question about the cub was all I was waiting for to turn and blast him. Had he thrown me the key to his place, I would have done it.

We cleared our way to the gates and found only one guard there. Of course he had to belt out, "You're back already? No bison I see! Where are the others?" Word traveled through the guards faster than what was conducive to our success.

Kanute hooked a thumb over his shoulder. "We found them. Killed most of the family. Now we just need carts."

"Let me help out with that one, then. I asked to be one of the guards going along, but nope! Wanted to see a man who killed two basilisks in action. I'll be right back with a team."

"No!" Even I heard the panic in Kanute's voice, and I wasn't really listening that intensely. Either we got to Aaliyah's or this blew up right now and I would just turn and bolt. I was only attached to the former option because of the cub. He was the one in all of this that didn't deserve to be hurt. The guard stopped and although I couldn't see his face beneath his helm, I was sure he was staring at Kanute as if he'd just sprouted a second head. "What I mean is, that there needs to be someone here. We saw what we think was an Ochari out there in the trees. Someone needs to stay here and watch the gate."

"True. Alright, when you get to the station, ask them to send another my way then. Don't need to take on those lizards myself if they do show up. Good hunting, you two."

Kanute thanked the man and seemed sincerely proud of himself. We moved on.

The city fell away and we were before Aaliyah's warehouse. Beard and One-Ear were outside. They each locked their emotionless gazes on us. Beard demanded, "You have some business with Aaliyah?"

"I do actually," Kanute responded.

"You selling those throwers?" he barked.

"That's the exact reason we came back actually."

"You're an idiot, Kanute. Those are guard-issued. Fuck off before I make you swallow your teeth."

"They're guard-*stolen*," Kanute corrected. "Look, just give me a moment to speak with her. We both know the majority of her shit in there ain't clean."

One-Ear said, "We'll ask her. Wait here. You take a step forward and he makes good on his promise."

"Of course. Heard you there, big man. Go now, please."

I was surprised by the balls on Kanute for that. He was looking death right in the face though. I guess he wanted to either get out of this a king or die a fearless fool. I just wanted out of everything.

One-Ear simply turned and he and Beard opened the massive door. Kanute pointed and fired and I followed suit, aiming for One-Ear's chest.

Both big men took the inferno square but Beard ended up with a face full of fire. We burst forward together, continuing our assault. We made it in and found that the warehouse seemed empty of other guards. The two giants still outside beat at their burning bodies and face and hollered. A moan of pleasure echoed from Aaliyah and through the warehouse before it turned into a shout of surprise.

Kanute and I took separate angles of attack, him moving right and me left. We snagged the corner of the first tarp we came to then whirled and blasted it.

Beardless staggered through the open door, the flesh of his face puckered and red. One-Ear trailed close behind and came after me while Beardless took to stomping after Kanute. I backed away and sent fire at him. It hit his chest again and he flung himself to the side to get free of its sharp embrace. I followed him with it until he stumbled into the wall. He bounced off it and hit the ground hard.

One-Ear rolled and roared as he attempted to put the cloth tunic beneath his armor out. I stopped spraying him and turned to run. Shelves, crates, tarps, chests, glass cases, and so much more filled the warehouse, creating a labyrinth. How did Kanute expect to find the stardust?

I saw him then, right before I disappeared behind shelves stocked to the point of breaking. I also saw Aaliyah standing in nothing but a robe that split open to reveal her chest and groin, screaming at Kanute. A third giant, bereft of clothing, with a large blade in each his hands chased after Kanute. This one was missing two fingers from his left hand. He shot fire at Two-Fingers and Beardless then ducked away into the labyrinth himself. Perhaps he knew where to go.

I darted around corners and behind shelves until I nearly smacked right into Kanute. I could hear the giants stomping around, coming after our heads. "Kanute," I whispered, "where the hell is it?"

"She would keep it in her personal quarters, I'm sure of it. It's on the same side of the room she was on. See, right there." I followed his pointed finger to a room tucked in the corner of the warehouse. "We need to get in there. Go!"

We took off and a metallic clang erupted behind us. One of the giants was right on our asses, his sword sparking off the concrete floor, and Kanute fired his flamethrower over his shoulder to cover our retreat. The giant yelled and I heard him pounding along after us which meant that Kanute was missing. I turned and added my own gout of flame to Kanute's to assist in stalling him to find One-Ear rampaging after us through the flames as if they weren't there. He couldn't keep a straight path with fire sheathing him and crashed into a stack of crates that he then swung his blade at. He smashed up the inventory with one hand while he swiped at his eyes and face with the other.

"Up and over!" Kanute yelled.

A thick, squat armoire sat before us, barring our progress. Kanute leapt, planted one hand on the top and then vaulted over it to land on the other side. All three giants raged and smashed through the shelves to get to us, their anger and pain driving them to disregard Aaliyah's precious inventory. Smoke was beginning to turn the air so thick that breathing it felt like swallowing syrup. I tried the same trick as Kanute but smacked one knee into the thick wood. I tumbled over it and landed hard on the other side.

The pounding footsteps of the giants got me up quicker than I thought myself capable of. Kanute and I weaved through the labyrinth and the giants smashed into things behind us. Their vision likely suffered from the billowing smoke above while Kanute and I were low enough to stay free of it.

We were about to clear the maze when the opening between two sets of tall shelves was filled by Aaliyah, her robe falling open again. I would have spent more time staring if she wasn't stabbing a dagger at Kanute's chest. The blade hit home, sticking in him.

I was going to blast her then flee for the exit when Kanute growled and drove his fist across her face. Her head snapped back and she fell into a heap on the floor, naked and unconscious. Kanute plucked the dagger from his chest and grunted. The tip had only a small amount of blood. Aaliyah had sold him strong, durable armor instead of deceiving him. She'd get to ponder that mistake when she awoke, unless the fire took her.

The open door to Aaliyah's personal room was before us and only steps away. We sprinted through and came upon a room mostly dominated by a circular bed. The blankets atop it were mussed up and clothes were on the floor.

"There!" Kanute hollered. He pointed at a glowing, orange rock inside a glass cylinder on a table. The rock seemed to breathe as the orange shifted color as if it were moving. Kanute darted for it, pulling his machete out. He swung his blade and shattered the glass.

"Shit!" Glass had exploded in all directions and sliced his hand. He paid it no more mind though as he used his bleeding hand to grab the rock. He turned and bolted back toward me and for the exit. I turned just in time to see Beardless a few steps from the open door.

The hard part was over now. All we had to do was get past them then keep running. I would cook him a bit more until he backed off or couldn't keep on coming. I raised by flamethrower. I pulled the trigger. Beardless roared and brought his forearms up to block his face.

The flames from my short burst went wild, spraying the wall. Kanute had shoved me hard enough to send me slamming into the concrete. I maintained my feet and saw Kanute sprint right into Beardless' massive frame. The former was wrapped up tight as he stood there dumbstruck for a brief moment. I heard him squeal as the giant must be squeezing the life from him. He dropped the stardust.

If Kanute didn't mind trying to get me killed then I didn't give a shit about him. I fired on them both. Beardless used Kanute as a shield but enough heat got to him to make him duck away. Two-Fingers was right behind him, still void of clothing, advancing on me.

I'd make him regret not grabbing some pants before coming after us. I aimed at his crotch and blasted him with fire. He covered up a moment too late and roared before throwing himself to the side.

Nothing else happened for a moment. I listened to my labored breathing and for what was transpiring outside of the room, my thrower aimed at the open door. I could hear Kanute resisting his capture. The smoke was thick now and I couldn't see more than a few paces beyond the door.

Aaliyah's voice pierced the tension, "Put that flamethrower down and we'll be nice to Kanute."

"I don't care what you do with him."

"Really!? Alright, go ahead and break his fingers."

Kanute pleaded, "What!? No! Just put it down! Gah! Damn!" I heard the snap of those fingers over his screams. From the cacophony of snaps, I was sure they'd all shattered at once. "Please no!"

Aaliyah called, "What's it going to be? Should we continue?"

I was silent for a while. Kanute's horrid cries were getting to me. I wanted them to stop. Why couldn't they just kill him?

She continued, "You put it down and come out and I'll make it quick. Come on, now. If we have to go get you things won't be pretty. I'll do to you what has been done to Kanute but so much worse."

I couldn't talk. Now that death was waiting outside of this room, I was terrified of it. Through the smoke I couldn't see anyone, but I could see fire raging across the walls and floor. No one in this place had much time.

"Fine. Tear his ears off." Aaliyah called.

"No! Don't!" Kanute wailed.

But then he lost it. He screeched louder than ever I've heard before. The way it sounded, the little breaks here and there as he sobbed, the insane noise he made, it caused me to press my hands against my temples and squeeze.

"Just kill him!" I screamed.

The tortured sounds coming from Kanute ensured that they hadn't nor would. I sat there trembling but managed to get past the madness seeping into my mind and let go of my head. I aimed the thrower back at the door just as One-Ear stuck his head around the corner. I pulled the trigger and a gout of flame had him ducking back behind the wall.

Growling murmurs pierced the air between Kanute's wails.

"Fine!" Aaliyah screamed. "Kill him!"

A bone-chilling crack echoed over the din of the roaring fire and Kanute squealed for a brief moment. His body careened in through the door and slammed to the ground then rolled. I looked down at his corpse, his head stuck in a nauseating position, reminding me of the way an owl spun its head around to look behind it. A key ring glittered in the light of the fires, hooked to his belt. I dove for it and snapped it from his waist then pocketed it.

I peeked out of the room and saw that part of the shelving was aflame now. Beardless appeared, part of his mass hidden behind a large, iron shield. The others lined up behind him as I let loose a blast of fire that struck the disk of black metal.

"Get him!" Aaliyah screamed.

They all began to hustle forward, despite the spear of flame that pounded the shield Beardless interposed between it and them. A booted foot came down on the chunk of stardust and shattered it, then I lost it behind their legs. I angled the thrower downward and the inferno skipped off the concrete floor to sear his shins, causing him to roar and change the angle of the shield. I blasted him in the face for good measure and he careened away from me and into the wall, curling against it and stomping his feet in rage and agony.

The others were right behind him and heedless of the fire. A single pace separated us. I switched the thrower to a one-handed grip and began to unlatch the machete from my belt. Two-Fingers raised his own massive blade, ready to slice me clean in half. "You want it!" I screamed in defiance. If they were going to kill me, I'd go out thrashing and would do my goddamn best to drag them down with me.

Fire caught Two-Fingers square in the chest as he brought his blade down. The sword, nearly as long as half my height, whistled as it cut the air near my head. I jerked away and spun, the blade actually caressing my arm as it passed, harmlessly, to my side and shattered the smooth concrete.

My fingers fumbled with the machete, however, and I failed to bring it to bear in time to slice into Two-Fingers hamstring. One-Ear paid dearly for my fuck up though as he grabbed me. Steel wrapped my arm, clamped down tight, and held me fast, pointing my thrower at the ground and rendering it ineffective. He had to lean down to reach me, placing his oversized, ugly, burnt, pockmarked face on the same level as mine.

The machete came free, and he was none the wiser. "Fuck you!" I roared as I flailed in his grip and sliced upward toward the ceiling. One-Ear had a moment where his eyes turned toward one another and aimed downward. But only the briefest of moments. The tip of my blade caught him square in the jaw, cracking bone and rending flesh as if it was no more resistant to the blade as I was to the brutality of the sun's rays.

His arm went limp, his grip faltering, and my thrower was free. I yanked on my machete like a beast tearing apart a meal before a scavenger could relinquish me from my hard-earned prize. As the blade left One-Ear's head, a fountain of blood and chips of bone followed out of the hole I'd created and he collapsed, holding his chin, on the cusp of unconsciousness.

I turned and sprayed the room as I ran for the exit. My arm didn't work all that well and a shockwave of pain told me that One-Ear's grip had torn or dislocated something. I hit mostly the floor, but stalled Two-Fingers just enough to escape the room and fly by a dumbstruck Aaliyah.

Shards of stardust twinkled on the floor and I slowed just enough to bend low and scoop up a handful, hugging my machete between my chest and arm. Awkwardly, I resumed my escape, my arms held tightly to my body. Smoke suffused the air so much that a single inhale of the thick stuff had me coughing. I lost my balance and slammed into a shelf piled with goods, flames licking across them.

I sagged against the burning wood, spun, and fired my thrower, catching Two-Fingers in the thighs. I ducked his wild rampage as he slapped at the flames and careened into the same shelf I'd been leaning against a moment ago.

I stumbled away then found strong enough footing to burst into a sprint. Aaliyah screamed and the giants roared in anger behind me while fire crackled and leapt about in every direction. I continued on along the shelving, ignoring the lances of pain that shot through my arm and shoulder.

I sped around a final bend and beheld the exit, drenched in flames. I ran over fire and through it then burst out into the light. The entire city stood before me, guards assembled with flamethrowers and blades at the ready.

"The Ochari!" I screamed and pointed at the burning warehouse as best as I could manage. All eyes turned to the entrance and I continued my escaped, shouldering past people, praying that they'd believe my deceit. Never once did I turn to look behind me as I fled for Kanute's home. I reached the entrance to the compound, fumbled with the keys until I found the right one, slivers of stardust falling as I did so. Finally, the tumblers clicked and the bolt slid free. I pushed it open and flew down the dark hallway to Kanute's apartment.

I repeated the process and burst into his room, the tiger cub looking up at me with feral eyes, coiled and ready to spring. There was no time for pleasantries. I dropped everything I held, then fell to my knees. My trembling fingers hooked the machete to my belt without conscious thought then stuffed the largest chunk of stardust into my pocket, a few flakes left behind on the floor.

Deep growls turned my head to the cub and I realized with horrific certainty that his eyes were locked onto something behind me. Fingers found the trigger of the thrower as I whirled around. I nearly roasted the animals I owed my life to. The orangutans were there, and obviously distressed. They hooted and hollered at me, waving their arms in a gesture that made me believe I needed to follow them. The younger female swung forward and grabbed my pants and began pulling.

"Wait!" I cried out as I turned and moved for the cub.

The floor began quaking as I scooped the tiger from the ground with my functioning arm, his claws sinking into my chest. Chips of concrete and slivers of wood trembled across the floor and the air grew thick with pressure as it vibrated. Screams from the orangutans brought me back to my senses and I took a single step toward them. Then, the wall at my back exploded, showering me with chunks of concrete and drowning out the cries of the apes.

I stumbled into them, the younger female catching me. Still leaning into her, I craned my neck to look behind me and beheld the knight standing in a cloud of dust, his sword leaking fire and his free arm sheathed in dark energy that slowly dissipated before my eyes. The knight took a step forward and the male orangutan roared in defiance, vaulting at him and slamming his feet into the knight's chest. He stumbled back a step then cut at the orangutan.

Breath fled my lungs like a bellows when the young orangutan pulled me away, and I barely glimpsed the flaming blade slice through the air right over the orangutan's head. The other joined the fight, offering her own war cry before doing so. I stumbled down the dark hallway, pulled along by the orangutan.

The exit remained ajar and we hit it with force enough to slam it into the outside of the building. A phalanx of guards greeted us, likely drawn by the knight. Several dead guards lay strewn about across the ground, the knight's victims. I dove to the side as a blast of flame came my way, the orangutan guiding me doing the same, albeit much more gracefully.

I hit the ground hard and landed on my arm, the cub screeching. I felt bones grind together and cried out, sure now that my shoulder was dislocated. I rolled over to see the knight, slowed to a walk by the fire that was engulfing him but otherwise unhindered by it, as he marched out of the exit. The monstrous being stomped after me and raised his blade up over his head. I didn't have anything left. I couldn't get up quick enough even if I tried. I was going to die like a coward. And I didn't care.

The blade, spitting flames, came down for my stomach. Strong fingers wrapped around my arm, the good one, and pulled. I slid across the ground and only briefly felt the heat from the fire as the sword slashed down and clanged off the stone. My savior continued to drag me away swiftly putting a dozen feet between myself and the knight. It was the momma orangutan. The smaller one was behind her and they both lifted me up with great speed. As soon as the bottoms of my feet touched down, the latter pulled me away again.

We ran several long strides before I turned to look for the orangutan we left behind. She, along with the male orangutan continued attacking the knight and avoiding the fire of the idiot guards all at the same time. The male leapt away from a blazing stream shot from a guard's thrower, hit the wall of the apartment with his feet, then bounded off it for the knight. He pumped both feet out and caught the knight in the back of his helm, sending him stumbling forward.

Before I turned away to continue my flight, I saw the knight stand tall and bat the female orangutan from the air. Did the one helping me see that? Was she just so committed to helping me that she wouldn't turn back for her mother even if she did?

We continued on, she pulling me along by my good arm as I cradled the cub in my other. We got far enough away from the battle for the sounds to become muffled and distant, the mind-numbing fear dulling enough for me to think straight for a moment. The gate out of town was only a few feet away, the forest encroaching upon the white stone that provided a plateau of security a dozen feet from the exit. I skipped to a stop, pulling her to make her stop as well. "Wait!" I hollered. "I can't go out like this."

I took the stardust rock, still gripped in my hand, and set it on the white stone ground. I unhooked the machete from the loop on my belt and used the hilt to strike the rock. It didn't even fracture. "Come on, dammit!" I did it again, and again to no avail. I looked back the way we had come and saw dozens of people, awestruck, slowly converging on me. They must not be so terrified of the knight that their lust for stardust was forgotten.

I put the flat of the blade on the rock then stood and stomped on it. It crunched and I quickly scooped up the blade and reattached it to my belt. Pebbles and shards of stardust were on the ground. I took one about as big as my fingernail and consumed it, disoriented for a moment by the unfamiliar burst of heat that blossomed in my chest and ran through my body. I scooped up what I could as fast as I could.

Screams tore my gaze back around. The knight was running after me yet again, this time with nothing to impede him. The cub growled ferociously. I didn't see the orangutans or the guards but the one guiding me yanked on my arm to get me going. I stumbled forward then broke into a run.

We left out of a gate that I had not seen before, now on the other side of the city and heading away from the caves. There was no chance that I could outrun the knight. It'd catch me soon. Perhaps the forest would move for it slower than it would for me. The orangutan and I bolted toward the trees and was forced to slow to a jog as the forest rippled away from me as quickly as it could, which wasn't fast enough to allow me an all-out sprint.

I suddenly remembered the map I had seen and this exit on it. Then, I remembered a river near us that the stream fed into. If I could get to that, maybe I could cross it. Perhaps water would be his anathema.

I hoped that I remembered the direction correctly on the map as I pulled the orangutan with me. She stopped suddenly, letting go of my shirt. We locked eyes for a moment and I understood what she was telling me. She needed to go back for her parents. I wished I could have gone back with her. We parted and I pumped my legs as if she were still pulling me. I heard her scream at the knight and imagined her harrying him to buy me more time.

No amount would be enough, though, unless my guess about the water was correct. I flew through the wood on the wings of the air, quicker than a galloping horse. The pounding steps grew louder and heavier. I just wasn't built right to deal with this and live. I wasn't made to survive this.

The trees before me fled and gave way to rushing waters, white and frothing. I dove in and came down on a round rock that I hadn't seen beneath the waves. Could this world not do any worse? I felt like it was all against me, aching for my death. The pain was terrible and I was sure I heard a rib crack. The pain hid beneath my terror and panic as I was dragged along by the current.

Raging water covered my head and swept me downstream. I surfaced and sucked in sweet air, making sure to allow the cub freedom from the water as well. I moved with the flow of the pristine water, keeping the cub clutched tight, although his claws ensured his perch on my chest, and the stardust rocks gripped in my free hand. I watched and waited. The current was slower than I had been running but I didn't try to speed myself along; if the knight could traverse the water without being sucked down by the weight of his armor, the quickest pace I could muster wouldn't be enough. I moved past rocks, somehow keeping from striking them as I stared at the bank where I had come from.

The trees were returning to their original spot slowly, the grass wavering as it walked its way over the loose soil. In a burst of motion, it all leapt away again and the knight appeared. He came to an abrupt halt, standing before the water. I had been right. I was safe amidst the water. His helmeted head deliberately turned toward me, the eyeless voids in his helm piercing me with a palpable aura of disdain. I wanted to smile at him, the fear he had instilled in me forgotten for a moment.

Slowly, as if he knew my mind and wanted to mock me, the knight lifted one leg. He set his foot down in the water, then did something that wasn't possible. he went knee deep in the surf before suddenly taking off as if he rode the water like it was some steed. Waves sprayed from around a cone of power that sheathed him as he cut across the river. His legs remained locked in a position behind him as he flew for me that made me wonder if he could accomplish this same amazing feat through the skies. I could try to get out of the river and run, but I was too tired. I was just done. I didn't even feel the fear as I looked up to the bright, starry sky. Those motes of light cast me in such bright light. They grew in intensity as death approached.

I kissed the furry head of the tiger cub latched onto my chest, then forcefully gripped the nape of his neck and tore him from my body. He screeched in surprised pain and I winced as his claws tore gouges of flesh from my chest. I surged to my feet for a moment before the water knocked me back down and gently tossed the cub out of the river and to the bank. He slid along the muddy shore, turned and locked eyes with me for a moment, meowed, then sprinted away as the knight sped near him.

I closed my eyes and the water pulled me down, submerging me. I held my breath. I felt the water roil as the knight came to my side. I felt with such agony and understanding when the blade stabbed through my chest, pinning me to the bottom.

My eyes snapped open and I saw that face of black metal, shimmering through the water and steam, menacing and hateful. I only wondered one thing as darkness crept in; why me?

***

"I know this is hard. So hard. Maybe I can't say that. You know better. I don't. You're right, I don't know. But I know this; I love you. We all do. We always will. I'm not ready to let go. I won't ever be ready. I won't ever let go... You can't let go now.

"It's like it used to be almost. Get up. Time to wake up, now. The day has only just begun. But it isn't exactly like that. Those were so much easier. Even when I would get so pissed off that you just wouldn't get up. I would think, why is this so hard? But no. Now that's what I think every day. That and why is this happening to you. Sweet boy.

"We might not ever see each other in this life again. That's hard to say... I... want you to know how much we all love you. How inspirational you are. But your spirit leads you. It always has. You've had such a strong soul. Time to get up now."

Chapter 11

"It's love. Love always does it. I don't know how much you know about that. But I feel it for a lot of things. That's why I can do this. I'm glad that I can do what I do."

The words came for me and pulled me from the black. I didn't know who was talking. The voice was familiar though. I couldn't put much together at that time. I just knew that I heard and what I heard was a woman's voice.

"There you are. So quick. Such a soul you have. So much love."

Darkness fled. I was looking up at a clear sky and a canopy of leaves from branches overhead barely reaching out over me.

"Hi."

I turned my head, which was apparently attached to a neck made mostly of stone. I groaned, "Oh, goddamn."

"Wow. Not what I expected."

I opened my eyes, not realizing until now that I had even closed them again. Jacquelyn was near me, lying on a rock, her hair covering her breasts this time.

"Sorry. I just hurt." It wasn't just my head, or my chest, or my arm, it was all of me. I felt as though I had been buried beneath hundreds of pounds of soil, compressing and crushing my entire body then had suddenly woken up outside of my grave. "What happened?" I didn't attempt to move any further. I just lay there, hurting, staring at those beautiful eyes.

"I was hoping you could tell me all that. Did you forget it all again?"

A wave of cold cut through me as it all came rushing back. Kanute's neck torqued up so bad that he had instantly died. Blasting the giants with fire as I escaped them. Abandoning the cub. The black knight and the horrible horns atop his head. How he had sped across the water. How he had killed me.

"I died," I whispered as if saying it too loud would take me from this dream between death and the afterlife.

"No. You're obviously not dead. How would we be doing anything we are doing? Here, take a deep breath. Fill your lungs, then push it all back out. Look around and see all the trees and grass. All the living things."

"The living things suck," I whined, immediately hearing the immaturity of my statement. I felt idiotic now, beneath her lovely gaze. Graciously, she didn't look at me as if I was an idiot. She just stared at me with that light smile. I looked away from her and to the trees and grass, swaying in a light breeze. I turned my head and saw that the rock we were on was smack in the middle of a pool of water. I saw fish, moss, seaweed, sand. I slowly inhaled as deep as I could. It hurt. I exhaled. That hurt too.

I looked back to Jacquelyn. "That sucked too." We both giggled at that and I smiled for the first time in a while. That breath worked though. I slipped into a more relaxed state, the pain mostly gone now.

"So, what happened to you? I found you floating along the river, a big hole in your chest."

My shirt was the only part of me that proved her statement to be true. The flesh beneath was perfectly smooth, void of the scar I expected. I ran my hand along my thigh and found that the canister attached to the thrower and the rod itself were both missing, likely swept away by the current.

I recounted what had happened to me then. Jacquelyn listened quietly, attentively. She wrinkled her brow a few times. "So I should be dead," I concluded. "The knight stabbed me through the chest with that massive sword. But I'm not. Which means it's your turn to explain what happened to me."

"Okay. Hold on." She rolled off the rock and slipped into the calm river with barely even a splash. She propelled herself out like a dolphin might and glided up back to her spot, splashing me with cold water that made me shiver. Her hair was now behind her back, and her supple breasts showing. I stared for too long. "I just needed some water. I don't like being out of it for too long. Oh, yeah. Sorry. I don't want you to feel uncomfortable." She pulled her hair back over her shoulders and covered up.

"Sorry."

She put a finger up and said, "Nothing for you to be sorry about. *I* just said that, didn't I?"

"Yeah, you did. You're beautiful, you know that?" I've no idea what compelled me to say that. I suddenly felt very uncomfortable. Being stark naked in a spread eagle position would have been less embarrassing.

But Jacquelyn saved me from my discomfort. "Thank you. That is very sweet. Now, I found you, bleeding all over the place. I just made you better. You never died." She said all this as if I was supposed to just get it. I sure as hell didn't though.

"How? Did you use the same staff that Morrissett used? Is that how you fixed me?" I tried to lift my arm, the one that had been ripped from its socket, and it responded. It felt stiff as stone, but it worked.

"With love. You probably don't understand it. I do. I understand it perfectly. You see, I love a lot of things; other people, animals, trees, the suns, the air. Why shouldn't I? This is how I see it; if there is something new in my life, why not love it until I have a reason not to? That's just how I feel. It makes me happy so I do it. So, I can heal people with love. I found you and held you close. I kissed you, and your body just got better. You were close to going though. I barely made it in time."

I was baffled, but I realized I really shouldn't be. There were stranger things in this world. "So you can save people with your love? Can everyone do that?"

"Not that I know of. You feel fine now?"

"Way better than I deserve to be, given a massive, flaming sword just stabbed me through the chest." I returned her smirk then continued, "Relieved to be alive. Still sore but okay. Thank you. What you do is a great thing." As I droned off, thinking of something to say, I was struck by the idea that the cub may have followed me after the knight left me to die. "Did you find a tiger cub?" I pleaded, scanning the banks although I was doubtful.

She reached out and placed a hand on my knee then shook her head. There was such compassion in her eyes that I wondered if she somehow managed to absorb my emotions, feeling them just as I did. Her touch and the care written into her face eased my pain-stricken heart.

"What do you think about love?" she asked after a moment, letting her hand slide from my knee. "I bet you don't remember much, but can you remember any love?"

"No. But I like what you said about it."

"Well then, if there was just one thing you could say about it, what would it be? And it can't be what I said." She smiled at me playfully, waiting for my answer with anticipation.

How did someone answer that when they couldn't recall ever having loved before? But I'm sure I had. I must have. Life just felt like it was supposed to have that in it. "I really can't think of anything. I'm trying. It's just..."

She waited patiently. I opened my mouth several times, intent on starting a sentence although I had no idea where it would lead. Finally, I said, "It's something that everyone should know."

Jacquelyn immediately responded, "That's it? That's what you would say about it? Come on, love is the stuff that life is made of. You have to have something better, even if all you remember is when you woke up in the woods. Your soul has something; you just don't feel it yet."

That all seemed very fluffy and soft. I just didn't feel it. It'd be nice to. "I just, I don't know, Jacquelyn."

My heart suddenly opened up and spoke. It pushed the words through my throat and between my lips. "If you love, then love out loud."

I didn't understand why I had said that. It was like I was possessed suddenly. I didn't merely speak it, I felt it. I said it with passion and my chest throbbed now. Tears swarmed my eyes, but I kept them in check. Jacquelyn smiled so wide, her lips a beautiful thing.

"See. I told you. Your soul had that tucked away all along. It feels good, doesn't it?"

It did. Although not as good as she thought. The throbbing in my chest became more intense, like I was holding something back. Like I had squeezed my hands down on the throat of my heart, shutting it up before it was done speaking. The good began to flee.

I wanted to keep myself bottled up but something burst in me. I slowly sat up and a tear fell down my cheek. "I'm supposed to remember something that made me feel that way. It isn't just my soul that knows it; my soul learned it. I learned it. But so far, all I can really remember is terror, pain, anger, and your love." Tears were leaking from my eyes now. I hoped that she was into the sensitive types of guys.

"I feel like I'm missing so much of myself. Why am I here? Why is any of this happening?" I suddenly stopped. My heart wanted to keep on going, but it was done speaking. It just wanted to feel now. So it did. My shoulders bounced as I sobbed. My eyes closed and my face wrinkled as I grit my teeth against the emotional pain. I let my heart out.

Hands wrapped my head and pulled me close. I felt her chin on my head, her warm chest on my cheek, her fingers running through my hair. I thanked all the gods and angels in heaven for her. I would have thanked the devil himself had he been responsible for her.

I cried for some time until I felt better, the throb in my chest dull and fading. I was tired. I wanted to sleep. I leaned into her a little harder and she laid back. We locked eyes for a moment and she looked so serene, so inviting and caring. I loved her.

I laid my head on her stomach and closed my eyes. I began to drift.

Her voice pulled me up from the clutches of sleep. "You can't rest. You have to keep going. The stardust isn't going to last forever."

I shook my head. "This is worth it all. Just a little while."

"Okay. Just a little."

***

Light cut across the nothingness and descended to float before me. He looked upon me with a sort of sad smile. He was sorry, I thought, and also glad.

The man of light was so close to me. He looked familiar, like I had seen him every day of my life. He was a piece of me.

And now, he was back. He was here to stay. I could feel it. The light swam toward me, losing his shape and becoming a cone. Whatever this part of me was, the part that wanted to get out of this place so badly that it had left, it rejoined my spirit. I felt warmth.

***

I awoke and sat up. Jacquelyn was there, holding me upright by my shoulders. "It's time to go."

She was right. I would be content if I just wasted away in her arms. "You think God is the only one who can help me now?"

"I do. But I'll be around. Do you still have my kiss?"

That woke me up completely. I winced. "I lost it. I'm sorry. I did everything I could to get it back."

"That's okay. Take this one." She suddenly leaned forward and pressed her soft lips against mine. Her hand stayed on my back. Once I recovered from the shock of surprise, I slid one hand across her cheek and to her head, resting my thumb near her ear. My other hand sought hers and found it as if they were two corresponding pieces of a puzzle. Our fingers laced together and I felt like I had just turned a key that opened a door onto a whole new world.

Then, it was over. She leaned back and looked into my eyes. I absorbed her. She smiled then dove into the water and swam away. I watched her go as long as I could.

Orange hair and dark skin drew my attention. In the trees above the water sat the three orangutans I owed my life to. They all looked down at me casually. I stared at them with such admiration. I did know love, more so than I thought before. Jacquelyn had helped me realize that.

The momma leaned heavily on the other two, one leg barely touching the branch they all sat on. The knight must have broken it when they were saving me. I loved them even more for it, and craved the death of that monster just as much.

The male nodded at me, his eyes soft and caring. I stood up and found my machete on the rock behind me. I bent down and scooped it up to find a shard of stardust had been sitting on the rock beneath it. It was small and the only piece left. I was amazed that I even held on to that and the machete. Perhaps the water had used some of the stardust up just as my body did. I pocketed the stardust and hooked the blade to the belt at my waist.

I waved to the orangutans then leapt into the pool. The water didn't pull me away like it had done before and the knight didn't appear on the other side, riding the water on his way to kill me again. I paddled to the edge then pulled myself up. The trees and grass retreated from me about ten feet. I didn't have long before I'd need to use the last piece of stardust. I'd try to get some wood before that to save the precious rock.

I walked just a few feet forward, intent on getting out of the mud on the bank. I stopped mid-stride when before me, running horizontally, was the road, the very same one that Morrissett had set me on when this all began. I only now realized that I was about to head out through the forest without an actual idea where I needed to go. I had forgotten about the path until now. I would walk it to Morrissett's friend, hoping that they would have an answer for me, but I was convinced that the knight would haunt it as well.

Chapter 12

The stiffness had gone from my body. Hell, my back even felt better. I could consider myself happy for the most part. I had hoped that the orangutans would walk with me, or at least cut a path through the trees that would trail me, but they didn't.

I kept thinking that each tree that moved before me would reveal the terrible knight, or the tiger cub. I oscillated between fear and anticipation with each step. I thought of Jacquelyn for a moment and my mind drifted to a happier place.

I smiled as I stumbled across a squirrel that was slamming an acorn on a rock. The rock had been turned over by the march of the forest and the squirrel had dropped the acorn then scampered away. It stopped dead after a few bounds then turned and looked from me to the acorn. It considered its predicament for a moment then darted to retrieve its bounty. I laughed aloud as the little guy shot me one hell of a funny look.

"What am *I* doing here? What are *you* doing here? That's the question, my nut-loving friend. Ah don't go now! Just because I caught you red-handed? Come on..." The squirrel had bolted a moment ago. I hollered after it once more, "We all do it!" I chuckled then. I suddenly realized with a swelling sense of pride that I was a funny man. People should be around to see this.

Allowing my inner self to do its thing, I busted out a few dance moves. I wiggled my hips back and forth while taking these quick little steps and bouncing my shoulders one at a time. It all felt great.

A smile still plastered to my face, I continued on, kicking a leg out or shimmying a hip here and there.

It wasn't long before something much bigger than a squirrel ended up on the short end of the forest-moving stick. An Ochari, wiry but tall, fell down from a branch as a tree suddenly shuffled to the side. Those trees plodded along heavily, their tops swaying and hitching all around violently when they moved. I'm surprised more things hadn't fallen out of there.

The green, lizard-like thing had a spear in one hand and the position it held the weapon in made me believe I was a few moments from a painful interaction with it before the Ochari plummeted. I halted as the thing crashed down on the soft soil. It rolled to its feet and launched its spear at me.

I tried to shrink down. I pulled my elbows in and put my hands across my face. I even raised one leg up really high. Air rushed past me, my right elbow tingling with the gust of wind, then a loud thwack came from behind me. I opened my eyes, let my mouth go slack. It had missed, but it had tried to kill me. After I felt so good about my journey and my life.

No. That wasn't going to sit well with me. Fear was pushed deep down into a little pit in my stomach. Then, anger transformed it into a furnace and burned the terror and weakness all up in a single moment. The Ochari was rushing at me, a knife held in its hand.

I didn't feel it, but I pretended to be terrified. I backed away quickly, waving one arm out in front of me and twisting my body. My other hand worked at the loops wrapping the hilt of the machete. They came free. I felt not the fearlessness of apathy for life, but the ferociousness of wanting so badly to live. This bastard wouldn't win.

It screeched as it leapt forward, unable to see that my hand, hidden from it, was wrapped tightly around the hilt of my machete. I threw myself to the side and slashed at the Ochari. I felt resistance, similar to when I'd sunk my teeth into that first pear back in the cave. The satisfaction that erupted within me as the substance of skull and brain gave way beneath the sharp edge was so grand that I craved a dozen more lizard skulls to slice through.

The blade came out cleanly. The Ochari spilled forward, the top of its head rolling away and into the brush. I wasn't even disgusted. I felt like my heart would hammer a hole in my chest, and reveled in it. I stared at the corpse for a long while, breathing, trying to get control of my body again.

"Holy damn," I whispered.

A thin coat of slick blood and other, clear fluid was on the blade. I walked to the Ochari slowly, trying my best to play the part of a good hunter. I surveyed my kill for a moment longer at this close range, the eyeless body with a wide open mouth, tongue lolling to the side between teeth. Brain oozed from the top, riding a stream of blood to the soil. I bent down and used the little bit of cloth that covered this creature to clean my blade. I did so thoroughly.

I then picked up the knife and found two extra loops in my belt to secure it. I put my machete away, then went to the spear in the tree. At least, I tried to. It scurried away. The shaft was maybe three feet long. I attempted to get close enough by running. That didn't work. It would be foolish to waste my energy trying to acquire something I didn't particularly require, especially now that I had the machete and a knife.

I rediscovered the path then continued on, passing the corpse once more. I didn't manage a smile like before, but I still felt good. I was proud of myself, and determined more so than ever. Determined beyond smiles and silly dances.

***

I had walked alone for hours and the fatigue and hunger were getting to me. Trees and vines had begun to sneak close enough to touch me, so I consumed that last sliver of stardust. The road maintained its random array of smooth, red, blue, orange, and black stone. It took me away from the stream and deeper into forest until I was travelling up and down hills. That's what got me so terribly tired. I couldn't stop. I needed to take advantage of the time I had.

Rustling and chirping noises stopped me. Somehow, I'd managed to hear them over the din of the constantly shifting forest. Animals. They sounded small, meek, high pitched voices that squeaked and chattered. I moved toward the noise slowly, away from the path at a soft angle. I found something I didn't expect.

An Ochari lay on its back, chipmunks surrounding it. The lizard-man was much smaller than the one I had killed earlier, and its leg was obviously broken. Deep breaths lifted and collapsed its chest, a knife was gripped tightly in its trembling hand, and its dinner-plate eyes locked onto mine. I pulled my machete out. The small creatures cried out and scurried away behind the Ochari a few feet.

The green creature seemed incapable from keeping from quivering. We stared at one another for a long time. It communicated with me through its gaze. It didn't want to kill me, but it didn't trust me not to kill it.

I backed away slowly, never turning my back. My feet found the road and the trees and grass moved back to hide the Ochari from my sight. We lost each other's gaze. I stood there for a moment, just knowing that there was a terribly wounded living thing without anything to help it. I didn't think of it like an enemy.

127

Not knowing exactly what I would do, I walked back to the Ochari. The chipmunks had surrounded it once more but they didn't run this time. The Ochari looked at me with that same intensity, its blade poised next to its hip, ready to thrust out if need be. I raised my hands slowly, still holding the machete. It must only be a kid by its height. "I'm not going to hurt you. I'm a friend." I used my free hand to touch my chest. "Friend. Good. Help."

I'd feel like a real ass if it suddenly began talking to me with perfect speech. It didn't though. I tried to relay my point even further by holding my blade out then dropping it to the soft soil. The Ochari's eyes followed it to the ground then snapped back up to me. It looked at my belt for a second. I took the knife in my hand, hoping that it wouldn't know the blade was one of its kin's then dropped it to the earth, grateful when it sunk down into the soil so that the majority of it was hidden.

"Can I see? Can I help?" I pointed to the disfigured leg, the knee pointing inward far too much and the thigh and calf a terrible dark color and the flesh swollen. I imagined that something very heavy had fallen down on the knee and shattered it.

The Ochari kept its knife cocked back and ready to strike, and something about the set of its jaw and the broadness of its chest made me decide it was a male. I needed to gain his trust somehow. I noticed that several chipmunks had moved several small steps closer to me. I stepped away from my blades then bent down slowly. I began making a noise by clicking my tongue against the roof of my mouth. The chipmunks all shot their heads in my direction, those big, beady eyes black and curious. "Come on. One of you at least."

Several of them scampered forward but stopped at my blades. My stomach growled, loud enough for them all to hear it and send them hopping back a few chipmunk steps to then stare at my torso, heads cocked to the side. I hadn't eaten in a long time. I wondered how cooked chipmunk would taste.

I derailed that line of thinking real quick. I was trying to do something selfless. I wouldn't pass out from lack of food just yet.

I rubbed my fingers together and continued my clicking noise until two of them came for me. They sniffed my hand warily and one even nibbled on my fingernail. I tried to pet them but they shot this way and that to avoid me. "Okay. My bad. You guys do what you want."

More of them came to investigate me. I let them run around, sniffing, nipping, pinching. They were odd, and I chuckled at them. I looked to the Ochari. His blade was resting on his stomach, still clutched in his hand. His eyes maintained that ferocious look, but I figured that was more because of fear rather than an urge to kill me.

I stood and the chipmunks all bounced away. The Ochari eyed me suspiciously, but didn't raise his blade. I approached cautiously, with my hands up in front of me. The Ochari suddenly leaned forward and sliced at my thighs. I threw my legs back and nearly fell on top of him. I barely managed to keep my balance and stumble away.

The urge to retrieve my machete and cleave that bastard in two filled me. I backed away a few more steps and nearly turned around to grab the blade. Something stayed my hand. I instead analyzed the wounded creature before me. He was terrified and acting on instinct. I wanted to do the same and kill him. That would only make me a murderer and an utter failure in what I was trying to accomplish. Killing him wouldn't be like what I had done to the other one; not even close.

"Stop," I said calmly. "I am trying to help you. I want to only help. Please, put the knife down." He stared at me, breathing heavier than before. It was likely that the movement he had made had hurt like a son of a bitch and was probably still in terrible pain. "Knife down." I held my hand out before me and made a fist then opened it up.

I made the motion several times until I grew too frustrated to continue. "Fine," I seethed. "If you don't want my help then you can die here."

Frustrated, I turned around to leave. I scooped up my machete and was reaching for my knife when I heard something hit the soil behind me. Grinning, for I already knew what that noise was, I stood and found that the Ochari had tossed the knife to the side.

Aggression had vanished from his eyes, replaced by what must have been defeat. He had given up struggling against the current of life and finally allowed fate to take its course, placing his survival in my hands. I approached once more, this time less warily, and knelt down right next to his wounded leg. I pointed to his knee then said, "Broken?" I made a snapping motion with two hands and he nodded.

"I need to put a splint on it. A stick to keep it straight. Do you have a spear?" I tried to mimic the motion of throwing such a weapon. He nodded then pointed deeper into the forest. I stood and set off that way. The grass moved and I found the spear just twenty feet from the Ochari. I also found a boulder, the same one that must have shattered his leg.

It must have rolled down the hill, hidden from the veil of trees, then slammed into him. Had he crawled to where he was now? The boulder couldn't have launched him so far without shattering much more than just one leg. He must have tried to crawl home, only to find that even going that short distance was nearly impossible. Like me, he just wanted to live. Well I'd be damned if I let my difficult predicament result in me forgetting compassion and the responsibility I felt to help others.

I picked up the spear by its stone tip then came across even more good fortune. Several trees had been felled because of the boulder and two of them were just several feet from me. Their roots writhed slowly as I came close, feeling the effect of the stardust and trying to escape. They must have been barely alive. I even felt a pang of sympathy for them.

I quickly remembered that they were nothing more than plants and began stomping on branches thin enough to break, each stomp sending a jarring sensation up my leg and through my body. I kept on though until it snapped off. I did this twice more and had three branches that were mostly straight. I hugged it all close then made my way back to the Ochari.

I piled everything near the him and mumbled, "A splint. Okay, that sounds doable. Two sticks and something to wrap it. My shirt would even work." The Ochari nodded at me and I felt like he agreed with my plan. I was sure he couldn't understand me but felt confident anyway.

The Ochari was on his side, gingerly resting his leg on the ground. I knelt before him and hovered both hands over the shattered limb. "Can you straighten your leg? Straight. Like this." I bent my arm then extended it. The creature nodded his head once then winced as his leg began to quiver. He straightened it maybe an inch, then screeched and shook his head, looking at me with wet eyes.

"Okay, no splint. On to the carrying thing then... Whatever it's called. You know, the thing that I can put you on then drag you across the ground." I was trying to make this creature understand what I was talking about when he didn't even speak the same language as me. I felt like an idiot for a moment.

***

A while later, I had my litter ready. The spear and one of the branches served as the outside while the part the Ochari laid on was composed of the broken pieces of another branch and my clothing. I was actually relieved to find out that I was wearing something under my pants. It would have been a little uncomfortable walking through the forest naked.

The Ochari figured out what I was doing quickly. And thank God for that. I had put all the pieces together then tried wrapping my clothes and my belts around it all to create the litter. It was pretty obvious that I wasn't any good at what I was doing. I only had a very general idea of what I wanted to do.

The Ochari had made a barking noise and asked for the pieces with hand motions. I helped where I could, holding stuff in place. He had torn the armor apart, using the thick leather cords keeping the armor in one piece and my belts to hold the litter together. When it was all done, we were both sweating but had a shoddy litter. The thing would barely carry the Ochari, and some of his body wouldn't fit but it would suffice as long as we weren't travelling far.

Together, the Ochari and I positioned the litter next to him. I then rolled him over onto the work of master craftsmanship, causing him to wince and grit his sharp teeth the whole time. He wiggled this way and that to find a suitable position. I laid my weapons on the litter next to the Ochari then handed him his knife. As he took the blade, we stared at one another for a moment. I could feel the gratitude in those eyes. They had changed so much since I first stumbled across him.

"Home. Where is your home?" I asked. The Ochari was silent for a moment so I stood up and splayed my arms out wide to encompass the whole forest. Then I pointed in several directions and put my hands back up. "Where is home? That way?" I pointed back to where I had found the boulder. He shook his head and pointed the opposite direction. I nodded and said, "Thank you," offering a smile.

I used two pieces of leather from the dismantled armor to wrap the parts of the litter that I would grab, saving my hands from blisters. "Hold on," I said as I bent down and gripped the two short handles. The Ochari was pleasantly light and I lifted him easily. He gripped the branch that ran across the top of the litter near his head to keep from sliding down while pulling his leg up away from the ground.

Cautiously, I turned and began on my way in the direction the Ochari had indicated.

We bumped over loose dirt and small rocks, the Ochari gritting his teeth when I dragged him over potholes that opened up as the trees moved aside. Both of us strained as I stumbled on, the Ochari's biceps flexing as he kept himself from sliding off the litter. Three chipmunks suddenly jumped on top of the litter and squeaked at the Ochari. I let them be, wondering if they were going to see their friend home. That is, if I could get him home. I might run out of stardust, but nothing in my head told me to stop. I didn't feel any remorse for helping the Ochari as opposed to continuing on my path.

I merely knew that what I was doing was the right thing, even if it required a sacrifice on my part. So I continued on doing it.

Chapter 13

Those little chipmunks stayed on their perch the whole way, bouncing and squeaking. The Ochari stayed where he was supposed to, hissing every once in a while as his knees hit together or his leg was jostled too much. I followed his pointing finger whenever he thrust it out and found his village without incidence.

That didn't mean I was home free though. Before we made it to the Ochari tribe, the creature barked and I stopped. "Whatsup?" I asked, craning my neck to look back at him. "Is it that bad now?"

He didn't seem to hear me as he kept on. A loud thud turned my head around and I beheld a much larger, muscular, thick-jawed Ochari was standing up from a crouch right before me. I thought about cutting it down, but then realized that would never work. This wasn't one that I could beat, and my machete was a full step away.

"Hi," I said, certain that it wouldn't understand me.

But it opened its maw and out came the voice of a throat as dry as a graveyard bone. "Well met. You helped Zerast?" He nodded his head toward the Ochari on the litter.

I was amazed that this one could talk. And more so that it spoke so well. "I did. His leg was smashed by a falling boulder. The knee is shattered."

"I see you have stardust. Who are you to be so important?"

"I'm not. I just got lucky is all."

A low growl and whistle came from between his teeth. I hoped that was a noise of contemplation, not one of suspicion and anger. "Come. We will get help for my young brother. Then we will talk more."

The Ochari took the litter from me but I kept the leather keeping my bare hands from the wood. Only then did I remember that my machete and knife were still lying next to Zerast. "Um, I left my weapons on the litter. You mind if I grab them?"

He stopped then asked, "What do you need them for?"

"In case my stardust runs out, or something else out here comes after me. I had a nasty run in with a few basilisks earlier and realized the importance of being armed."

He nodded and I skipped forward and scooped up the weapons. Zerast caught my forearm and gave me a stern, grateful stare. I nodded in return, then fell back and walked behind them as the litter continued moving.

Instinctively, I began putting my blades away on my belt and recalled that I wasn't wearing that or anything else other than tight undergarments. I felt self-conscience for a moment. Until I recalled that the Ochari wore nothing more than a harness for gear across their backs and a piece of cloth or leather to cover their genitals. I'd fit in just fine... besides everything else about me.

The trees cleared before us. The Ochari beside me said, "That is nice. A straight path every time."

I smiled and kept on. After several silent minutes, tepees of sticks and animal skin appeared as the woods moved. The Ochari gripped my shoulder with one strong hand, his claws poking at my flesh. I stopped cold, my heart pausing.

"Stop. The trees could trample our homes. Just sit." I nodded and backed away a few steps, the trees and grass inching back to their original position.

The two Ochari continued on and Zerast stared at me with wide eyes. He suddenly squawked and the older one came to a halt. The chipmunks leapt off the litter and scampered through the village.

The large Ochari looked at me over his shoulder and said, "He thanks you."

I nodded to Zerast and offered a smile. They disappeared into the village and I heard a cacophony of screeches, clicks, and hisses. Leaves rustled and branches creaked behind me. I whirled around expecting that there really was something else coming for me. I began to adopt a fighting stance as best as I knew how, staggering my legs and brandishing my weapons, when I realized it was just another Ochari moving through the trees. She leapt from the tops and fell a dozen feet to land lightly then spring up to her full height. Cloth covered her groin and chest, providing scant cover that failed to do its job often as she moved.

She held a spear to her side, her eyes turned to slits and trained on me like I was a piece of meat and she was a starving predator. Perhaps I did need to stand and ready my blade. Other than her breasts, she was obviously different than the other Ochari I'd come in contact with. She was far thinner, the features of her face at sharper angles to give her a sleeker look. Her belly was covered mostly by soft flesh while the large one I'd met earlier was wrapped entirely in rough scales.

"Can you speak?" I asked.

She tilted her head to one side slightly. I became extremely conscious of the fact that I held one of their knives in my hand and that I'd killed the creature for it. I transferred it to the same hand that held the hilt of my machete and pinned it between my palm and the blade grip, hiding it from view. She kept her eyes on me as we waited. And wait we did. I felt awkward just standing there so I sat and kept my eyes on the soil as the fingers of my free hand played in the loose dirt. I found a dozen worms and had them squirming around atop the soil by the time the other Ochari came back.

Several others were with him, one of them a female as well. "You found him and just brought him here? Why? That confuses us," he said.

The others all looked on with obvious interest.

"He was hurt. What else was I to do?"

"Nothing. Most people would have done nothing. We are grateful, but still unsure as to your purpose. Are you looking for something from us now?"

I didn't have any kind of reward in mind when I decided to do it. Sure, I expected to be greeted by gratitude, but that's not why I did it. "I didn't help him to gain anything. I just did it because it was the right thing to do."

"Thank you. You need to go though." The Ochari said damn near everything in a dull, monotone voice. "Your stardust is a danger to us if you come too close to our home. Before you leave though, are you from the city?"

"Not exactly, no. I came here from there, but I don't live there. I was only stopping there for a time."

"What are you doing then? These are stressful times between us and those in the city."

The others seemed far more interested in me now. They shuffled forward and their hands brushed spear tips and knife handles. I suddenly felt as though I wasn't so safe. "I'm just following the path. I was injured and woke up downstream some time ago. I am travelling through the forest down the path of stones."

"I see. You seek the one they call God. We will leave you to your journey then. I will have a torch brought to you to protect you as you walk. Your stardust is not going to last much longer."

"Thank you. Could I also be given the litter as well? I used my clothes to make it and would like them back."

Before he could reply, a tremendous screech came from behind me, shaking my bones and setting my hair to stand as if I had been struck by lightning. A hand clapped the back of my neck and forced me down. Another groped my wrist and applied a lock on it that had me cry out in pain. I glimpsed green fingers rip the blades from my hand.

Soil filled my mouth as I sucked in terrified breath. I turned my head away as best I could beneath the crushing grip of the Ochari and spit dirt and a worm from between my lips, the urge to vomit barely quelled.

The creatures conversed in their tongue for some time before the one I had spoken with earlier put his head down right next to mine and said, "You have Genrak's knife. How is that? Was he with the other?"

"No," I croaked, tears filling my eyes as the Ochari ground its claws into my skin. "I'm sorry. He tried to kill me. I couldn't do anything else."

"You killed Genrak?" he accused breathlessly, disbelieving.

"I had to. He was going to kill me. I'm sorry!" I couldn't keep myself from continuously apologizing. If I didn't earn his forgiveness, I was certainly dead.

"So you kill one of my brothers then save another? Why? To discover where we live? Is that it? You were going to leave and tell the others then?" He was roaring his words and they were difficult to understand. I caught the gist of it, though each shout caused me to cringe. He was just a word away from killing me.

"No! You have to believe me. I found them both on accident."

"You are a hunter, and a liar! You came looking for us and used one of our own to find us!"

"I didn't! I am going to see God. That is it. I swear to you."

"How can I trust you? How!"

"Ask your brother! The one I saved. Ask him what you should do."

Everything was quiet for a moment, as if the entire forest was waiting for the verdict that would determine my fate.

"I will. You will stay here. Do not try to stand up."

I nodded slowly. He turned and marched off. Hours seemed to pass that I spent there lying there on my stomach, watching as the vegetation inched closer to me, Ochari with weapons standing around, ready to kill me. He returned and the first thing he did was snatch the knife from the Ochari holding it.

"Sit up," he said.

I was sure that he was going to run the knife across my throat. Only this time, I didn't have Jacquelyn near and nothing would bring me back from death. He brought the blade up over my head. Then, it came down terribly fast. It was going to crack through my skull and scramble my brains.

But it sliced through the dirt instead and stuck in the soil. "You took it, you stay with it. You live for now. Where is Genrak's body?"

"Just follow the path back toward the city. You'll find him."

The Ochari turned and left, barking at the others.

I wasn't sure what was going to happen. He had said that I would live, but for how long? What would he do when he came back with his brother draped over his shoulder, missing the top of his head?

There wasn't much else to do but wait though. I swallowed and tried to stifle the adrenaline running through my body. I looked down at the knife before me, but I wouldn't dare touch it. Several Ochari stood around me. And even more were certainly in the trees.

I should have left Zerast in the woods to die.

***

The litter I had constructed was on fire, burning and crackling before me. The stardust had run out and the Ochari watching over me had used the branches from the litter as fuel to keep me from the clutches of the forest. I tried asking them why it didn't come for them but they didn't understand me. That, or they just refused to acknowledge me.

A pile of squirming worms lay near me by the time the Ochari returned with Genrak's corpse. I stopped plucking the wriggling, thick, purple things from the earth when I heard the rustling in the forest.

The Ochari who had decided I was to stay here came up to me and laid Genrak down in the soil. "I found his spear in a tree. I believe that he was trying to kill you. But I can't trust what you will do now. I need more time. No person would so cleanly kill one of ours unless they were trained. You are a hunter."

I shook my head but wondered if I should keep denying it or not. There was nothing to prove that I wasn't. The evidence that I was one lay before me though. "Fine. I am someone who can use a blade. But I didn't come here for the reason you think. I wouldn't have killed him if he hadn't tried killing me first."

The Ochari hissed and barked. The others suddenly grabbed me and I was being pulled by my biceps, my feet dragging through dirt.

"Wait! The fire. I need the fire." They all stopped for a moment and another Ochari carrying a flaming branch walked around the ones carrying me and waived it before my nose. I recoiled from the heat of it. We kept on.

We moved away from the tribe until we came to a piece of wood that didn't flee. It was a thick post set in the ground with two shackles on it.

I didn't need to wonder what was going to happen next. There was old blood on the post and even fingernail marks near the shackles. I was latched up to it and didn't have to wait long.

Fire tore across my back three times. I kept my mouth shut until the third. I cried out when the whip lashed me the final time.

"You are not lying to me? If you are, this will be your life," the Ochari said. This one must be some kind of leader. He had called the shots so far and was the only one who had spoken to me.

I only needed to convince him.

"I'm not lying. I will not go back to the city, I swear," I cried, punctuating my plea with sniffling, cracking words, and grunts. It wasn't pretty. But it worked, at least for now.

The whipping stopped but I wasn't freed. The Ochari all left, leaving me alone with a single branch burning near me.

***

I was left in a void, alone with my thoughts. As the burning branch near me grew weaker, no longer singing my flesh, I felt the void close, soon to swallow me whole and bear me away from this terrible journey. I didn't quite know if I cared whether or not this was when I died or not.

A single sob and tear had escaped me, then I had cast those emotions from the abyss, refusing to wallow in self-pity. I'd been put here. My path had been cemented in concrete and I wasn't allowed the will to stray from it. There was no haven from my hell.

Instead, I filled the hole I existed in with thought. I contemplated the significance of what I had done, the puzzle still hidden in the brainfog, hoping to unlock more and understand my decisions thus far.

Determination to discover the answers to those questions had brought me this far. Relentlessness in my pursuit to discover myself presented me with another piece of my memory as I agonized over the shit hand I had been dealt in Haven Sprawl and the effect Kanute, Aaliyah and her giants, and the knight had on me. The memory stole me away from this world. I was barely learning how to walk, but I wasn't a child; I was a man.

My long, thin arms shook as my hands gripped wooden bars with so little strength. I felt a sickness rise in me. The calm, inspirational face of a lady standing at my side attempted to motivate me as I began to shuffle forward. Decay grew inside me, however, and I felt it worsen. I continued my shuffling, determined that the foreboding feeling that an infection was devouring me from within was merely a figment of my imagination.

Men and women in long white coats stood around me suddenly. I drifted in and out, seeing them appear and disappear with each flashing vision. Learning how to walk no longer mattered in the least. By the way they spoke to the others not in similar uniform, their backs turned to me as they sat on the edge of my bed, I knew that there was something terribly wrong with me. Sobs shook the ones sitting with me, and the face of an angel turned to look at me. I slipped into the black again, and the image along with it disappeared, hiding back within the fog that clouded my past.

The present returned, and I realized that only a few inches separated me from the nearest vine creeping toward me. Instinctively, I pulled away from it, then stopped. I wanted to find the angel in my dreams again. Perhaps I would if I just subdued and gave in to this world which craved my death so desperately.

A will to live I hadn't felt several times in the past had pushed me to survive and achieve feats I didn't think myself capable of. Had it finally run dry? Did I come all this way only to give up to the thing that had come for me in the first place?

No. "Fuck no," I growled.

Tears again sprung to life before my eyes, blurring the world into a painting of running and blending colors. These were not borne of pain and sadness though. An inferno raged within my soul, cementing the hope which seemed so terribly frail at times. I imagined the orangutans, the cub, Jacquelyn, and their sacrifices for me. Chords resonated within my heart, urging me to continue my fight, for them and for myself. They were the solid rocks that allowed me reprieve from the waterfall of life I'd suffered through thus far. And their love and care was worth every ounce of pain.

Nothing I did would have prevented any of this, I realized. If I had made the choice that placed me in this predicament, then I would have accepted it and given myself to death long ago. Instead, life imposed its brutal hand upon me, asking that I fall before it and be crushed. Well, it had no idea how strong I truly was, and how hard I would rail against it.

This wouldn't beat me. I would live.

I stomped on the encroaching vine and ground it beneath my heel. I would live.

Chapter 14

Every so often I would hear some kind of commotion. Either it was a noise from the village that was loud enough to reach out to me, or it was an approaching Ochari bringing another branch to keep the grass and trees at bay by a few feet, or it was something moving out in the wild. This time, the racket was louder.

Screeches, hisses, and other chatter came at me from behind in such a volume that my naked back trembled, the three cuts there stinging with a fresh wave of pain. The noise grew louder and I eventually heard leaves and grass rustling as the Ochari coming after me stomped through the forest.

I turned as much as I could before the short chains stopped me. Dozens of Ochari marched toward me through the trees, most of them holding some kind of weapon, some of them swinging and jumping from branch to branch high above. So they had decided then, and I was going to be slaughtered by them all.

Zerast was among them, a long staff under one arm to support himself as he hopped on his one usable leg. Even that looked painful and his leg flopped sickeningly with each lurch. He held a short spear in his one free hand. He screeched and growled as he moved, jabbing at the others when he could.

I swear I could see the pain in his face as he moved. I could read it off his body like a page with writing on it. He seemed terribly upset. What could have driven him to get up and hobble over to me, obviously defying his tribe's wishes as they barked and wailed at him? I knew what drove him: emotion. I just didn't know what kind. Was it anger? Was Genrak his brother? Did he come to kill me as recompense for his brother's death while the others wanted him to stop and rest? Or was it something else?

The others stopped Zerast before he reached me but he looked into my eyes as he argued with them. They spoke in their own language with each other, obviously upset. The one that had put me here suddenly stepped before Zerast and steadied him to keep him from moving. Zerast snarled a word alien to me then pressed his forehead against the larger one.

Not all went silent, but most did. Some murmured in their hissing language. The two Ochari I was fixated on stood there for a moment. Finally, Zerast spoke a stream of words with undeniable intensity, his eyes blazing, his voice strong and deeper than I'd heard it thus far. Everything went quiet at that. A blanket of calm that had been waiting for its time to descend suddenly fell over the entire forest it seemed.

The larger Ochari replied with a nod and all the others breathed for the first time in a few moments. I hadn't even noticed that they had been waiting so eagerly. The two clapped each other on the shoulder firmly, Zerast nearly toppling, then the larger one helped him to my side. I tried to stand but the shackles kept me down and I was only able to come up to a crouch.

I flinched as Zerast placed a hand on my cheek. He squeezed it gently then smiled at me. Then, he turned and the entire tribe went back with him, all but the large Ochari who stayed before me.

"We're letting you go."

I nearly plopped down on my ass. "Really? You aren't lying to me?"

"No. You can go."

"Is that what all of that was about?"

"Yes. I'm coming with you though."

"Coming with me? I don't get it. I'm not going back to the city."

"I can't trust that. And my people's survival can't depend on something I can't trust. If you are telling the truth, however, then we should have no trouble. Where are you going?"

"Down the stone path. Straight to its end. That is all."

***

We were back on the narrow, stone path shortly after that. My back was sore from the whip. However, I had come to find that the cuts were superficial and had already stopped bleeding. I nearly thanked him for his restraint, as it was plainly obvious from the swelling muscle twisting along his arms that he could have torn into me deeply. He had given me back the tattered remains of my shirt and pants. I put them on and found several new holes and that they sagged from me now.

A torch blazed in my hand, pine resin cracking at its end, the machete in the other. Genrak's knife had been taken from me, and I was glad to be rid of it. I wasn't a hunter. I didn't want trophies for my kills. I merely wanted to survive, and things kept getting in the way of that.

The Ochari walking with me stayed in the forest, out of the range of heat my torch put out that pushed the foliage away. A spear of wood and metal rode his hand and I was keenly aware of the weapon, lest he turn it on me once we were far enough away from his people.

The dense forest was beautiful in its colorful glory. Light shone through the openings in the canopy above, caressing bright flowers of red, pink, purple, blue, and yellow. Petals flared out and curved inward, some as large as my head, others the size of my fingernail and all sizes in between. Animals scurried amongst the tree trunks, skipping from place to place, many of them an enigma to me. Despite the exquisite scene all around me, I was more preoccupied by the questions I had.

"Would you mind us talking?" I asked.

"Speak."

"You mind coming a little closer so we don't have to yell?"

"I can hear you fine."

"Alright. Why does this all come after me and not you?"

"What makes you think I can answer that? Does anyone know why the trees and grass try to kill your kind?"

"I don't know. I am not from here. At least I don't think. Has it ever tried coming for you?"

"No." I saw him run his hand along the bark of a tree as he spoke. "Where are you from?"

"I don't know that either. I awoke in the forest some time ago. My memories are scattered and make little sense to me. I know I was sick before all of this..." I trailed off, searching through the fog once more before quickly giving up. "I recognize stuff and things make sense. At least some things. Morrissett told me to follow this path. There's a friend at the end who will help me. So I've been on this journey to do that since. I bet you don't believe me."

"It is an odd story. We will see what I come to believe."

I nodded and we were silent for a moment again. "What is your name? I never caught that."

"Ardetii. What is yours?"

"I don't know. That has to be believable right? There wouldn't be a reason to keep that to myself." Ardetii didn't remark, he just kept his eyes forward and walked. "What happened back there? When Zerast put his forehead against yours."

"That is a contest."

"What do you mean?"

"When one Ochari does not believe the other, the one in question can wager his life against his honesty. It is also applied when arguments are unable to be ended. Zerast gave me an offer that either I would take, or I would have to kill him for it."

"Why would you do that?"

"Because that is what we do. Why do you not survive without fire in the forest? Because you just don't."

"But what if you didn't believe him and were forced to kill him? What then?"

"That doesn't happen often. The contest removes emotion and we think logically. When we connected," he placed the knuckles of his balled fists against one another to symbolize the connection between their foreheads, "there was no more emotion. Our anger was replaced by reason. Did it make more sense to slaughter my brother when I could simply escort you away from my village?"

He let the question hang in the air and I got the impression that it wasn't actually meant to be answered. It was far too obvious. I wondered, however, why the same solution didn't apply before Zerast wagered his life for mine. Ardetii had let his anger control his mind when he decided to kill me, unable to see the simple alternative until Zerast contested him, forcing him to think clearly.

"Before that," he continued, "I wanted you dead to atone for Genrak's life. Zerast had heard that we were going to kill you. We were both enraged. He hurt the woman trying to mend his leg in his escape. He was beyond reason though."

"You were going to kill me?"

"One life is not as important as the many lives in my village. No life is so important that it outweighs the lives of hundreds. It is better to live that way then to hold one thing as being so important that there is no circumstance in which it should be sacrificed."

I quietly absorbed that, thinking about how wise those words were. Ardetii sure as hell had a handle on the language. He must be important in his tribe.

"There was an alternative suggested," he said.

"What?"

"To pick up our entire tribe and move. We decided against it. That would have been an incredible feat and we would have had little time to complete it. The time we live in just wouldn't allow for that."

"But I am a living thing. Why *wouldn't* killing me be the last resort?"

"Because it just wasn't. Not to us. It'd be easier and quicker to simply kill you right then. You're only alive thanks to Zerast."

"When I saved Zerast," the alien name slipped between my lips cumbersomely and I knew I butchered it," I didn't have to. I wasted the stardust I had in doing so. I should have continued along the path. But I didn't. Because I thought that he would die if I did nothing. That's all it took. Life is sacred. I've learned that in my short time here. I've seen plenty of people die and never once had the ability to do anything to stop it. This time, I did. That's why it's sacred, to me at least."

Ardetii walked up to the path and tread alongside me. "That is an interesting thing to say. That must have been where Zerast's mind was when he came to you. He was going to lie down with you until we moved the tribe. He wasn't going to let us hurt you or heal him until you were let go. He believed in you. It is hard for us to do that. Whatever you did, or however you did it, it impacted him."

A flower of pride bloomed in my chest. I hadn't saved Zerast so that parades would be made in my honor or my name praised by him or his people. The only thing guiding me was my sense of right. I was amazed that my nature was enough to do that to a person... well, an Ochari.

"So, you're going to walk with me until I reach the end of the path?"

"No. I am going back to my tribe as soon as I am sure you are doing what you say you're doing. We are on the verge of war."

Kanute had said something similar. "Why?" I asked. "What is supposed to be gained?"

"Asking why doesn't make sense. War is a part of life. After it is over, all is better."

"Couldn't things be better without it? I just don't understand it."

"Many don't. And I am not one to give the perfect answer. It is natural for things to progress to that. The people in the city start to rely on us less and things tend to no longer turn out in our favor. They know that war is inevitable as well. After, we all work together better. We all know how war affects us. Everyone takes that into consideration on both sides. But after a time, the past is forgotten and it repeats."

"Wouldn't it make more sense to simply be able to compromise?"

"You say it like it is so simple." Ardetii was grinning at me.

"Well shouldn't it be?"

"I never said it shouldn't. Only that it isn't. There are things that should be, but aren't. Or that shouldn't be, but are."

Another one. I was beginning to like this creature.

"Oh!" I suddenly thought of the knight. The trees before me had shuffled away and had revealed a wall of rock to the left. It was dark, not completely black, but nearly. "The knight. Have you come across the black knight?"

"What is a knight?"

"You don't know that word? You know a lot of others. You even make me feel dumb."

"I've learned how to speak well because diplomacy is needed sometimes. But I have only learned words that are used by the people I speak with. Knight is not one I have ever heard."

"Well, he is a man, or a creature, covered in thick armor from head to toe. He has a flaming sword. He's the reason Morrissett put me on this path. He's tried killing me since I woke up in the forest. He nearly succeeded too. Stabbed me right through my chest. I was saved by a friend though."

"I have not ever seen that. Nor have I heard of it."

"Let's hope you never do. That'd make me one happy person."

***

Ardetii and I passed the time talking as we walked. I asked questions that he didn't have great answers for. They weren't philosophical, otherwise he would have had plenty to say.

I was beginning to ask what his people thought of God, whether they believed in the same one as everyone else or if they believed in one at all, when he raised a hand to my chest to stop me. "Come," he said. I would have obliged him willingly, but I didn't have the chance to make that choice as he pulled me along by my shirt, ripping it even more.

"Hey, I don't need to be pulled around all the time!"

"Quiet!" he hissed.

I shut my mouth although I was getting worried. Why were we leaving the path? Where was Ardetii taking me? Why did we have to go so far from the path? We might lose it!

But then he stopped me again and kept his eyes trained in the direction of the path.

"What are we doing?" I whispered.

He held up a hand and I rolled my eyes. I wanted to be as alert and intense as he was. But I didn't like this secrecy. I felt like screaming just to piss him off.

The sounds of ambling trees and slithering vines came to us even though what was around us was still. Someone else was doing that then. They were moving through the forest with fire or stardust, which meant they were human. The forest allowed everything else through it without a care.

Sure enough, two men in thick tunics came into my limited vision. I saw their heads bobbing as they trudged along the path, flames dancing before them. They moved slowly and laboriously and I knew that they were pulling something.

"They're hunters. Why did we have to hide? It's not like they're hunting us."

"I know they aren't. They don't even know about my tribe. They wouldn't be out here hunting normal game if they did."

"Then what are we doing? Couldn't we have just talked to them when we crossed paths? You speak perfectly well. They're just people."

"They are never just people. Haven't you ever had people act like they weren't people? Or treat you like you weren't? No one is ever just that simple. Stay here."

Ardetii took off before I could reach out and stop him. I whispered after him as loud as I would dare, "What are you doing? Ardetii!" Either he didn't hear me or he didn't care that he had. I knew what he was going to do: the same thing that Genrak had tried doing to me.

If humans and Ochari would just give each other a chance, then maybe things wouldn't be the way they are. They wouldn't need history to repeat itself if they just learned from it.

Fear tried to stop me from doing what I wanted, but I stuffed it away. I'd save it for when Ardetii turned on me. "Run!" I screamed. "An Ochari is coming to kill you! You need to run now!"

Ardetii disappeared into the trees with one great leap and I began running toward the hunters. They stood still, one holding a blade at the ready and the other with an arrow notched, looking around for the danger.

"He's in the trees! Just run!" But they didn't budge; they'd rather stay and fight. They didn't believe me and likely thought I was trying to scare them so I could take their bounty.

Their eyes found me quickly, the flame of my torch giving away my position, and the one with the bow aimed at me. I ducked but the arrow never leapt after me. I rose slowly, keeping myself hidden behind the trees before me as well as I could. I was just in time to see the archer fire an arrow into the trees.

It was as if Ardetii had caught the arrow and threw it back immediately. Only, it had multiplied in size tenfold. The spear cut through the air immediately after the arrow disappeared into the leaves then slammed into the archer's chest, knocking him to the earth. The other hunter turned and began sprinting back down the path, his torch held out before him. I heard Ardetii giving chase as he swung and leapt through the trees. He moved terribly fast.

I slowly crept up to the path. The trees finally parted to reveal the cart and the dead hunter. The former held a massive creature with shaggy fur and wide, dead eyes. The latter was lying on his back, the spear lodged deep in his chest where his heart resided, blood seeping from him and around the stones that made up the path.

A ragged scream tore my head in the direction of the path. I couldn't see much through the thin tunnel created by the trees on either side, but I didn't need to see anything to know what had happened. The hunter had run until Ardetii had caught him. Then, the Ochari had fallen on him and murdered him, his victim's last noise one of surprise and terror.

I felt very tired now. I walked several yards away from the cart, the dead hunter, the carelessly and needlessly spilt pool of blood, the direction of the scream, then sat down. I didn't look at anything other than the stones beneath my knees.

It wasn't long before Ardetii came back. I knew he would be back quickly, and that he would be angry. I wasn't even surprised when he grabbed my neck in one crushing hand and lifted me up. I gagged and coughed but I didn't fight too much. If he wanted to kill me then he would. Ardetii was skilled and one heartless bastard. It was his decision whether I lived or died. I had no say.

We stared at one another for a while, anger in his eyes, defiance in mine. Black spots swam in on me. They rimmed Ardetii's face making his stare that much more intense. Just moments before the abyss took me, he let go. I staggered away, and not because my legs were weak. But goddamn was it difficult coughing and trying to suck in breath while my head felt like it was floating up above the trees.

"You shouldn't have done that. Don't do it again," Ardetii commanded.

I was hunched over, my hands on my knees. "No, you shouldn't have done that. What was the reason? No, I know what it was; you didn't want them to find your village and bring the city down on it. So you killed them. Don't you think that your people could have handled those two? You're all quick as hell. They would have seen the hunters first. And what if the hunters would have just walked on by without even noticing your tribe? They didn't need to die! You just didn't give them a choice or even a chance!"

Ardetii seemed taken aback for a moment, but then, with ice dripping from his lips, he said, "They weren't as important as my tribe. I did what I should have done, and what any other Ochari should have done. You think with too much emotion. You'll end up dead because of it, believe me. From now on, we don't talk. We don't rest. You get far away and I go back to my people. War is coming.

Soon, you will not be important. Get far enough from my tribe or I'll kill you."

That was supposed to light a fire under my ass or perhaps I should have dropped to my knees and groveled for mercy. I chose neither. I wanted to reach the end of my journey, to find my answers. This much shit so close together... It was too much, and it caused me to hesitate and take stock. My whole life, at least what I remembered, was a real short occurrence of terrible events.

I wondered if these were the kinds of things that sent people spiraling into depression, forgetting the good things that they once possessed and lived through. Forcefully, I changed my line of thinking. Because I knew I was right. I thought of the orangutans, of Jacquelyn, of the cub and his soft fur against my chin. I started moving down the path.

***

A massive pit had opened in my stomach, yawning wide for sustenance. I cradled it as though I could contain the pain somehow, my attempts made in vain. My gut screamed, twisted, turned and slammed against my insides. Ardetii walked up to my side, out of the forest he had been stalking through hidden from my sight until now. A freshly dead blue bird was in his hands and he was holding it out to me as though I was supposed to know what to do with it.

"Eat it," he said.

"How? I can't just shove a whole bird down my throat."

"Stop and cook it for a moment then peel its skin off and eat the meat beneath it. It isn't much but all I care about is you moving a little quicker. You're far too slow and far too empty."

I wasn't any good at this. I took the bird between two fingers as if it was diseased. Shit, it just might be. My worry over its cleanliness was such that I nearly chucked the carcass out into the woods. My distrust didn't hold much water as my stomach yelled, "Eat it!"

"Do I pull the feathers off? And the stomach, what do I do about that? Can't you do this for me?"

"No. I'm going to keep a look out. Make sure there aren't any other hunters around here. They come in groups sometimes. The feathers will burn off. You don't have the time to spend cleaning it. Just cook it and eat what's there."

Ardetii disappeared as he fled into the forest and leapt up into a tree. I marveled at his athleticism as he cleared such distance with a single bound and was in the branches and moving across them.

I knelt down and put the torch on the path then tossed the bird onto the flame. It crackled and popped and the feathers caught fire. I stared at the eye until it exploded, turning my head, repulsed.

A few minutes passed and Ardetii was back. "That's enough," he said.

I pulled the torch away, the carcass of the bird flopping onto the stones, still aflame. I blew on it until I nearly passed out, black dots swimming at the corners of my vision. The stink coming from the burnt feathers was nearly enough to make me vomit. I stood and tapped on it with my foot until the flame was finally extinguished.

The black, charred thing looked like a meal fit only for a raving beast with an insatiable hunger for flesh. I bent down and pinched its burnt flesh between two fingers. Immediately, I let it go. Somehow I hadn't realized before touching it that it would be hot. I sure as hell knew it now though. I blew on my fingers then stuck them in my mouth and found little reprieve. The bitter taste of charcoal was on my fingers and I spit them out.

"You're making this difficult."

"And you made me no longer hungry. Let's just go. I'll be fine."

I didn't wait for a response as I continued on. I looked over my shoulder as Ardetii picked up the bird. He threw me a look of disgust. Fuck you too, then.

He moved back into the forest, out of my sight. "Pick it up!" came his voice from somewhere in the trees. The next thing I would hear would probably be the whistle of his spear before it slammed into my side.

I started taking bigger steps, but the hunger immediately caused a pain in stomach.

"Some fruit would be nice," I hollered into the trees.

I kept my eyes toward the trees Ardetii was leaping through for a while. I continued watching the trees until I felt all hope for something edible to be thrown my way run out. I turned my eyes back to the path and stopped thinking that Ardetii would do something human for me.

***

"We've gone far enough. You can go on without me. Don't make me regret this." Ardetii said as soon as his feet dropped down on the stones behind me.

I whirled and had to remind myself to keep on breathing. That cold shock shook me from my stupor. We had been going on in silence for some time now. I couldn't put any amount of time on it. I was drifting in and out even as I walked.

"God, Ardetii. You couldn't just walk up next to me?" I sucked in a deep breath then blew it out in a sigh. "This is it then? We've gone far enough?"

"Yes. Here." The Ochari extended his scaled arm and in his hand were two bananas, the peels green but still the most appetizing thing I had seen in a long while. I took them as if they were going to up and jump out of his hand then scurry off to be lost in the woods.

"Thank you. So we've gotten far enough from your people? You believe me?"

"Not completely."

"Then why are you letting me go? Wait, forget that I said that. I'll just shut up and go this way, you go that way. I hope your brother's leg heals well, that your next war isn't so terrible, and that we never see each other again."

If I had the energy, I would have run away from Ardetii. I was too tired, and too busy working on one of the bananas while still holding the torch and keeping the flames from burning the hair off my face to manage more than a slow walk. I only hoped that the kingdom was close, and that these two pieces of fruit and my torch would be enough to get me there, although the pine resin was beginning to run out.

"I don't think you'll make it. That's why I'm letting you go. I believe that you aren't from here, because you aren't strong enough. People as weak as you die. Something will take you."

Nothing else mattered for a moment. I had one of those epiphanies one usually has after something had already major had occurred. I was reminded of when Kanute had said things that were supposed to break my spirit and I had remained passive and ignored it outwardly even though I would obsess about it inwardly. Then, once I tossed it over a bunch of times, I'd discover a great retort. Well, I did all that in the span of a second.

Turning, I said, "You don't even have the strength to stand up to something threatening. You throw your spears and knives from the trees. Or you jump on someone's back and kill them that way. You don't have the balls to go and try to fix a problem that has existed between you and the people of the city for as long as you can remember even though you know how to solve it. If I really was weak, I wouldn't have made it this far. I would have given up before I even began down this fucking path.

"No, you don't get to call me weak. I stood up to this whole hellish world. I've done things the hard way because it was the right way. You have talent, you have brains, you have power, but you still act like a savage. You are a waste. Me, I'm going to use what I have to change things. Enjoy your pointless wars, you lizard fuck."

Death stared me down, the promise of violence written plainly in Ardetii's gaze. I met it without balking. I felt powerful because I knew I was right. I knew I had balls. I knew I had gone through shit and come out the other side still able to fight. I hadn't been broken yet, and that was my biggest victory.

We held the stare down for another moment. I tried to communicate my power, my anger, my purpose through my eyes. I turned and put that bastard behind me and out of my mind. He wouldn't come for me. I'd made a stand, placing myself on the same pedestal he stood on and held my own. Before I turned away, I saw respect in his eyes, hidden within the fury.

Chapter 15

Glorious and beautiful, a valley sprawled out before me. I had been walking through the forest when the trees before me suddenly shifted away from the heat of my torch to behold this low land of long grass. I was amazed mostly by the absence of trees. This was the first time I had stumbled across a land that wasn't bursting with all kinds of vegetation.

I had a strong urge to drop the flame and just run out into the field. My better judgement beat out my joyous mood and I realized that grass as long as this would wrap me up better than the webs of a thousand spiders. So I simply stood at its edge, the flame held low at my side, and marveled.

Stalks of golden wheat pierced the glade of green grass, reaching up to the sun here and there. Lone trees speckled the valley claiming dominion over large swaths of grass and wheat. Dozens of those large, shaggy animals roamed the valley, munching on the grass which tried getting away once they closed their teeth on it. A river ran to my left, bending around the edge of the valley, separating it from the forest on the other shore. The glistening water, reflecting the sunlight in blinding flashes of light, flowed on in until it was lost behind the trees that suddenly sprung up from the far side of the valley.

I scanned the treetops beyond the valley until something stopped me right above where the river disappeared. That didn't look right. It was interesting, and even a little daunting. Was that one massive tree? But it was shaped oddly, all sharp angles and square tops. It couldn't be just a tree. The kingdom. That must be where God was. I *was* nearly there.

I tossed the banana peel I had been holding into the air and screamed, "That's it!" I didn't even know why I had been holding onto the peel this whole time. Throwing it now felt like a great way to celebrate. I took off at a run, holding my torch before me and close to the ground to move the grass. I cut a path through the field, over the thin path, as the grass slithered away.

The valley bounced with my shaking head and I was careless enough to veer close to a tree. A branch began reaching for me but I swiped my torch at it and it recoiled, "Not today, tree!"

I ran by one of the creatures lumbering along the valley and it barely even noticed me. They looked harmless enough. It was a sight to behold the grass wiggling between the large, blunt teeth of the animals as they chewed it up.

Such immense joy lifted my spirit that I didn't even consider stopping myself as I ran to the side of one and gave it a big hug with the arm not holding the low-burning torch. I felt the creature rumble as it mumbled a low, deep groan.

With big, slow, careful steps, the creature tried spinning toward me. I caught the gaze from its big eye between long strands of thick hair as it turned its head to me. "Come here, buddy." I let go of it and then wrapped its head up with one arm then kissed its nose. "Oh, you smell terrible. And your nose is wet. Tastes salty. Ugh. Nice meeting you. Have a good life."

Skipping, I moved around the creature and it swung its head slowly after me. I waved to it then continued on jogging. I got winded pretty quickly and had to slow to a walk. Still, I felt great. I breathed the sweet air and looked at my destination over the trees, uplifted.

***

Flames from my nearly exhausted torch began cooking my hand. The leather straps from the torn up armor I'd used for the litter provided scant relief. I considered trying to break a branch off of a nearby tree, but decided against it. The tree would run until I got a hold of it then it would start smacking me around and I didn't look forward to that. I still had a few minutes until I absolutely needed to try that trick out.

Thick forest was all around me again, the kingdom lost to my vision because of it. I must be at its doorstep though.

I'd reached that critical point now. I lunged forward to grab a branch, holding the flame behind me as its heat hurt my skin. The tree was playing it safe though and scrambled away. I reached again and this time I caught the branch. I put as much weight as I could into breaking it off but wasn't so successful with just one hand. The tree bolted to the side suddenly and I barely kept my grip. I let go of my own accord immediately after I figured out why it had changed direction though.

A place void of anything green was before me. It reminded me so much of Morrissett's place. There was a circle of empty dirt and a house within that, the latter a sight that set this place apart from Morrissett's. That was the thing that really stood out. The house was much nicer. It wasn't a hut so small that I could barely fit in it. It had walls of brick, a roof of a mixture of long grass and dried mud, and an actual door made of wood with a handle. A small chimney even popped out of the roof a few feet with a thin, waving stream of smoke coming from it.

I stepped onto the holy ground and smiled. I let the torch slip from my fingers and fall to the dirt to burn itself out. I lay down on the dirt and looked up to the bright sky above. I could have fallen asleep, such relief washed over me, but I was too energetic.

"I'm here!" I yelled to the sky. "I made it!"

"You made it where?" came a voice.

I turned to the sound and found a woman standing at the open door of the house. She didn't wear an odd mask like Morrissett had. Despite that, she reminded me of him somehow. She had a rod much like his.

"Here," I sang. "Did you know I was coming?" I was still on my back, twisting my head to the side to hold her gaze.

"How would I know that?" she asked. An aura of warmth resonated from her, the smile on her lips contagious. Her hair was twisted into a bun on the back of her head, a swirl of auburn and grey. Her eyes were alive, shining amidst the deep lines and wrinkles on her face.

"I don't know. It was just a wild guess. A hope maybe. Do you know what I have been through? There's so much. Is it okay that I'm here?"

"Too many questions at one time, young man. Why don't you just relax for a time? I don't know what you've been through, but I know it must have been one hell of a journey."

"Can't just relax. I have too much going on. It's nearly all over. Let's just talk for a little."

And we did. I told her my story. She said, "Ah, that old idiot," when I mentioned Morrissett. Then she said, "I'm only kidding. He's not so bad. Looks like he got you here."

After I was all talked out, I asked her, "So what am I supposed to do now? Morrissett said you would help me. Do you know who I was?"

She flashed that comforting smile and shook her head. "I'm not a fortune teller, young man. But I can help. Come here."

I had since turned over onto my side and was holding my head up off the ground by resting it on the palm of one hand. I scrambled up quickly and jogged over to her. She watched me with a light smile as I made my way to her.

She was still for a while, just staring at me with something that looked almost like love, so I asked, "What? Is something on my face?"

I wiped the side of my cheek expecting there to be dirt on it. She shook her head and said, "No. You just have such life. I wonder why you're here."

"Because I had to come here. There was nowhere else to go really."

"For some that is true. This is their destination regardless of what choices they make. But you are so young. Too young to be where you are."

"What do you mean?"

And then I wondered if maybe I had taken some really good, or really bad, drugs. Time skipped forward I think. She was suddenly walking away, and she hadn't just turned. She was ten feet away from me, nearly around the house.

Time played a second trick on me, it seemed, as my mind was suddenly usurped as a fragment of my memory broke loose from the haze shrouding it. I was sitting before a desk, someone seated next to me, his hand resting on the arm of his chair. A woman sat behind the desk, a name too blurry to make out etched into a block of wood on her desk. She wore a white coat, and her features seemed so similar to the woman I was even now speaking to. She was looking upon me with sadness in her eyes, and I got the feeling that she'd done something wrong and was apologizing for it.

"Aren't you coming?" she asked, the memory now played out.

I shook my head and said, "Wait. Didn't I just ask you something? You said something just a moment ago."

She looked at me strangely. "I asked you to follow me. You've been standing there ever since. You should have rested more, young man."

Now I knew what had happened. Or at least what had taken place. I knew that she had just told me I was too young to be here. Despite that, I didn't understand how things had just changed all of a sudden. I shook my head and let it go, only because of how fixated I was on what she was going to show me.

Excitement had me skipping after her. She continued shuffling on and we moved around her house. We came to the end of the patch of dirt, trees lining up before us like a well-trained army.

I was about to ask what I was supposed to be looking for when she lifted the rod. I knew this trick. "Here comes the fire. Those trees just don't learn, do they?" I said, smiling at her.

"They're almost as stubborn as people." Fire erupted from the rod, sending the trees smoking and scurrying away. One ended up with a few leaves aflame and it dragged that branch across the trunk of another to extinguish the fire.

Smart ass things wanted to come from my mouth about the tree's behavior. As it was, I couldn't speak all that well. A big, furry, pissed off cat had my tongue and held it fast.

Blue, shimmering water calmly moved in the stream before me. There was a lengthy drop from the edge of the earth I stood on to the water below, but not so far that one would die if they dove in. It might hurt like a son of a bitch. I just barely saw the end of a wide, wooden bridge with thick beams holding it up. That bridge led to the entrance of a black citadel of stone.

The kingdom of God looked a lot less inviting then I had imagined. It seemed like a single slab of rock chiseled into rough angles, studs, towers, and parapets, a labyrinth from this distance and angle.

"God is in there, isn't He?" I asked.

"Safety is in there. Some people call it God. For some that's all that can protect them."

"What do you mean?"

She turned to me, drawing my eyes away from the immaculate structure. "The knight doesn't just chase you. The trees don't only come for you. Many have gone down the same path you are on, or some version of it. Some have managed to survive, while others... haven't."

I was reminded of what Jacquelyn had told me when I first met her about the many souls who had failed to make it past the Sentinel. "The knight can't enter there?" I wondered aloud hopefully.

"Not exactly," she responded. "The Sentinel is a test both you and him have to get past. If you can manage that, you'll have something between you and him. If you survive the test, you'll be better warded against him. But there is no guarantee he won't be able to follow you in and take you anyway."

"Why does he come for some of us? Does he come after you?"

"No. But I've seen him come for many, and I've helped them as best as I know how. I am not sure how he picks who he comes for, only that he is a terrible affliction."

"How do I get in?"

"Not just yet. I want you to stay with me for just a little while. I don't know you. But I want to get to know you before you go. What is your name?"

"I don't know. I have no memory. Young man seems to work fine. What is yours?"

"Bernsinger. Young man it is. Come inside and we'll talk."

"I would, but the knight could be coming for me even now."

"Young man, I'm sorry to tell you, but he is coming for you. Be calm though, you have some time at least before he arrives. It's important to come to grips with your own mortality and to reflect before you undergo this last leg of your journey. If this works, you might make it out of here alive. Either way, you need to be prepared for what might happen. Watch."

Bernsinger aimed her rod a bit more left. The fire left in its wake a hole that showed me that immaculate bridge. I squinted at it but couldn't pick up whatever it is I was supposed to see. "What am I looking for?"

Even as she said, "The man there at the middle," I saw him. He moved slowly across the bridge.

"It moved!" I exclaimed as I thrust my finger at the bridge. Sure enough, the side was lifting up. What kind of bridge was this?

"Not the bridge. The Sentinel."

She was right. What I had thought was the bridge moving, was actually the water being disturbed in odd way. From thin air, there appeared the Sentinel. It was a great thousand feet tall and as wide as the bridge. A massive appendage ran from each of its shoulders and along the sides of the bridge, the source of the disturbed water. It stood on four squat legs.

It is difficult to explain it right. Most of what had me so awestruck about it was its presence, an aura that spilled out from it and washed over me. I felt like that was God. That thing could be the end of me, or my protector. I imagined that the knight would have no chance in hell against it.

Its body was white, green, and brown. Greenish crystalline structures seemed to explode from places along its back in random disarray. The appendages coming from each shoulder looked like tails, thinning to a point. I couldn't see eyes from this distance but I did see slants, menacing. I saw the white of teeth within its grinning mouth. Its head was otherwise smooth.

I wanted to speak. To ask Bernsinger what was happening. I physically couldn't. Absorbing the glory of the Sentinel was all I could manage.

The appendages rose from the water and hovered to each side of the man. Bernsinger blew out a sigh, but I didn't turn to look at her. The man dropped to his knees. I was shaken to my core when one of the appendages swept across the bridge, smashing into the man, sending him careening through the air, causing me to recoil and cover my mouth in horror. He was aimed in our direction, but he would have never reached us. We were too high above the bridge. He didn't make it that far anyway. He splashed down into the water then his body actually skipped several times before he sunk down below the rippling surface.

I looked back to the Sentinel and I could have sworn its head swiveled ever so slightly toward me. Then, it vanished.

Swallowing all of that was difficult. I wondered if another anomaly had occurred and none of what I had seen was actually real. But I didn't skip to a different time.

I had to accept what I had witnessed. A colossal, ancient, mysterious, wondrous, all-powerful being had just crushed a man. He'd came face to face with his fate and just fell to his knees to accept it.

Bernsinger's soft voice pulled me back, "I'll make sense of it inside. Come now, young man. There's nothing more to see."

***

We were both inside her home, sitting down before a table. She was rolling marbles across the wooden, uneven surface. One fell through the planks that made up the table and she let it roll away, rolling another now. I was busy staring at the wall, fighting a battle with my stomach so that it wouldn't explode. I felt like I was losing.

I sipped more of the hot tea, hoping it would push more of the stew I had inhaled deeper down into my stomach, helping it to shut up. Rather, the hot liquid mixed with the viscous meal and my gut burbled aloud in protest, pleading with me to put the damn cup down for an hour or ten. "You must be out to get me too, Bernsinger. That stew was so good I couldn't stop eating it. Now I'm sure I'll pop in a moment or two."

She rolled a marble across the table that bounced and hopped until it got stuck in a groove and rolled its way to her other hand. "I'll take that as a compliment."

"You're being awfully normal. Especially after what I had just seen. You saw it too. It can't be a normal thing for you, right? That was... It was terrible." I hiccupped and felt stew rising in the back of my throat. I winced and pushed it back down.

"I don't see it all the time. But I've seen it enough. It troubles me, but not so much. I can watch a hundred more and be fine soon after. A person just gets that way."

"Well, could you explain it?"

"What you saw was the Sentinel."

"I've heard of it before. It protects the kingdom."

"Correct. You see, there are a few brave souls that face the judgment of the Sentinel in an attempt to get into the kingdom."

"And have any made it yet?"

"Some."

"To escape the forest and the knight?"

"Exactly."

"Isn't there an alternative?" I asked as I swirled the tea in my cup.

For some. But for most who travel this far, it's a last resort. They stand up before it, knowing that they might die because of it, and that they certainly will if they aren't permitted to enter."

"But why does any of this *have* to happen? That's the part I don't get."

"Because you aren't supposed to, young man. That part is a mystery, and it always will be. Some people have to face it, others don't."

"Do you know how to get past it?"

"Not particularly. The result varies from person to person, and I am not sure why. The Sentinel chooses to accept some and reject others."

Anxiety welled in me as I agonized over how the Sentinel would receive me. "Bernsinger, I don't mean to sound ungrateful, because that stew really was the best thing I've tasted since I woke up in this place, but what else can you do for me? You know my story, how hard it has been. If I have to face the Sentinel anyway, then I'd rather just get it over with. I want my answers. I want this to stop, to live normally. And I know the knight is coming for me. Sitting idly is not something I am accustomed to."

Although I was fearful that I'd come off as being impolite, Bernsinger showed no indication that she thought such. "Well, young man, you're right. You've been forced to undertake a journey arduous, long, and completely unfair. It very well may be that this is the end of it for you, one way or another. Coming to grips with your mortality is difficult. What do you recall of your family?"

"Nearly nothing at all. I am sure I had one, but that's it."

"I'm sure that they are eagerly awaiting your return, and that they love you dearly. I want you to think of the good you've done in this place, the brightness you shined even though you were faced with such incredible suffering. You're a strong man, and your fight is commendable, regardless of the outcome."

I imagined the face of the angel I had seen in my memories while waiting for Ardetii to return to me at his village. She must have been part of my family. The family of orangutans came to me next, and I thought of how desperately I wanted to run through the forest with them without having to worry about my immediate death.

The choices I'd made so far all rushed me in a single moment and I smiled as I thought of them. I felt pride for the strength I possessed. I wondered if I would have reached this point if I wasn't the person I was. Had my past experiences, even though I couldn't recall them, been different and the makeup of my character arranged differently, would I have been strong enough to reach Bernsinger?

She reached out and placed her hand on mine and said, "Just know that nothing that happens is in any way your fault and that you and everyone who cared for you did everything they could before you go. The Sentinel's choice in no way reflects who you are. Either way, it will be difficult to pass its test." I wanted to relish in this comfort for just a bit longer, but the way she spoke made me believe that it was time to go soon.

"Do I have to leave soon?" I asked.

Bernsinger lost her smile suddenly and gripped my hand terrible hard. She bolted from the table, ran to the door, and threw it open. Stepping down from the forest and onto the holy ground surrounding her home was the knight in a full sprint. "Run!" she screamed at me.

Fear propelled me and I surged to my feet turned, and sped for the open window. I glimpsed Bernsinger aim her rod at the knight and a column of glorious light shot from it with the speed of a bullet as it exited the barrel of a gun, crashing into the knight and sending him careening back into the forest. I leapt out of the window and hit the ground hard, rolling awkwardly.

"Go to the Sentinel!" she yelled as she leapt down onto the empty holy ground, taking a defensive stance between me and the knight who was even now pursuing me again.

"I want to help!" I responded as I pulled my machete from my belt.

"You can't, young man! This is what I am here for. You need to get away. You need to live!" She sent another blast at the knight only this time he thrust his empty hand at it and caught the spear of luminescence in a net of darkness. Still, it slowed him enough.

I looked to Bernsinger one last time, thanking her with a nod, then turned and ran. The path ran through the holy ground then widened enough for me to not need fire to keep the trees at bay. I sprinted along the stones that sloped down and toward the kingdom.

Chapter 16

I stood just feet from the first giant piece of timber that made up the bridge. I had reached it quickly in my terror-induced sprint. The sounds of Bernsinger fending off the knight had been lost some time ago. I sucked in breath and spewed it back out like a bellows.

The sight of this immaculate construction was enough to cow me, despite knowing that the knight was near. Forty of me could have stood shoulder to shoulder and walked across it. It would be a walk that would take several minutes though. The kingdom was on the other side, its doors open but the inside shrouded by shadow. I knew that I was looking straight at the Sentinel, and that it was regarding me, judging.

Such a thing set my bones to quaking. Having an invisible, all powerful thing so close to me, knowing what it was doing and what it was capable of terrified me. Did the others always feel this way?

But my urge to get past the Sentinel and to God was enough to smash my terror to smaller pieces. It was still there, just not as intense. I took my first step onto the bridge. The wood didn't sag at all, or creak. No, it was sturdier than the very planet I was on. A meteor could fall on it and the planet would be saved from destruction.

I was able to fool myself at first, so far from where I knew the Sentinel stood guard. I thought of the knight as he came for me and that was enough to push me toward what I knew was staring down at me, which could be far more terrible than him.

Halfway to the other side, I stopped. I turned and looked at the forest and was momentarily stuck. The land looked wonderful and beautiful, a bounty of life and color. For that moment, I didn't think of the murderous tendencies of the trees and grass, only of how inviting nature could be. Something about that felt right, like I was having déjà vu. I despaired when I looked to where I believed Bernsinger's home was and no longer saw flashes of light. The knight must have bested her and was closing on me even now.

Fire leapt from the trees, spreading them apart higher up the land and to my left. I looked to the side of one of the few thick beams at the bridge's edge and saw a hole in the forest. I tried to make out Bernsinger but could only see a brown shape amidst the shade. I thought that was her, or it was the side of her home. Either way, I knew she was there, watching me, and I was glad she hadn't been killed by the knight. It seemed to ignore others as it came for me with such tenacity.

I took a deep breath then turned back to the kingdom.

As I closed the distance, certain that I was coming to the point where the Sentinel had appeared and crushed the man before me with each new step, I began to feel myself detach from my body. I was distancing myself from the fear of meeting my fate as I prepared for it. It was so close now. I faltered and considered turning back. I only persevered by latching onto the numbness that had claimed my body and fed my mind with the same stuff. I needed to do this, there was no other way.

I didn't feel myself as I moved, I just did it as if I had no choice. Had I asked myself to turn around, or veer this way or that, nothing would have happened. I couldn't even think that far, because my mind wasn't mine either. I had put myself on auto-pilot with just enough function to breathe and walk.

But all of that was eradicated when the Sentinel appeared. It was suddenly there, its body only a hundred feet from me, its eyes pinning me to the bridge. I couldn't breathe any longer but I could feel. Awe and fear poured into me like molten lead, filling every inch of my being.

I thought that I was going to be ready for this, but now I knew that nothing I ever did would have prepared me enough. This wasn't something that anyone could be ready for. So I stood there, inert.

The Sentinel and I were locked in a gaze so intense that I felt my head begin to ache. Its eyes were a cascade of blues, greens, browns, and points of black. They demanded that I be awestruck and they were not something anyone could defy. It was judging me even now.

How would I know when I had been judged? Would it speak to me? Should I try to say something?

My legs grew weak and darkness flashed before my eyes. I barely kept myself standing but staggered forward as I caught myself. I had stopped breathing and locked my legs, nearly casting myself into unconsciousness. I lost in the staring match with the Sentinel. I looked back to it only after I sucked in a gallon of air, my legs wobbling terribly.

Something in its face looked different, and my heart lifted. It accepted me, and as I thought as such, it disappeared, leaving the bridge empty and the entryway to the kingdom open for me to pass into it. Fires now lit the hall that fed into the citadel and I began my trek to salvation.

Something whistled off in the distance, a high pitched burst of noise that turned my head toward the tree Bernsinger stood behind. A jet of flame extended from where she stood and aimed at something behind me. I whirled around just as the knight broke the tree line. He was far from me though, and I knew I could make it into the kingdom before he reached me.

As the thought occurred to me, he stepped down on the bridge then took flight. His glide through the air was exactly similar to how he had closed on me in the river, only much faster. I wouldn't make it in time.

I turned and ran anyway, hoping that the Sentinel would appear to protect me. After a dozen steps the knight was halfway across the bridge and the Sentinel remained absent. "Please," I screamed. "Help me!"

Nothing answered my call.

I spun around and prepared myself to meet the knight for the last time. Fire engulfed him, however, and he seemed more an embodiment of destruction than a living thing. I had no chance against him.

The machete slipped from my hand but I didn't hear it hit the bridge, I was too intent on the knight. I wondered if Bernsinger would save me somehow. Would Jacquelyn or the orangutans do it? I realized that I was alone. I was going to die with nothing and no one.

The air vibrated and the bridge quaked as the knight closed. I accepted that my salvation from death at his hand lied in my own actions this time and turned and sprinted for the side of the bridge. I shouted as I leapt out into the open air, dozens of feet above the water.

As I fell, I twisted. My eyes locked with the knight's once more as he dove down after me. Oh, he was pissed.

I spun back to face the water and did what I could to move to the side while in the air to avoid his plunging blade. Truthfully, I didn't really manage to do anything.

An arm's length separated me from the water. I planned on hitting it then immediately kicking to the side. A face emerged from the blue. It was beneath the water for only a second, obscured. Jacquelyn's arm shot up and reached for me. I felt her fingers as they clamped down on my shirt.

I then felt other hands grab onto my legs, hips, chest, and neck. I fell into a moment that only people seconds from death could understand. I just gave up. Not because I was done, but because I had found relief. This was out of my hands. And I was in the best that I could be. If ever I had a chance of making it out alive, this was it.

Jacquelyn's face was just inches beneath the water when I felt her eyes lock onto mine. I felt our love pass through our gaze and into each other. Not a romantic one, necessarily, but one that two people shared who would do anything for each other.

Cold shocked me as I hit the water, then I was jerked to the side. I sped through the water until an enormous wave of force shot through me, dislodging all the hands from my body. I was stunned, stuck beneath the waves, my eyes shut against the quick current pushing me along. Then, I ceased moving, and the wave stopped accosting me. I opened my eyes and saw several mermaids swimming for me.

They gripped me once more and I was wrenched away yet again, on the wings of these angels of the sea. We hadn't gone far by the time I felt myself needing breath. I held it as long as I could manage, then held it longer. My head was expanding, pushing against the bed of sand at the bottom of the river. A terrible pressure asked me to suck in a breath, but my mind fought it, pleading with the desire, trying to make it understand that there was no air for me down here.

The knight cut through the water not far from us, a large, blurry splotch now void of fire. He turned on us and I felt his regard like a hammer blow.

The urge to suck in a breath was unbearable and I gave in. Only, it wasn't air. Water filled my lungs and blackness closed in quickly.

I fought it away for a brief moment, screaming at my body that I couldn't go into the black just yet. The knight continued its pursuit, closing the distance faster than the mermaids could bear me away. My body disobeyed me once again, trying to fight logic. I sucked in another lungful of water and the darkness devoured my vision this time, and refused to recede.

***

There was no light, but there was no darkness either. My eyes blazed with something. A thing that let me see all. I knew then, as I sailed over the land below that I was the being of light.

167

To my left, was the kingdom. To my right, a crater in the earth that reeked of death. I didn't control myself much, but I could think. I found it odd that I had decided to go away from God and toward the crater.

I came down in the crater and on the other side was the knight. It came for me, sprinting. I took a defensive stance and raised a sword I didn't know I held until now.

Chapter 17

Acid shot through my veins, speeding through my organs and out of my throat. Color snapped back, dispelling the black. I was vomiting my soul from my body; nothing else would explain the pain that came with expelling whatever was in me.

But then I drank in clean air and my insides cooled, the knives stuck in them slipping free of my body. I heard plenty of voices around me, a loud and chaotic racket.

I remembered it all: the acceptance of the Sentinel, the knight taking that from me, drowning as Jacquelyn bore me away from him.

"He's up!" I heard a voice near me shout.

I opened my eyes finally and saw a pattern of shafts of light and deep shadows. The maze of shapes and light vibrated and little fragments broke off and fell down.

"Are you alright?" asked a female voice near me.

"Jacquelyn, we need to go now!" called another I didn't know.

I knew that first voice had sounded familiar for a reason. I attempted to roll over but my body suddenly convulsed. More acid swam through my chest and throat. Water shot from my mouth and then splashed back down on me.

The worst of the pain came then. I was sure that the bones in my chest had collapsed. I did roll over in pain then as I tried curling myself into a ball.

After the pain dulled enough, I could look around and actually take in what I was seeing. Mermaids swam this way and that in a cavern, some shouting, others quiet but all of them obviously terrified. The pattern I had seen above me was actually dim light reflecting off of stalactites dripping from the ceiling, reaching for the rock and water. I found that I lay on a large rock among only a few. A half-circle of light blazed at one end of the cavern. Jacquelyn was floating in the water before me.

"We made it? You -"

169

A dull roar shut me up and had all the others in the cave squinting in confusion and looking around. They darted about haphazardly as they tried to understand what was happening. I sat up, pushing my upper body off the hard rock I was lying on with one arm, and cast my eyes around. The noise was growing. The rumbling began. We were all dead quiet.

A loud crack announced the falling of the first stalactites. Then, dozens of others fell. I rolled off the rock as one came down for my chest. I hit the water and saw the mermaids surging side to side as they avoided others.

I kicked hard and my head shot out of the water. A stalactite struck the surface near me and a wave cascaded over my head again. There was no way in hell I'd be quick enough to get myself out of here. "Jacquelyn!" I screamed.

She looked away from the ceiling, gave up on trying to avoid the falling spears, and her body arched up then dove down beneath the water. A stalactite narrowly missed drilling right into her back as she sped through the water to my side. She cradled me close with her arms and used her fins to propel us toward the exit from the cavern.

The other mermaids were already making their move, escaping for the exit. Claws of terror shredded my mind as a mermaid just a few feet before us was hit by one of the falling stalactites. It crashed down on her back and I heard bones break. She screamed, one last final, brief noise. I saw the tip burrow through her skin before she was lost beneath the water, driven to the bottom.

Horror suddenly became my closest friend. Four other mermaids went down in the same fashion in the next few seconds, one of them suffering from a pulverized skull, another screaming as a thin stalactite had stabbed right through her back and out of her chest until she sank down out of sight. I turned my eyes to the exit and tried to shut it all out.

But I couldn't. I screamed. I didn't know why, I didn't understand it, but something inside me, something animalistic forced me to.

The half-circle of light suddenly darkened on one side. It was like a massive tooth had grown inside the mouth of a terrible beast, and we were in its throat speeding for the exit. I quit my terrified whimpers as I realized that the exit was collapsing and that Jacquelyn was bringing up the rear, slowed down by me.

"Let me go!" I yelled. "You won't make it!"

She acted like she didn't hear me and continued on.

More darkness crashed down on the exit, taking a mermaid so close to deliverance with it. I felt Jacquelyn's body tremble as we surged forward even faster. The exit was thinning to just a few openings. The last of the mermaids made it out. It was just us.

All at once, the small remaining expanse of light shut off. Absolute darkness swallowed us up. The earth took on a new noise, us stuck in its belly. It rumbled deeply, only the sounds of falling stalactites there to break it.

Jacquelyn stopped and I slipped from her arms. I found that my feet could touch the bottom, the water just up to my neck. Neither of us spoke. I turned my head around this way and that, searching for a light in this darkness. There was nothing. I was disoriented. I didn't know which way was Jacquelyn and which was the blocked exit.

I suddenly felt like I was falling, lost in this dark world. I slapped at the space before me frantically. My fingers brushed something hard and I lunged for it. I leaned against rock and said, "Jacquelyn? Are you there?"

"Yes."

"What do we do now?"

We both had to speak loudly over the din and I could just barely hear her. I did, however, hear hopelessness in her words. "Nothing. There is no other way out."

Not after all this. After I was so close. The kingdom had been opened to me. The Sentinel had deemed me fit to pass into it. I had come so close. And now I was supposed to die in the belly of the earth knowing full well that I was the cause of Jacquelyn's death too?

My thoughts were suddenly stolen. Not to a different topic really, but a broader one. The others. The five that I had seen die. The plenty of others that must have also met their fate inside this cavern; had I been the cause of their death too? What was happening outside of the cavern? Was the world falling apart? Was the knight ripping it to pieces? Were countless others dying?

I needed to know that I wasn't the cause. "No. I'm not going to just stop now." I was whispering at first, my words lost even to me under the rumbling. But then, something forced me to shout, "This isn't happening!" I struck the rock with my palm, ignoring the shock that came with it.

I shuffled to the side. "No!" My palm slammed against rock again. "It! Wasn't! Me!" I hit the rock with my fist like it was a hammer with each word. "I didn't ask for this!" I hit it again. It didn't yield to me. I couldn't bear this responsibility. If I didn't get out of this, I'd die. Not because of a fucking rock falling from the ceiling or drowning in this piss water. I'd die because my heart couldn't take all that.

Fingers gripped my shoulder but my hand was already balled up in a fist, reared back. I roared once more, an incoherent noise, as my fist collided with the rock. Things gave. Bones snapped. Fingers cracked. My wrist shattered. Lightning shot up my arm, arced through my body and shut off my brain for a moment. But rock gave way as well.

Light and pain brought me back. Sunlight was streaming through the head-sized hole, painting my face. Blood was leaking from my hand, the flesh ripped and torn, bones stabbing through. I rolled away from the light and leaned against the rock. I grabbed my mangled hand and cradled it close.

I tried to dull the pain. Failed. "Ah, fuck! Goddamn!" I kept on cursing as the urge to smash my head open and end it all infected me. I could barely understand the thing I saw through my swimming vision. I did notice when the light streaking through got bigger.

Turning my head, tuning in, I saw that Jacquelyn was pushing with her thin arms against the rocks trapping us in here. Several had rolled away. A final one fell over and the exit was large enough for her to fit through. She grabbed the sides with both hands, propelled herself with rapid beats of her fin, then slipped out of the cavern.

I stumbled to the hole and simply leaned through it. I let my body do the rest as I tipped over and fell down into the water and sunlight. But sunlight wasn't normally so hot. Jacquelyn pulled me up to the surface as I had been content to just lie there beneath the water focusing only on my pain.

Fire rose from the water. Flames danced on it as if it was actually a sea of oil. But I wasn't allowed the time to gawk for long. Jacquelyn bore me away from the fire smoldering all around us, weaving between gouts of flame until we came to a shore. Beyond the sand, I glimpsed the forest, wreathed in flame as well, the trees staggering about madly under the hellish onslaught.

I sat up on the shore, water lapping against the sand and up to my waist. I brought my mangled hand up and held it to my chest gingerly. Sharp lances of pain reminded me of needles stabbing into my skin while the aching throb that accompanied it was reminiscent of the agony I'd suffered through with my dislocated shoulder. Had I not known what had happened, I would have guessed that I had pissed off the devil and he was stabbing me over and over in my arm with a red-hot pitch fork.

I let out a loud sob and exhale at the same time as I leaned forward. Jacquelyn pulled me into her arms and I felt a warmness come from her that was different than the fires around me. I felt her lips touch my forehead and a sensation that bewildered me spread from there. My entire body shuddered and I gasped, my eyes widening in wonder. The tingling spread down into my hand and I felt it twitch as bones reset themselves.

The pain all vanished and I breathed in like a bellows. Jacquelyn pushed me back though then slipped back into the water a little deeper. "We don't have much time."

I stood up and asked, "Did I do this? Was it the knight?"

"I don't know," she despaired. "Look."

I followed the direction of her finger across the water and behind smoking trees. The sky was distorted, as if I was seeing it through a bubble, a massive one at that. "What is it?"

"It is whatever is doing all this. Right after we got away from the knight everything started to tremble and break apart. The water caught fire. The trees lit up like fire had suddenly grown from their bark."

The knight wanted me, and it would destroy this entire planet to have me.

"I'll stop him," I vowed, unsure of how to accomplish such a feat.

"How?" she asked, looking to me in disbelief.

"I don't know, but I did this. It's my responsibility."

She nodded solemnly. "I have to go," she whispered. "I can help others."

She turned to leave but I hollered, "Wait!" She stopped and looked over her shoulder at me. This might be the last time I would ever see her. I wanted so badly to just hold her and communicate my appreciation. There wasn't time for that. This wasn't how I ever pictured saying goodbye would be. She'd done so much for me already. "Thank you. Please, be safe. I'll stop him. I promise."

Jacquelyn nodded, her green eyes shimmering, reflecting fire and love. She then spun and dove into the water and sped away. I took a moment to watch her go, flexing my hand and marveling out how it functioned perfectly.

I now had a mission. It went far beyond my own wants. I was responsible for not just my survival, but the survival of this whole world. There wasn't time to spare.

I turned and sprinted up the shore. The trees had receded from the burning water and were frantically dancing away from those that were already aflame. They all seemed to be losing in their attempt at avoiding catching fire. I witnessed several become trapped by two trees fully engulfed in fire and haphazardly darting around. The branches slammed together, ashes and smoke erupted from the trees and sped upward.

The sandy shore curved along the perimeter of the burning water far off into the distance. I sprinted along it, safe from the fire on both sides. After several minutes, all that stood between me and the obscurity in the sky was a straight shot through the raging woods.

I would need to dart through it, keeping from the deathly clutches of the flaming trees. A tree avoided another, lending me a small opening, and I burst forward into the woods, past flaming branches that swayed and jerked.

Smoke and cinders accosted me immediately. I began to cough as the ashes filled my lungs. I stopped in a very small clearing as three towering trees danced around me, shedding fire like a dog might shed its fur after winter. I nearly gave in to the awe of dancing walls of flame, my jaw loose and hanging. Smoke seeped into my lungs and I coughed anew. A red ember fell on my shoulder and seared a hole through my shirt. I slapped at it then burst forward.

The heat of the flame hit me with such intensity that I could barely keep my eyes open. I just wouldn't stop. Ever. I'd keep on going until I found the knight. Although I realized that I had already lost my sense of direction.

My lungs burned in protest of my staggering run, my face sweltering from the towering flames. I choked down my hesitation and just ran as well as I could manage. The trees not aflame didn't bother trying to snatch me up or smash my head open. They just weaved, much like I was doing, to stay clear of the marching infernos.

I heard the crack over the rumbling earth and roaring fire. The tree came next. It splintered as it fell, coming down for my head. I slowed only for a moment. Another tree was right before me, on its side, spitting up flames ten feet tall. I burst forward as blistering pain engulfed me from above. I felt smoldering pine needles and twigs scratch my back and I leapt.

I dove into the flame, sailing through the inferno, my mouth shut, my breath held, and my eyes squeezed tight. The flames I passed through felt like a physical force for a moment. I thought that maybe I had gotten trapped inside them, snagged by some web that would hold me fast as the fire cooked me. After an excruciating moment, I broke free of the choking heat and was rolling across the ground.

Visions of fire and earth briefly flashed past me as I tumbled, a kaleidoscope of chaos. I sprang to my feet and danced to the side, avoiding the reaching claws of a towering blaze. My hands lifted before my face reflexively to ward off the threat, and I beheld flesh red and blistered, bleeding even. I ignored the damage then sped on, past it and all the others that came my way. I ran my hand across my face and scalp and found that my eyebrows had been singed to almost nothingness.

I cast my eyes skyward, between the burning tops of the trees, but nothing besides smoke was up there. Stopping meant death, so I merely put my head down and ran in whatever direction held less fire.

A deer surprised me, or I surprised it. It was hopping back and forth, surrounded by fire. The few openings were narrow and it was likely too scared to pick one. I skidded to a halt and it reared up and kicked at me. A hoof nearly smashed into my face, an inch of space saving me from a shattered nose.

"Whoa! Whoa," I said. "Calm down, now. You can get out. There!" I pointed to the widest avenue between the flames. "Go!"

The deer huffed, shook its head and backed away from me. Its flank was nearing the fire and it must have been bitten by it for it cried out and lurched back toward me. I ran to its side, before it could get away and smacked its backside. It took off like an arrow from a bow, speeding in the direction I aimed it, between the flames and out of my sight.

Now it was my turn to pick a way. I didn't give it much thought. I didn't try to figure out which way was correct. I just picked a path and sprinted.

Luck was in my favor this time. I had picked the right way.

I burst between two pillars of fire and was in a clearing. Short grass sprung up from the earth all around, broken up by grey, flat rocks flecked with blue. The clearing was nearly a perfect circle, three hundred feet across, rimmed by fire. A black sword stuck out of the ground in the middle. The blade curved to a sharp point in several places along it. It seemed as though whoever had forged it had purposefully curved and twisted the blade, lending it a menacing look. It was the knight's blade and he stood on the other side of the clearing.

Dark slits in his helmet peered at me. His chest faced to the side though. The sword wasn't in his hand, nor was it on fire. The black knight was responsible for all of this. He hadn't been able to destroy me yet, so he was going to rip this whole world apart to finally achieve that. I didn't fear him any longer. As far as I was concerned, if I could reach the sword first, I'd have the advantage.

Before the knight turned, and turn on me he did, I burst forward. We were in a race for the blade. Getting to it first didn't mean that I would prevail against the knight, it was just an edge that I hadn't had before. And, I really wanted that thing dead.

I wasn't sure if ever before I was a great runner. Now though, I was the fastest being on the planet.

My vision bounced as I cleared ten feet at a time, over rocks and dips in the ground. Ashes fled past me, caressing my cheeks. Wind billowed around me. The knight and I closed terribly fast. I felt fire build in my throat. I had to let it out.

Monstrous in sound and pitch, a roar ripped from between my teeth, drowning out the clacking of the knight's armor. Just a few more strides. I reached out and dove. The knight was only a step away.

The world seemed to slow. I watched as my fingertips brushed past the hilt of the blade. Then the metal slipped comfortably into my palm. My hand closed around it. I looked up to the knight as I was carried beneath its splayed hand. I felt the blade resist me for a moment, but then it gave in and on we went, past the knight in a tumbling heap.

I bounced across stone and ground. I sprang to my feet as soon as I came to a halt. I didn't feel the pain from whatever injuries I had sustained. I didn't have the time. Fear blossomed in my chest, a cold burst that wracked my whole body instantly. The knight was there and swinging for my head with one spiked fist.

The killing metal skewered only the air above my head as I ducked. I came back up with the heavy blade in two hands, ready to run the knight through. Only, a crushing grip found my throat and I was paralyzed. My feet left the ground and I struggled just to understand what was happening.

The knight was before me, one arm cocked back and ready to punch a hole in my chest. The hand gripping my throat was just moments from pulverizing my neck. I still held the blade in two hands, and it was above my head.

With force born of my will to survive, I brought it down. The blade collided with black metal then sheered right through it. Sparks exploded from the metal as it was torn apart. The force crushing my throat subsided and I fell. My legs hadn't been ready. I spilled to the ground, on my hands and knees with the knight's severed arm right next to me.

Blood didn't leak from the appendage. Muscle and flesh didn't dangle from it. Bone didn't jab out from within it all. There was emptiness inside the armor. I surged to my feet, grabbing the hilt of the blade again, and poised it to run through the knight's chest.

I expected him to be reeling from the injury. He wasn't.

His remaining palm smashed into my chest and the weight of a thousand mountains caved it in. The same odd shimmering that marred the sky above flashed from the knight's hand. My arms were splayed out, my hands opened wide, the sword falling from my grip. My head snapped back and I looked up into the obscured sky.

The sensation of being crushed left and instead I felt myself being folded up a thousand times. Blasting white light assailed me. The wavering sphere above, however, was pitch black. I watched it dance within the pure whiteness for a brief moment. I realized I was screaming, a ragged noise that stretched on for far too long.

Then, all the sounds droned out into one drawn out whine that grew terribly deep in moments before it vanished with a whir.

***

I felt nothing. There was no sound. The white was still around me, the black shimmering sphere hanging in the sky, or what used to be the sky.

I was here though. I moved my hands up and they were before my face; numb, but there. I began to wonder what had happened, how the knight had sent me to this place.

Darkness flashed as if a black bolt of lightning had arced through the sky. I looked up at the orb of blackness and found myself looking through a hole in space. I saw motes of light I knew to be stars, shades of dark red, orange, blue, and purple smeared in with the blackness, and twisting, milky spirals. This was a sky that looked familiar, but not exactly like the night sky. It was a place removed from all worlds.

The orb began to grow, becoming oblong. It stretched out and rolled over, the image of the sky within it shifting as if it had decided to swim to another place in the darkness. It was descending on me. I was so mesmerized by what I was seeing that I hadn't realized it until it was so close, just an arm's length from me.

Fear didn't bloom in me, asking me to turn and run from the thing. Instead, I felt wonder. I actually reached out for it. My hand fell through the veil as if it had went through calm water. I then felt my fingers as I wiggled them in the darkness, the numbness now vanished. I reached for a star as it engulfed my whole arm but I couldn't grasp the twinkling speck of light.

Soon, all of me was within the darkness, but I could still see the white to either side of me. I realized that I was in a column made up of deep space. It touched the invisible ground and expanded, spreading out as though it were water spilling across the ground. Waves of darkness invaded my vision higher up, and I found the same phenomenon happening above, spreading outward as though the column had struck the ceiling.

New stars and shades of color blossomed inside the darkness as it expanded. I turned around, watching as the waves of black ate up the light. Eventually, all the white was gone except for the shimmering brightness of the stars.

I took a few steps forward before looking down. My feet stood on nothing. Beneath me was more of the sky. I was in space. I was above the ground, the clouds, and the atmosphere. This place seemed vaguely familiar, like something I'd seen in a book long ago but never chanced across in real life.

How had I gotten here?

Before I could continue my thoughts, a ghost passed right next to me. I saw a shape much like a human, but it was all smooth, no definition in its face or body. I watched it jog away before it was gone from my vision, vanished in space.

"Hello," I called weakly. My voice didn't echo like I imagined it would. It was small and lost immediately. I wondered if my words had even gone a few feet past my lips.

I wasn't comfortable walking in any one direction. Each time I looked down I got the idea that I should be falling. I was afraid that I would walk off this invisible ground and plummet through space. I spun around in a circle several times, searching for anything.

Vague lines suddenly dragged down the space before me. I squinted at them as they moved. It was as if worms were painting lines all around me with semi-translucent paint. "What is this?" I asked the nothingness before me quietly.

Lines expanded, becoming sheets of ghostly gray. Sheets became three dimensional, unfolding over my head and all around me. One large sheet came for my feet. I lifted one foot right before it got me only to watch dumbly as it went beneath my other one. I immediately felt a warmth set in that I hadn't felt before.

Something about what was happening made me feel small. The world was building itself around me. It could make itself in any shape it wanted. I could wind up stuck in a small box. My skin seemed to contemplate jumping off my body, my muscles twitched, and my bones vibrated.

The ghostly shapes began to take on more substance. I couldn't see through them as well as before. Other details sprang to life on them, studs and corners and whatnot. Lines carved themselves in the shapes. Soon, noises came after me.

I looked up, searching for the sounds and found ghosts all around me. They had more shape now though, their heads angular and sporting horns and other things that looked like wide mohawks. Entranced, I watched until I was in a new place entirely.

Someone was speaking loudly and with vehemence. I was sitting on a wooden bench that was nothing more than slabs of wood nailed to other slabs, the burns I'd sustained flaring angrily on the backs of my hands and arms. A dozen others sat around me on the benches too. They all wore armor, some bronze, others silver, a few gold. No one helm seemed the same, each with something to make it distinct. Weapons and shields of all kinds were in hands with white knuckles.

I found a shield strapped to my left arm, a thick-bladed sword in my right hand, and a helm resting on my lap. I wore a bronze breastplate, a long skirt of thick leather straps, and bronze boots.

Where the hell had the knight sent me?

A screaming voice tore my attention forward. I found a grizzled man in regal armor with badges galore on a sash that ran across his chest. He addressed all of us.

"... The Matriarch says we can't do a damn thing to stop this. She's been right every other time. Well that means that after tonight, everyone is fucking dead anyway. So when these gates go down you hit the ground and you do it running.

"You split as many skulls as you can. These fuckers are dying with us tomorrow, or they die by your hand tonight. Me, I want to wash myself in their blood before this ends!"

Everyone around me hollered agreement, beating their fists against the sides of their heads and their chests. A terrible cold fear shot through me. What was he talking about?

The soldiers calmed down once he continued screaming, "Your mortality will be seen tomorrow, when our world dies. But tonight, as a group, you're all goddamn invincible! You fucking run through those bastards out there as fast and hard as you can. You know what I hope? I hope that this is the first time the Matriarch screws up. That means that we have a shot at stopping this shit.

"You fight like you can. Kill and kill until you get to the source field and then find a way in there. Murder the thing responsible for this."

Now that the men and women had been quiet and I had gotten a better grip on what was happening, I realized that whatever we were sitting in was moving. It lurched and creaked as it rolled forward.

"You could have stayed home and curled up with your family and waited to die but you chose to come fight. So fight like killing enough will save their lives. Because it just might. You were all born to fuck and fight, but not to die. None of us were born just to die. Unless we figure something out, that's exactly what will happen tomorrow. Me, I'm not too keen on dying. But fucking and fighting? I could do with a few more years of that!"

He continued on but I tuned him out. I was at the end of my bench, a walkway to my left and another bench on the other side of the walkway. I turned to the man to my right, a brutish person with a helmet that resembled an upturned bucket. I found his eyes beneath the Y shaped hole in the face of the helm. I nudged his shoulder with my elbow and asked, "Hey, what is happening?"

I thought he was going to eat my face off for a moment. The look he had was beyond threatening; it was carnivorous. His features softened slightly, albeit turning to that of annoyance, and I realized he only adopted such a demonic look in the first place as a result of the commander's savage speech. "The fuck do you think?"

The world was ending. This one was at least. There was something that was going to kill it. I should have asked a less stupid question. To him, my question was about as mad as I found this whole scene to be. I tried a better tactic. "I mean what is the plan exactly?"

"First, listen better. Second, we get out when the gates open and you fucking lose it. That's the plan."

"Hey!" The commander had caught me. I faced him and saw hatred in his eyes. He marched over to me and continued, "You two all of a sudden lose your spine?" Spit flew from his mouth and coated my face.

The man next to me boomed, "Fuck no, sir!"

I jumped at his outburst and the commander saw. He spit in my lap then said, "Stand up!"

It took everything I had not to piss myself. The shaking, that was beyond my control. I trembled to my feet until I was nose to nose with the commander. My helm had fallen down to the floor and clattered on the wood, but I barely noticed.

His face suddenly screwed up in a snarl and he barked, "How are you going to die?"

I couldn't respond. A lump of fear had grown in my throat and gummed it all up. I could barely think.

Without warning, the commander smacked me. And it wasn't some little wake up call. Stars exploded before my eyes. Stinging pain seared across my cheek. I fell into the soldier sitting next to me. He shoved me to my feet and the commander stopped me from bumping into him with a palm to the chest.

"If you want, I'll fucking open your throat right now." A knife was suddenly poking my jugular. "You don't have the balls to get out there and fight then I'll just end it now. How are you going to die?"

I needed to say something. I'd die if I didn't. And I didn't know what would happen if I died here, wherever here was. "Out there," I managed to mutter. My voice was weak and I stuttered.

He shoved me back down into my seat then screamed, "Anyone that has the fear this boy does is already dead! You all watch, he'll go down in moments. Wash that fear from you right now, or die without making a difference." He'd kept his eyes on me the whole time.

A cacophony of shouts and curses aimed at me rose from the soldiers. I didn't know what this place was or what was outside, but I sure as shit wouldn't be the first one to go down. Not anymore. Now, I was going to do exactly what everyone else was going to do. I'd do it better than most too. I knew what I had been through. I could handle it.

Wood exploded, shooting slivers of shrapnel at all of us. A massive spear tore through a corner of the room we all sat in and its edge caught one soldier. The man was ripped in two before the pieces of him went along with the spear. A large hole yawned open to reveal hard, dry earth ten feet down.

All around the siege engine we rode in, sprinting across the ground and leaping at our engine were these dark being. They wore armor and brandished weapons and shields, but otherwise bore little resemblance to us.

Dozens sprinted for our engine and then I lost them beneath it. They must have jumped onto the rocking tower of wood, for I heard them climbing. The soldiers stood and got ready, dozens rushing over to the hole. I snatched up my helmet and jammed it on my head, the piece of armor sitting at an odd angle. I was jostled forward then and ended up in the flow of soldiers shouting war cries.

I moved with them but angled myself away from the hole. I ended up out of the soldiers' way just in time. The dark creatures, spikes of metal jutting from their helms and shoulders came up in the first wave. One pulled itself up and leapt high. It was near coming down on the wooden floor when a woman kicked it in the chest and sent it back out of the engine. Another one caught her leg as she set it down and she was pulled from the engine and down beneath it.

The battle quickly grew there and I watched. My mouth hung open as axes, spears, and swords split metal armor and grey flesh. I caught glimpses of circular eyes, the pools of white broken up by several rings of black, small bumps instead of noses, and mouths so big that it seemed as though their lower jaw may be completely unattached from their head and full of sharp teeth.

The commander stabbed one more through its spiral eye then screamed, "Get out! The wheel is coming apart!" He then cut a rope anchored to the middle of the wall. He and a dozen others slammed their shoulders into the wall and the whole thing came free.

What I thought was a wall was actually a gate. It swung down then picked up speed before hitting the ground with enough force to rattle the whole engine. The majority of soldiers were on the left side of the engine. I had a clear sight out onto the battlefield. It was just like standing on the bridge beneath the regard of the Sentinel all over again.

The light of the day was nearly gone but enough rays from the dying sun came down to paint the miles of land in all directions in orange and pink. Hundreds of thousands, millions maybe, of figures were on the field. A mile off, atop a cliff set in the middle of a mountain was a large dome of green energy that crackled like living lightning. I had to look away from the rolling hills and endless waves of dark creatures as those before us began to close on me.

Dozens of those things were sprinting up the gate at us, and I was standing between them and the other soldiers. I shrank back from the snarling faces of the demonic creatures as they came for me, spit and blood flying from their mouths. The jagged swords in their hands jerked side to side as they ran, and I was sure that once they got close enough, those blades would run right through me.

Silver and gold armor blocked my vision as a few soldiers filled in the gap I stood in. They vaulted down the gate and threw themselves at their enemy, cutting them down and screaming all the while.

The engine I was in came to an abrupt halt and tipped toward the direction of the hole. The wheel. It was going to break apart and anyone still in here would end up beneath a whole hell of a lot of wood.

My instinct to survive, that thing I had come to rely on so heavily, kicked in and I sprinted after the hundred soldiers that were already halfway down the gate or on the ground fighting. The gate shook and jerked as the wheel splintered. It lurched once more and a loud crack let me know that I was out of time. The gate lifted up and I fell to one knee. It tipped to the side slowly.

I had to get off it now. I got up and ran, as hard as I could. I was near the end but I couldn't see the ground I was going to come down on. I jumped. I sailed out into the air, several feet above the heads of the fighters beneath me. The gate missed clipping my foot by a handspan.

Creatures saw me coming down and thrust their swords up so that I would fall on them. My comrades cut them down just a yard before I fell on their blades, shedding lines of their black blood. Wildly, I slashed at the dark beings beneath me. Metal hit metal then lightly scored flesh. I crashed down on several and we fell to the ground in a heap, weapons flailing and fanged mouths grunting.

Foul odors, steel spikes, and the growling faces of these alien things forced me up. I didn't need a grappling match to tell me that rolling around with these ugly bastards was something I wouldn't enjoy. A hand gripped my neck and pulled hard. I nearly swung around with my sword leading my turn until a spear plunged past my shoulder and into the gut of one of the creatures beneath me.

It was the commander, the man who had nearly made me piss myself, who had picked me up. I wasn't afforded the time to thank him. Partly because he wasn't giving me another shred of thought, mostly because there was a hell of a lot of these dark creatures ready to cut my head off.

More sprang forward at us. I chopped at one, the tip of my sword slicing a divot in its face. The commander stabbed another. We both retreated as more came and other soldiers pushed forward to take our place. The man who had jumped into my spot ran right into the point of a sword with his eye. Not a good look for him.

The creatures swarmed forward quickly. A sword came for me and I wasn't quick enough to get away, mostly because of the men and women behind me pushing to get up front and fight. Steel collided with my bronze-covered chest. Vibrations surged through my body but no piercing pain came with it. The sword glanced off and I slammed my shield into the creature's face, staggering it back a step.

This couldn't have been right. Sure, killing these things was the priority of most everyone. The commander had said that there was a better way. A way to end this. The vibrating field of green energy sat a mile away and hundreds of feet up. That was it.

Purple flashes suddenly turned my head to the right. The commander was there, a sword sticking out of his back. I was still squirming to get away, taking shoulders from my comrades. They too saw the purple strobe and ceased pushing forward into the ranks of the dark creatures. It came from the commander's hip where his hand gripped something, pulsing from these fist-sized things that looked like ominous blood-orange fruits covered in tiny spines of thorns.

I saw the commander's face one last time, a look of defiance and hatred. I saw the soldiers all around throw a kick or bash with a shield the enemy before they leapt away to hide behind cover or flatten out on the ground. I just watched it all.

The commander must have saved this just for me. It was like he had slapped me yet again, but this time harder, and all over. Oh and the light, that blinding flash, never would I have thought that something could be so bright. Had the sun just fallen on me?

The commander exploded and I was blasted back. I felt my feet leave the ground and my body career backward. Whatever kept me upright normally had just taken a major hit because I had no clue as to which way was up. I didn't know what was happening. I didn't realize I had hit the ground until I was finally able to breathe again and inhaled a mouthful of dirt.

I coughed and each spasm hurt my chest. There it was again. I was flying, spinning around. Another explosion? But then my head immediately ended up against the ground. I hadn't moved at all, I just thought I was up in the air flying around again.

I opened my eyes, I think. Everything was still white with little purple dots. I heard some muffled noises. What was going on? The fight!

I rubbed at my eyes furiously. I needed to get my head back together. That or I'd lose it, literally. I scrambled backward until I ended up with my back against something big and hard. I rubbed my eyes and ears, checked my body for holes. My chest surely hurt like it might be missing a big piece.

Everything started to make sense. I came back to the battlefield. A large area was mostly clear before me. A big circle of nothing but dead bodies blasted away. A dozen of our guys got up, a little disoriented, dents in shields and helms, but alive and ready to fight. The enemy had been like me. The ones that hadn't been taken out in the blast but close enough to get back into the fight quickly were rubbing eyes and casting off helms, defenseless.

Soldiers ran forward and cut them down but an endless stream poured in to fill their ranks. I watched as I recovered, still unsure of what had actually happened. My eyes drew to a soldier running between friends and foe, no weapons in hand. He jumped, posted a leg on the back of his kin, then launched himself over them and into the enemy. Before he came down, I saw his hand on the red, spine-covered fruit at his hip. His fingers twisted a small knob then pushed it in. The purple lights started flaring.

Boom.

A few dozen creatures went flying, plenty of them already dead.

I looked to my hips and found two of those things. Spines ran along the outside like veins but none were very sharp. The knobs were right there, ready for me to twist and push, ending my life for the reward of a bunch of dead bastards.

I'd consider those later, when I had a few swords sticking in me. Right now, I needed to get out of here.

Hundreds of other siege engines rolled along the ground all around, plowing through fields of the creatures on extremely wide wheels, spikes jutting from the middle of them that spun and gutted any who attempted attacking them from the side. The towers of wood and metal reminded me of the structures from Haven Sprawl, some nearly four stories tall. They tapered to a thinner top, stabilizing their massive weight. Every so often, I'd catch a glimpse of arrows or spear tips shooting from between holes in the engine to lobotomize one of the enemy.

There were soldiers here and there, little armies fighting within the sea of dark creatures. They wouldn't make it though, no matter how many explosions went off.

I needed to get out of here and back to the world I came from. Was it possible? Could I get out? I didn't think that killing a bunch of the dark things was my ticket out. Maybe taking out whatever was behind that field of green energy would do the trick.

My sword had stayed in my hand somehow. And a damn good thing it was. My back was against the fallen siege engine. Through the racket of battle, I heard wood creak and splinter above me. I looked up and found one of the enemy atop it, staring down at me. Its wicked mouth smiled then it jumped.

I rolled away, but not as gracefully as I wanted. I ended up on my back still. The creature brought its sword down. I lifted my shield just in time. The tip of the blade rang off the bronze and sent a shockwave up my arm.

I kicked, slamming my heel into its knee. It buckled and fell down onto its back. That was good enough for me. I didn't have the same bloodlust that the other soldiers had.

Ground and sky mixed as I stood, a vertigo that threatened to send me sprawling again. I pushed through it, finding my path despite the rocking ground beneath me. A siege engine was rolling by. If I ran, I could maybe make it. The enemy, however, was everywhere and I'd need a lot of luck.

To my left and stretching out before me was the toppled siege engine. To the right... well, and everywhere else I could see, were the creatures. I took off straight ahead, making sure to give the rising creature with the injured knee a wide berth.

A sheathe slapped against my thigh and I thrust my sword into it. I needed as much of my hands as I could use. Explosions of purple lit up the field left and right. So many were so willing to throw their lives away. They'd all resigned themselves to the idea that they were all dead tomorrow anyway. I wasn't that way. I still had my hope.

Stairs made up of shattered wood and the toppled wheel of the engine provided me a path atop it. I sprinted across the front of it then stopped at its edge. The creatures were everywhere. The moving engine I was aiming for was going to come close. I could reach it if I timed it right. If I didn't though, I'd end up coming down on the metal spikes shooting from the engine.

I'd seen what those spikes had done to the enemy. I didn't relish the idea of being cut in half.

I waited, time flowing far too slowly. I attracted the attention of plenty of bad guys in the meantime.

A hundred eyes looked up at me. I still had a while to wait until I could jump. It was time to improvise.

The side that the other engine would roll closest to was to my right. I ran left, drawing the crowd thirsty for my blood. They were slowed as they jostled one another, running in a pack. The fruits bounced against my hips. Perfect.

A vine coming from the fruit was tied around a belt weaved through my skirt. I stopped running for a minute and tried to untie it in vain. The vine was dead and stiff, hard to work with. Eventually I wiggled my fingers beneath the fruit and pried it off. I held one in my hand and looked down over the engine at a dozen creatures climbing up the side of the engine. Now it was my turn to introduce these things to the bitterest fruit they would ever try.

I found the knob, twisted it, then pushed it in. The purple light flashed once and I started as though it had suddenly shocked me. I chucked it down. It hit the side of the engine, then bounced off the shoulder of one of those things. All of those with their eyes stuck to me followed it intently.

From what I had seen so far, I knew that the thing would go off in just another second. I waited in anticipation of the blast and concluded that mine must have been a dud. The purple flashes ceased once it left my hand, the depressed button extending back out. The creatures and I all stared at it as it bounced along the ground, me with terror, them with a smile.

Realization came in a rush. The others wouldn't have ended their lives so quickly unless they had to. Had these things been mobile, they would have been lighting up the sky until they fell upon the heads of the dark creatures. But a finger was needed to hold the knob in. It all made sense. It worked with every aspect of this war of attrition. It couldn't be accidentally tripped. The enemy couldn't take them and use them against us. It was a suicide or nothing. Go out with a bang or just go out.

Staying in place seemed fine for a moment. I almost thought that the creatures had forgotten about me. Maybe the dying light had finally grown so dark that I blended in with the night.

Wishful thinking.

They snarled, black spittle flying from between their grinning lips. Time to run.

I now needed to go the other way. The engine was still a hundred feet from me, but it moved quicker than I did. Besides, I needed to beat the creatures too. The latter would be far harder than the former.

I picked my path, a line straight to the end that involved a few leaps over upward stabbing slabs of wood and certainly a moment or two to swing my sword or implore my shield.

In my head it all played out fine. I took actions as if they were lines I had studied plenty of times. The others just needed to play their roles the way I saw them.

Right hand on the hilt of my blade, I bolted forward. My steps were true. I didn't falter on my path. A creature shot one hand up and gripped the edge of the engine. I stomped on its fingers, felt satisfaction flood through me at the crunch beneath my boot.

I was halfway to the end of the engine. My target was now fifty feet from me. A creature made it to the top quicker than I could run. It spun on me and I was at it. I pulled my sword free on the run.

It readied its blade, holding it in two hands cocked back and ready to swing. I lifted my own and kept on my charge. The creature shifted its grip and rotated the blade so its point was aimed directly for my chest. I expected a slash, not a stab.

I twisted, steel plunged past me. I nearly fell, but somehow managed to dance over splintered wood and holes. Stopping now to deal with this creature would slow me far too much, and I'd likely die in the process; I wasn't a fighter, only good at playing parts that placed me in advantageous positions.

Another of the enemy leapt up onto the engine. One before me now, and another pounding its heels behind me. Only this time, it had jumped up right as I was about to run into it. Its feet touched down and I opened a hole in its throat on the run. But that slowed me just enough. I heard the ragged breathing of the thing behind me.

I turned mid-sprint and knew that it would be impossible to keep myself up on my feet. I brought my shield up, blocking the descending blade from my view. It glanced off my shield, then I was tumbling. I landed hard on my back but continued on with my momentum, rolling over my shoulders and then up to my feet. I backpedaled a few steps before I was able to turn and continue sprinting.

I'd lost a few moments, and I hadn't had a single one to spare in the first place.

The shield had saved me several times, but it would be my death in just a moment. A dozen steps separated me from the end of the engine. I flung my arm out, casting the shield off my arm for it to bounce along the wood behind me, harrying the thing behind for a moment and buying me back those lost moments.

I ran with such intensity that I was sure that I was flying, my feet only an inch off the ground. Each stride I took ate up space as if they were starving for it.

My target was rolling past me and it seemed that I might lose this race. I put my all into one last burst of speed as the back of the engine bumped right past the ledge I ran on.

The perfect step put me on the absolute edge of the engine beneath me. I pushed off that leg so hard I'm not sure how I didn't hit the engine hard enough to knock it over. A large beam ran from its bottom all the way to its top at each corner. I hit the beam at its back corner.

The impact would have sent me back off the engine and down to the ground below. Desperately, I gripped my blade in two hands and thrust it at the space between the beam and the planks of wood that made up its side. Steel slipped in and wedged deep. My grip was strong. I kept my perch, but goddamn did I hit the side hard.

Finding breath took a moment, my eyes shut tight and a ringing in my ear. The discomfort and pain abated once I sucked in that sweet air. My body trembled as I inhaled and I opened my eyes.

Thirty feet below was the ground, swarming with the dark things. Several saw me and tried jumping on to the engine. It moved too quickly though. They smacked their heads into the spikes, sometimes falling back with a chunk of brain spewing forth from a crack in their skull.

Nearly twice the distance upward was the top of the engine. The ledge I was on only stuck out far enough to hold half of my foot lengthwise. With the rocking of the engine as it pitched on hills or rolled over bodies, I'd probably find myself splattered to pieces on the battlefield below. I couldn't keep a strong grip on my sword forever.

Up was the way to go then.

Horizontal beams spanned the side of the engine every eight feet or so. I reached up but my fingertips only barely touched the ledge I sought. Slowly, painfully, I wiggled my sword free. My arms were on fire when I got it out from being so careful. I hugged the beam to my left with one arm and poised my blade with the other.

I stabbed. Wood splintered. Steel sank somewhat deep.

I tested it. The blade slipped right out. I pitched backward, hollering, "Shit!" as I nearly fell. I gave the engine a bear hug as though it was a child of mine whom I hadn't seen in years and anchored myself to it.

Take two.

***

Wind blew past me, setting my bones to shaking. My grip had frozen on my blade, the knuckles white and without blood. Hell, it felt like most of me had run dry of blood.

Nearly half an hour had passed. The climb to the top had taken only a few minutes once I got the hang of scaling a moving engine. I had watched spears sail by my engine and hit others, punching holes in most and toppling others. Masses of enemy bodies had piled up before some engines, stopping them completely, forcing the soldiers inside to come out and fight their last.

It was a god-blessed miracle that I was still up here.

Still, despite all the dead soldiers and the endless dark things killing them, there were plenty of engines rolling along, nearing the mountain finally.

Cliffs stretched out before me. I stood up on unsteady feet, ready to make my leap in a few moments. The darkness hid what was on the cliff waiting for me, but only during the ride over. Now that I was close, I could see the creatures massed there, blades bristling in my direction.

The odds always seemed to be stacked against me, a monolith towering over me that said, "Go ahead. Try to climb on up here," with a wicked grin. I'd ran from most of my problems so far. I'd like to start smashing through them with deadly efficiency.

I prepared myself to jump. To hit the ground with my shield and sword out before me. I'd run as if the devil was on my heels, tearing at my soul. Maybe I'd get past them somehow. Maybe I'd end up blown to pieces in an explosion of purple destruction.

Hellish noise came from the demonic creatures, tearing at my sanity. Something rattled behind me, metal chains snaking across wood. I turned around, hoping that I wouldn't sprout a very painful shaft of wood or metal from the back of my head.

Soldiers were coming from a hole in the top of the engine, a square latch flung open to allow them access. I hadn't noticed it before, thus it was probably cleverly hidden. Or I was just half-blind. The few that had made it out by now gave me quite a scornful look.

"Why the hell are you up here?" screamed one. "All those fucking things probably saw you and got up there to wait."

I tried to respond but we were out of time for that. The engine was slowing. That meant is was about time to jump.

I felt like I had just two options. Go first, or get kicked off by the pissed off soldiers. I didn't fancy falling a few dozen feet to hard-packed earth crawling with demonic creatures.

But I didn't want to go alone either.

"Come on!" I yelled. Then I turned and broke into a sprint. I heard a roar come from behind me, the battle cry of the soldiers. Good.

191

What was not so good though, was the fact that I was right now running toward a horde of nightmarish creatures with blades and teeth aplenty aimed in my direction. I'd be fodder. That monolith gave me its biggest smile. I swear I even heard it laugh a little. *I'd found a way to slip around you before. Time to do it again.*

I jumped. Blades hungered for my blood. I reached down with my sword hand. My fingers lit on the knob of the exploding fruit. I twisted and pushed. I hoped I had the timing of these things down, and that these ones had seen how the exploding fruit worked by now.

One flash. The enemy lost its ferocious look. Another flash. They dropped their swords and started shoving one another to get away. A third flash. My feet touched down on the cliff and they were all scrambling away from me as if I had the head of dragon with fire spewing from my mouth.

I let go of the bomb. It stopped flashing. I stood still and couldn't help but grin at the things. Well, until they rushed me again, thoroughly upset at me for forcing them to nearly piss themselves.

Like a wave they came for me. And, like a wave, they crashed against the rocks that were my comrades. Dozens of soldiers came down on the cliff, ripping swords and axes down at the creatures, slamming shields into chests and faces. They pushed forward, I followed, blocking a strike meant to open my forehead, and a dozen more soldiers landed on the cliff behind us.

We advanced like this for a while, me just using my shield to preserve my life, the others fighting hard to spill the blood of the enemy, and in turn winding up with theirs spewing from gashes and severed limbs. I didn't really need to multitask. I was just fine with hiding behind my shield. Besides, I didn't have the courage to start swinging my sword right now. I was in the thick of it. And "it" was some terror-inducing madness.

I kept one eye on the things in front of me and another on the soldiers around me, aware of any purple light. Eventually, swords stopped slamming into my shield and the soldiers around me took up a cheer. My eyes poked up from behind my battered shield and I saw the backs of the few enemy remaining.

We'd routed them, the few that were left.

But soldiers chased them down and cut them apart. I looked down the jagged line of cliffs and saw dozens of siege engines butted up against them. Some still had groups fighting on them, bodies falling to their death every so often. And a few lit up with purple flashes.

It was hard to not join in as those around me roared in victory. In fact, it became impossible. I raised my sword and barked like a dog. It felt good.

Green light pushed up into the dark sky above coming from the dome of energy higher in the mountains. Trails wound through the multitude of jagged outcroppings and ledges, leading up and side to side. We really weren't all that far from the target, given the trails didn't lead off in the wrong direction. Our soldiers had let a few of the enemy escape. And on purpose.

We all watched a dozen of them sprint along the trail before turning right up a steep rocky hill. We knew where they would be going.

"Never a better time to whet that blade on the enemy's bones! Follow them to the top!" one woman hollered.

Others grunted and murmured agreement because we knew that it was time to move quietly. We would get to the top, and hopefully find a way to end this.

Our group was nearest the target. After what felt like a few breaths, we were there. I had fallen deep into my role, committing everything to my character. Time had gone quickly as we neared the top. I hungered for this just like the others.

A few boulders stood before the dome of crackling energy, obscuring our view. We couldn't see much inside anyway. The bolts of lightning that zapped across its surface flashed so bright that only glimpses of what was happening within could be seen.

Standing before it all though were dozens of the creatures, a laughably small force when compared to the rest. Why would there be so little to defend the endgame? This would determine the winner of this whole thing.

I don't think anyone was willing to dwell on all that for long. They saw their target and reacted like a ravenous beast that had been starved for weeks then thrown out in front of a big pile of blood-soaked meat. I jumped on the bandwagon.

The creatures came to meet us. It went really badly for them. I even bloodied my sword. One of the things had gotten lucky, or my compatriot too overzealous. As the former speared the latter, I cut into its neck. It reacted like I had been a ghost just a moment ago, its widened eyes flicking to me in surprise more than anything, glaring as it fell to die beneath the feet of the soldiers.

Then, the fighting was over. We crept toward the green energy slowly, scrutinizing every inch of it.

We passed the boulders. It was so close now. All we could hear was a loud buzz. Someone reached out and touched it. Lightning flared at the point of contact. He pulled his hand back with smoking fingers, blistered and bloody already.

Others did the same. They looked to each other and found that they too received the same treatment. I was close enough to look inside better, but I wasn't going to touch that thing. I saw something standing within, arms stretched out.

The pained roars of a man broke through the continuous whir of the green energy. He'd slammed his fist against the dome and came back with a broken arm, the flesh sporting dozens of terribly deep lacerations. Others moved to help him but he cradled his broken arm close and beat them back with his good arm.

I backed away with them. We double-timed it once he put his good hand on the wicked fruit at his hip.

Twist. Push. Flash. Flash. Flash. Flash. Bang!

This time, I actually saw the body within the purple for a moment. It had begun coming apart in a bloody mess before the light blinded me momentarily. The wind carried the smell of the explosion and that of what made up the inside of a person. It was a sickly sweet smell mixed with something hearty. It stuck in my throat and nose when I inhaled it, causing me to hold my breath until I coughed it out.

Green pushed away the purple and nothing but a few bits and pieces of man remained. The bomb hadn't done a damn thing.

But that wasn't going to stop the others from trying a few things. They'd made it this far. Either the Matriarch was right and they were dead anyway, or she was wrong and they could survive. The only way to figure that out was by being a little reckless with experiments.

And by a little, I mean belligerently so.

Soldiers screamed and sprinted for the dome. They hit it like a solid wall but when they bounced back off, their bodies didn't fall the right way. They slunk to the earth as if their entire skeleton had just turned to water. Some seemed void of a single bone intact beneath the skin, plenty of them shooting through flesh. Hundreds of deep cuts wracked their flesh.

A few swung swords and ended up with broken forearms and shattered shoulders. One man slammed his shield into the dome and the reciprocating impact killed him, cracking his skull wide open to spill brain down.

Now, it was time to throw things. Rocks, spears, swords, everything we could find hit the dome then rocketed back at us fivefold in speed.

We all seemed to get it then. We just accepted it. Somberly, but with certainty, everyone gave up. I walked as close as I would risk and looked in.

Between bolts of jagged lightning, I saw the kin of my nemesis. This black knight, however, had both arms intact and a skirt of metal links that flowed between his legs in the front and back. The horns were slightly different too, and there wasn't a weapon to be seen. He looked right at me.

I'd nearly beaten the other one. He was going to die by my hand, so he had sent me here, to another world where his kin could kill me because he was already in the process of destroying an entire world.

The knight looked away from me and then it began weaving his arms in an odd pattern. The dome stretched toward me and the others. We jumped back and ran.

Some continued down the mountain. Many more finally stopped running at some point and turned to face their doom. I was of the latter group.

I sat down on a waist high rock in the darkness and watched the green energy come for me. Another man took his station next to me on his feet. He let his sword drop to the earth then pulled his helmet off and let that fall too.

"This is it then. The Matriarch was right. Goddamn that bitch!"

I merely nodded. What did you say to a complete stranger when you knew you were both going to die? Nothing.

But he continued, "You know, it's kind of beautiful. The way the green lines jump this way and that. That's what I'm going to think about now. Dammit am I mad and do I feel hate. But I think I'll go out this way, with something good to think about. What about you?"

"Yeah."

"Think of family. Friends. The good shit."

He obviously was. I doubted he was really even talking to me. It seemed like his mind had taken complete control of his mouth and was merely speaking to itself. I, however, couldn't. I didn't have any good times to think of.

But then, as death closed, I was able to recall a few. The orangutans. Jacquelyn. The cub. Morrissett.

Then it came.

I watched in silence as the knight within locked his gaze on me again. He flung his arms out for the final time and the dome ceased its slow crawl to adopt a tsunami style attack. It came fast and I watched it the whole time, fear in my heart and a cold pit in my stomach, but the reassurance in my soul from knowing I had nothing to do, nor any right to try. To be honest, it was beautiful. And going out with those thoughts seemed alright.

Chapter 18

Fire covered everything. I could see for miles. It raged through the forests, polluting the sky with smoke. Steam billowed up from the river below, its surface spewing writhing flames.

God, there wasn't a place safe from the fire. Nothing could survive there.

The Sentinel suddenly appeared before me. Its long, white neck, sprouting green crystalline masses sloped up and away. I was behind it. I'd gotten past the Sentinel somehow.

Black stone was beneath my feet and to both sides of me. Towers and parapets stabbed the sky to all sides of me, and a kingdom of buildings sprawled in all directions to my sides, below the massive structure I stood on. I was atop the tallest citadel within the kingdom the Sentinel guarded. I'd made it, somehow.

But the mountain, I had just died there. The dark creatures. The black knight's kin. I remembered it all. Could that have been my previous life? Had I died there in a past life then ended up here?

A deep rumble came from the Sentinel and reverberated through the stone I stood on. I looked around and found that the stone was free of any fire. I stepped back as the Sentinel's two appendages lifted high up into the air. Its long neck twisted around and one eye caught my gaze. I saw malice in that orb, but it didn't seem directed at me. The Sentinel looked away as something appeared far off in the distance.

A black shape shot up into the sky from the forest. It was miles away, just a speck. Despite the distance, there was no mistaking the black blade stabbing upward, fire dripping off it.

The knight. He must be coming for me. When I had first come across him, he had only walked after me, like he wasn't all that concerned with my death. Then he had sprinted for me, even cut across water like a god. Now, he was going to destroy a whole world to kill me. He'd grown tired of my resistance, and wanted me eradicated. And goddammit did it seem like he was going to achieve his purpose.

The Sentinel locked its gaze onto the knight and angled its appendages in challenge. The knight cut a pattern in the air with his sword and the smoke swirled as if a tornado was forming. Then, the smoke exploded outward as the knight thrust his sword upward. It was as if a massive bubble had suddenly come to be in that space, pushing all the smoke away. And that bubble was made up of the same stuff I had seen obscuring the sky before, the same field of black that I had gone into.

Hell came through that bubble. It was a portal to the sun.

Fire engulfed the knight in a torrent. It came from the portal as if it were water falling from a cliff. It hit the forest and swallowed everything. Then, the fire washed out in all directions, a wall taller than the kingdom I stood on coming for me.

I turned and ran. I didn't know where I was going, but anywhere was better than standing here while an inferno devoured me. The roof I was on was primarily flat, four small pyramids the only thing that broke the monotony. They weren't large enough to provide me with the protection I would need to keep from being swallowed by the conflagration.

The kingdom was massive. I wouldn't have the time to scour the entire thing before my flesh was blasted from my bones and turned to ash. I aimed for the middle of the roof, relying completely on luck.

The stone beneath my feet soon began to shake but I didn't risk a look back. It whined and rumbled. The fire must be close.

A handle rose from the roof a hundred feet away. That was my way in. I glanced back briefly and saw as the fire actually hit the structure, setting it to trembling so terribly that I thought it was collapsing for a moment. I even saw the Sentinel writhing in the flames. The kingdom trembled and I felt the heat at my back.

Hell nipping at my heels was the single greatest inspiration I had ever felt. It motivated me to move with the speed of a jaguar intent on catching its prey, lest it succumb to starvation and perish. It persuaded my legs to go numb and my lungs to work double time.

I was there. I slammed my feet to a halt then reached down and grasped the handle. I pulled with all my might and my arm nearly tore free of my shoulder. "Come on! Fuck!" My hand had slipped off. Just seconds separated me from the worst possible death I could think of.

I gripped it again and my thumb found a lever on top of the handle. I pressed that down then pulled and the hatch opened. It was heavy and I screamed as I wrenched it open. It probably creaked, but I couldn't hear anything other than the roar of the fire coming to consume me. Dust billowed out of it and I leapt in.

Complete darkness raptured me as I slid into the gullet of the kingdom. A flash of red and orange lit up my world for a brief moment then the darkness returned. I plummeted a short distance then my back slammed down on something hard and smooth. The falling, however, didn't seem to stop. I was still descending and twisting, only I felt myself sliding along something. The disorienting descent lasted a short while, but I had also been moving at incredible speed. I felt myself slow suddenly and dim light washed over me.

I slid from a chute and then crashed down on my back once more. I was in an open chamber, the chute I had come from a few feet above me. I lay on my back for a moment, just looking around at the inside of the kingdom and collecting myself.

I'd made it in. My body hurt as though a ton of brick had been dropped on it, but I was alive. Despite being crushed by the dome of death magic. Even though a mad knight with the power to set a whole world aflame had tried his damn hardest to kill me. I was alive.

***

Gone. Everyone. I'd survived. But no one else had.

Another tear fell down and landed in my lap. Jacquelyn was gone. The cub. Morrissett and Bernsinger. The orangutans.

I had come to accept that I'd likely never see the others again. This wasn't the same. This was me knowing that they were gone, dead. Bernsinger had been preparing me to die in the event that I failed the Sentinel's test, not for the grief I'd feel for the pain I caused the ones I loved. Why hadn't she?

My shoulders bounced as I sobbed. Worst of all was Jacquelyn. She had done so much for me. She had counted on me to stop the knight. I had let her down for the last time.

Coming here had meant more than just not seeing any of them again. It meant the end of whatever life I had before. It might have been a journey filled mostly with pain and anguish, but at least there were silver linings. People I loved and counted on, imagined seeing again, existed. Now, there was nothing besides this giant tomb I sat in. I hadn't thought this would be a problem before. Now, with everything gone because of me, I felt like I shouldn't have ever come here. Morrissett should never have saved me. I cost others so much through all my struggles.

Something skittered and clacked on the stone floor off in the distance. I heard the noise bounce between walls as it echoed past me. I imagined some creature stalking the winding halls of this massive place. It must have heard me... It was coming for me.

The noise continued and grew more frantic fairly quickly. It was closer. In the dim light cast by spears of brightness that came in through holes as big as an eyeball high up in the walls, I could see a large threshold at the other end of this plain chamber. The thing was going to come from there.

I remained seated, tears still winding a path down my cheeks. I didn't have the hope or energy to get up and run this time. My life didn't mean what I thought it did. The fire that swallowed this world should have taken me too.

A yelp accompanied the clacking and I grew very interested in it. It sounded vaguely familiar. A dozen more came and I knew what it was. Something clicked in me. A piece of the puzzle that was me slipped from the fog and suddenly found its correct spot. It locked into place a picture formed. "Neo," I breathed.

A dog sprinted into the room, his paws sliding and doing very little actual turning as he tried to orient on me. He finally got a good grip, his nails no longer scratching the floor madly. He came for me like a bolt of lightning. Life surged through me and I rose to my knees.

"Neo!" I cried out. He collided with me and I wrapped him in a tight hug. I knew him. I'd known him for years. He was a piece of my life before I had come to this world. He rubbed his head against my neck and whined. He pulled away to assault me with a thousand licks and I ended up on my back. I blocked my head from the onslaught for a moment before embracing him again and pulling him down on top of me.

This was my dog.

I spent an hour with him, petting him, hugging him, sniffing his golden fur, scratching his floppy ears. We played and talked. Well, I talked while he barked and yipped. His tail never stopped wagging.

I recalled the day he came home. It opened my mind to so much: him sprinting across white carpet covering the first floor of my home and the stairs that led up to my room, parties with dozens of people playing with him, many of them kids. I found happiness in those memories, even if they didn't create a full picture. They still inspired me and pulled me from the depths of depression.

I'd lived. I'd loved.

"Boy, I wish you could talk, Neo. I'm more confused than ever. None of this makes any sense. You could tell me about the other things I can't remember."

Faces had flashed before my mind's eye, here and gone in an instant. He could tell me their names, and their importance to me, if only he could do more than pant, drool, and lick. "Come on. Why don't you show me around this place? God is here, right? Maybe you've met him even."

I stood up and Neo got on his back two paws, putting his front two on my stomach. I rubbed his head and we held each other's gaze. "I know, buddy. I missed you too, although I didn't remember until I saw you. You've been here waiting for me haven't you? Just had to see me again. I'm glad you're here." I leaned over and kissed his nose and got a tongue across the face for it. Dog love, such a wet, scratchy thing.

Neo popped down and led the way. I followed him to the threshold from this room. It was large enough to fit ten of me hip to hip and another ten stacked atop one another. The hall I stared down was long, shafts of light at its end. I expected fire to be shooting in from the holes, but it didn't. Just bright sunbeams.

Neo stopped when he realized I'd slowed to a halt in my inspection. He half turned and padded the floor with his paws in anticipation. I smiled at him and then we continued on. Neo led me through the kingdom. I gawked at each inch of the ancient structure. There were sconces with burning torches in some rooms, spears of light in others.

201

It all started looking the same after a while. We passed a tall block of stone sitting in the middle of an empty room and I was sure that I'd seen it before. I ran my hand along it and said, "Neo, are we going around in circles?"

He came and sat next to me, his head nudging my other hand. I scratched behind his ears then said, "I'll take it from here."

Halls and rooms fell behind us as I tried walking the structure in lines that would keep me from missing anything. I felt like I lost my direction several times though. This place was so massive and empty. There was nothing here. What was the point of it?

Hours passed and I grew sick of the lowlight and same black stone. The stone made up everything. Stairs, rails, decorative moldings, blocks, plateaus. Sporadically, I'd find these winding stretches of stone that looked like low walls without a purpose.

"We better find something soon or I'm going to rethink this whole God thing. Do you think we should start yelling for him?" Neo cocked his head to the side and closed his panting mouth. "Yeah, that would probably piss him off. Alright. Come on."

Finally, a room like nothing before. It was different, mostly because of the opening above that let in a flood of light. It was less an opening and more a raised ceiling. Light greedily spilled through the long slits all around the roof above, raised about a foot or two. It was hard to judge that from here but that's what I guessed.

"We've landed somewhere good. I hope so at least."

Neo agreed with a yip then took off. He bounded up the stairs that rose from the floor right in the middle of the room. Now standing atop a plateau with sculptures of different, simple shapes, he turned and looked at me. "Come on," his eyes begged of me.

"Alright. You should have told me about this place earlier. This is... different. Something has to be here."

I followed Neo up the steps. In the corners of the room along the back wall there were vases of black stone with flowers and vines sculpted into them. It was the most decorative thing I had seen so far in this bleak place. I crested the stairs and came to stand next to Neo on the plateau. I absentmindedly rubbed his head as I looked around at the shapes. Pyramids, cubes, and even spheres were here and there, seemingly growing from the stone.

"Now what? There has to be something."

My words didn't have the magic this time. Nothing just appeared. I took some time to look at the sculptures, investigating them, looking for hidden buttons or levers. I then went to the vases and took a look in them. Nothing.

Thresholds into darkness leading from the room could have taken me deeper into the kingdom. Despite the new territory spreading out before me, I'd lost my drive. Neo was here. He seemed to want to stay here. That was fine by me. If I was going to waste away inside the kingdom, at least I'd do so with someone I loved.

***

There was a great light before me, one that encompassed everything, dispelling any darkness that might have been. I felt one with it.

It felt comfortable and familiar. I'd been here before. I was traversing the space toward it, floating calmly and nonchalantly like I was like a cloud slowly riding the winds above the land.

But I knew that I had some time before I reached it. Not much, but at least a little. A divine message reached into my head and caressed my mind, telling me that this portal was an exit into finality.

There was no fighting it this time, and I allowed it to pull me in without resisting. I touched it, and became one with it.

***

A bone chilling bark sparked me to life. My brain overflowed with a sense of danger, although it moved stiffly, lethargic from the nap I had taken. Neo stood on all fours, his tail smacking against me as I staggered to my feet.

As I tried to control my breathing and stifle the cold feeling of terror in my heart, Neo barked at the ceiling. I looked up and saw three creatures. The brightness coming from the long opening above hid most of their features. They were hairy, human-like, but all dark with the light behind them.

They moved down the wall, using the irregularities in its surface as handholds. I retreated as they descended. Neo stayed beneath them, barking up a storm. "Neo," I said, "get over here. Come on, boy." He didn't care to listen.

One of them leapt down and landed atop one of the spheres. "You!" It was one of the orangutans. "How the hell did you fit through the gap up there? And how'd you survive the fire?"

As I spoke, I looked up to see the others, the females, coming down slower. The younger one helped the older one down. Seeing them again, after expecting them to have perished, brought tears to my eyes. They failed to fall though, a smile plastered to my face that I felt from cheek to cheek and mind to soul.

The male orangutan was fixated on Neo. He reached down and held a finger out for the dog to sniff. And sniff he did. Then, he rubbed his head against the orangutan's hand and he reacted by bursting with this loud noise that resembled a laugh. The orangutan then leapt down and began playing with Neo, batting him around, hugging him, pinching his front paws, and laughing with that loud, obnoxious noise as Neo reacted by barking, licking, and stomping his paws.

"It's like you two know each other." They both even looked at me for a brief moment at that. Shit, they must have somehow. How could that be possible?

The other two came down then, with a lot less jumping though. They too embraced and played with Neo. I let them be, just watching them all interact. I felt very close to them, and I was so relieved that they had made it through the fire.

Soon, they all came around me. They just stared at me, sometimes running their hands along my chest and arms as if they were trying to figure me out. Their eyes, however, were less curious and more affectionate. It's profound all the things I picked up from just looking into their eyes. Songs with the deepest meanings and paintings with more life than reality wouldn't rival the emotion those orbs inspired in me. I would love them forever.

The male finally grabbed my hand in his. We locked eyes and I felt safe and comfortable.

"What do I do?" I asked him, hoping that he understood me somehow.

He splayed both arms out wide and looked from wall to wall. That must be ape-talk for something.

"Um, the walls... Something about walls."

He shook his head. I turned on my creative orangutan side and really focused as he poked me in the chest then pointed to the stone beneath me. Then, he did the open arms thing again before pointing at me again.

"Mine?"

He nodded vigorously.

"This is mine? Why would this be mine?"

But he didn't answer that. Instead, he pointed at me again and then pointed to the ground.

"Stay?"

He replied with a vigorous nod and an outburst that reminded me somewhat of his odd laughter from earlier, a wide smile communicating his understanding.

This place was mine then, and I was supposed to stay in it. It was my home, an empty shell full of air that tasted like it hadn't been disturbed in years. I didn't want this though. What good was staying in this place of nothingness? I felt like I would shrivel away here. I looked around, hoping to see what he was seeing, some kind of reason and a glimmer of hope.

He grabbed my hand again in a firm grip and I found his eyes were sad, watering even. "What?" I asked weakly. Something about his sadness made depression settle on me.

He pulled me in and hugged me tightly, his head leaning into my stomach. There was so much comfort there, in his strong arms. He could have carried me through any trial, up any mountain, over any ocean. I dropped to my knees and embraced him just as tightly. His smell was familiar and calming. I never wanted him to leave. Our moment drew to a close as he pulled away from me.

The others were right next to me now. The younger female gripped me suddenly. Her embrace was lacking though, and I felt her sadness through that. Something occurred to me then. I was saying goodbye, and they were too. I pulled her closer and she found strength in that. In our connection I found a want to make her feel better. I wanted to take away whatever sadness she felt.

We shared a final look then she turned away to find Neo at her leg. The older female's hand was on my cheek. She turned my head and I found the most caring eyes looking at me, spreading warmth in my soul just from her very presence. She gave me a light smile before she pulled me in to her. I leaned my head against her chest and wrapped my arms around her. She stroked my head and hummed a light tune. Tears fell from my eyes, and I didn't know why. What I did know, was that I never wanted any of them to leave. Or if they did leave, I wanted to go with them.

That wasn't in the cards. I could have stayed in her arms forever. The male gently pulled her away until she willingly let me go. We had said farewell. Now it was time to part.

The three orangutans, my guardians, smiled at me then stroked Neo once more. Then, they walked to the wall. The females began their climb, the younger one helping its mother. The male had stopped at one of the spheres. He placed a hand on it as if he were thinking. Then, his hand slid down it and a finger poked it in just the right spot. The smooth stone caved in beneath his finger and a large, orange-slice section of it suddenly fell free and crashed onto the floor.

Within, I saw a sliver of something golden.

The orangutan looked over his shoulder once more, catching me with his fatherly gaze. Then, he too leapt up onto the wall and began his climb. I watched them go. *Stop. Stop*, I said with my thoughts. They didn't, and I couldn't bring myself to utter the word out loud. They were smart. They had made a choice, or had helped me understand that this was the only choice.

They reached the top at the same time, the intense light turning them into simple black shapes without features. They stopped, and I knew they were looking at me, longing to stay, or for me to come with them, but then they disappeared.

Neo whined suddenly, bringing me back to the now. I would always remember them, in this life and any life after. I rubbed Neo's head and wiped the tears from my face. "It's okay, boy. It's okay." I was speaking to both him and myself.

Gold pulled my eyes down, reflecting the light that came from above. I walked to the sphere and knelt down to look at it. I felt the light from its reflection on my face, warming my skin. I reached out and lightly touched it to find it pleasantly warm.

The same trick must work again. This is what I was here for. This is what was mine. I knew it.

I began running my hand along the surface of the sphere. I couldn't even find the point that the orangutan had first pressed to unveil this sliver of gold. I searched the entire thing twice without success. Oddly, once I got back to the front again, I didn't feel frustration. I simply tried again.

This time, however, I ran my hand across it differently, coming down at different angles and swiping across, light pressure always on one finger. A seam suddenly came to be in the stone. The seam made an oval shape and I pressed on one side of the shape. It went in while the other side poked out. A click sounded and another large section rolled free to reveal more of the gold shape within. Whatever it was, it was made with a purpose, curves and angles of it crafted with a reason. It was more than just gold.

Neo beat his tail against my leg as he sniffed it. "I know. Me too, Neo."

Together, Neo and I continued our search.

***

I hadn't slept. All of the shapes were now splayed out in several pieces, massive flowers of stone that had started as a bud until I had opened them up to the light, helping them bloom and produce the fruits of my labor.

Days had passed I think. Countless hours surely. I had stopped feeling hungry or tired. Neo had slept most of the time, as dogs do.

Now though, he was awake, sitting at my side. A pile of gold, silver, and white was before me, but that isn't what I saw. I saw hope, a chance. Armor and weapons sat in a neat line. All of it gold and reflecting the light with brilliance.

I'd tested the sword's golden edge against my skin, it was a razor that drew blood from my finger with ease. None of this was mere gold; it was something more.

A suit of plated armor with gold and white curves of metal sat next to a skirt of the same material, large golden slabs resembling dragon's teeth overlying one another and sitting atop chainmail. The shoulders of the suit were domelike in shape, angled along their edges to give the appearance of flowing water almost, a mix of gold and white. Wings, like that of an angel, extended from the back of the armor suit, and I felt a divine presence exude from the miraculous artifacts. A

207

cape of pure white with golden trim laid on the dark stone in stark contrast, the backdrop declaring its beauty further.

The shield was larger than my torso, and the creature emblazoned on the front by angled steel and gold inspired strength in me. The profile of a roaring tiger stood out from the front of my shield, defying all threats from damaging me. I felt unimaginable power in its weight and image.

I spent an hour getting it all on, snapping buckles into place, hooking pieces together. It all felt like it was made for me. It was mine.

I stood in a full suit of armor that moved with my body fluidly. It was light, the gold thin. I pulled a helm on that snuggly wrapped my head, hiding my cheeks and nose. I thread my arm through the straps and grabbed the handle of my shield. I scooped up my sword and held it out, pointed at the wall.

A roar suddenly echoed through the corridors of the kingdom. That devilish sound bounced through each hall, coming at me from all sides, sounding as if it had come from a hundred demons. I knew it was just one being; the black knight.

His pounding footsteps followed next. He knew where to find me. I wanted him to.

Neo snarled and barked, ready for a fight. But this was mine, not his. I knelt down next to him, the clinking of my armor a beautiful sound. I put my sword down and rested a gauntlet-clad hand on his head. "Hey, this is my fight. You've got to get out of here for now. I don't know how you found me, but I've enjoyed every second with you. You helped bring me back. I'm supposed to do this. I don't know why, but it'll all end up alright. Go on and hide. Wait for me somewhere safe... You can't understand me. What am I doing?"

Neo would leap into the fight and he'd be killed so fast for it. That was it then, I needed to kill the knight before he could lay an evil finger on Neo. I'd cut that fucker in half as soon as he came around the corner. The knight may want me dead, badly too, but I wanted to live until I found God, and my will was much stronger than anything else. I persevered through hell so far, and would manage again somehow.

I gave Neo a moment, hoping that he would sprint off into some deep hole and hide in the kingdom. Contrary to my wishes, he kept his feral eyes trained on one of the thresholds, the one the knight would come through. He would stay. I hugged him close, felt his trembling body. He was scared. I was too.

But a blue light opened my eyes and I had to catch myself as I was suddenly hugging nothing but empty air. The light faded as quickly as it came, and Neo went with it. He was just gone.

The only thing keeping me company now was that damn knight and his pounding footsteps. I immediately wanted Neo back. I hoped the orangutans would drop from overhead and come to fight by my side.

I was alone. I couldn't do this by myself. I needed something, someone else to do it for. All of my vigor, my courage had been sucked away when Neo left, leaving me stuck in a stone cage alone with a demon bearing down on me.

I stood and faced the threshold, a good hundred feet from where I waited on top of the plateau. My grip on the sword and shield felt weak. My stomach grew queasy, my body cold.

I saw the light from his flaming blade before I saw him. The threshold from this room was the mouth to an enormous hallway. Fire bounced at its end as the knight came for me. He was closing fast.

He was halfway down the hall when I found my strength again.

The flames dancing from his blade reflected light off his body and head. I saw his face of black metal, his crimson cape billowing behind him, and was ready.

Ardetii, Aaliyah, the giants, Kanute, the phantoms, the basilisks, and finally the forest itself, every goddamn piece of grass. I saw all of them in the knight. I knew I wasn't alone. For if those things trailed the knight, my trail was longer.

Behind me stood Neo, the orangutans, Bernsinger, Jacquelyn, the Ochari I had saved, the tiger cub, and Morrissett. My guides were grounded in good-heartedness. Evil would not win.

I stood there, waiting for the knight. Hell, I even hoped that he would find a burst of speed and come to me sooner. As he neared, I saw that he was missing an arm. I could beat him. I'd chop him to pieces.

"You don't fucking know what I've been through. You don't know what you're fucking with," I whispered between my teeth. He entered the room and continued his sprint, never slowing even once. I roared with righteous fury, "I'll fucking kill you!"

He shrieked in response and bounded up the stairs. Then, he was upon me.

Fire came for my head, arcing down in a path to split me in two. I interposed my shield and dropped to one knee. The sword slammed off of my shield, pitching me forward. I rode the momentum and drove my blade into the knight's stomach. Metal screeched as it split. The knight slammed his knee into my chest before I could pull my blade free.

I took flight, spinning around to crash down on my stomach atop the orange slices that were once the sphere. My armor saved me from most damage, but the pressure from the strike still left me gasping for breath. I wasn't allowed the time to find it though. The knight was coming for me.

I bolted to my feet and turned to dash away. I jumped and heard the blade slice the air right behind my head. I came down at the bottom of the stairs and somersaulted. I turned and the knight was sailing for me. I pivoted to the side as his sword plunged down at me. The blade rent stone and sunk down into it. I slashed at him and cut a large swath of metal from his arm then danced away.

His arm worked awkwardly now and he barely managed to pull his blade from the stone. He sprinted for me again with his blade held high. I raised my shield to block and set my base on my heels. The strike from the blade never came. Instead, the knight collided with me, his head slamming into my chest. Before I folded, a horn pierced my armor and stabbed through my flesh. The impact drove me back but the knight stayed with me. I screamed until I hit the wall and white flashed before me.

The knight wrenched his head back and I felt the horn leave my body, tearing skin and raking against bone. Blood dripped from the tip of the spike of metal. I banished the daze afflicting me and went on the offensive. I swung for his head and he leaned away. I swung again and he dipped to the side. I stabbed at him over and over and he backed away. He swung at me and I used my immaculate shield to preserve my life. He kicked at me and I sidestepped to only take a glancing blow that spun me to the side.

"Come on!" I screamed as I faked high then cut low. My golden blade slashed the black metal of his leg and he fell to one knee.

I didn't even see the blade coming until fire was in my eyes. A great force slammed into my head, my helm ripped from its perch to clatter away into the shadows, and a sharp ring took up residence between my ears. I was rocked to the side, stumbling until I fell, my sword on the floor in front of the knight. I couldn't fight the daze this time. I tasted blood though, and that helped bring me back a little. I turned my head in time to see the knight hitching after me. Blood spilled into one of my eyes and I lost sight of him. I used one hand to wipe away the blood and when I could see again, he was over me, his blade held high.

There was no other choice besides to react on instinct. I raised my arm as the greatsword descended, only it was not the one bearing my shield. Black steel and fire bit through my armor and into my flesh, then into my bone. The blade sank halfway through my forearm and I felt my arm snap in two. I screamed, not because of the pain for I was numb from too much adrenaline, but from the fear. I was terrified. It seemed like it was my time to die now, but I knew wasn't ready.

I nearly passed out as the knight twisted his sword to the side to dislodge it then yanked it from my arm. My screams of pain and anger kept me awake, and alive. I desperately wanted to kill this thing. Now, my instincts decided to work in my favor. I kicked out and my heel collided with the knight's already damaged leg. The metal snapped beneath the gold of my foot and the knight pitched to the side, his leg from knee to foot a lifeless artifact on the floor.

I rolled away and barely escaped a sweeping sword that grinded across the floor. I pushed myself with both arms and the pain came then. White hot fire lanced through my forearm and scrambled my brain. I was up and it began to fade, enough so that I could operate. The armor I wore, or perhaps just the way my arm had broken, allowed me to put weight on my arm.

I ran to my blade then scooped it up. I turned to find the knight scrambling to his foot, struggling to push himself up using only one hand. I took my chance and darted in. I swung my blade down at his head. My arm shuddered with pain as the gold sheered into the black metal. I would have gone straight through the helm had my arm not been so weak. As it was, I simply cut through one horn before ricocheting off the helm.

The knight fell back down but swept his blade at my ankles. I jumped over the greatsword and, as I was coming down, used the edge of my shield to bash the knight at the back of his neck. A satisfying crunch sounded as metal crumbled and I did it again, driving the knight's head to the stone.

Fiery steel didn't come for me and I knew that I had won. I screamed a war cry of victory as I smashed his neck with my shield over and over again. Eventually, my shield struck the stone and I kept on, adjusting my aim to his back. I would have sat there for hours, pummeling the dead thing, only, I felt an immense wave of fatigue come over me as a sudden surge of pain exploded in my arm.

Throbbing pain cut through my thoughts, resonating in my head. I came to an abrupt halt, lying down on top of the knight, breathing with such intensity that I thought I might pass out. Somehow, I managed to stay awake.

Blood spilled from my arm, down my armor and dripped off my golden fingers. Streams of it wound around my eyes and down my cheeks. I wanted to inspect my head to find out what kind of damage was there. Was there a wide gash across my forehead, a hole in my temple, or something worse?

But I was stopped dead. Everything stopped. Time stopped. My organs stopped working. All of it because of the shock that came with the knight shifting beneath me. I surged to my feet and backpedaled. I watched the creature look up at me somehow and realized that he had reassembled his neck. Then, his leg writhed on the ground until it rolled its way to the rest of him. Metal met metal and wrapped around one another to form a solid bond. The large gap in his arm closed as the metal pulled itself together.

What was this thing? I had killed him, and nearly died in the process. And now he was back up and nearly restored completely. He began to stand and I knew I was out of time. I turned and ran. There was nothing else to do.

I could try to get out. But what good would that do? He would still come for me. In fact, he would catch me before that. He was faster, and didn't tire like I would. Besides, the orangutan had made it clear that I was supposed to stay and fight. Goddammit I wished he was here to protect me.

I ran hard, not knowing where I was going as I left the room through a side exit and wound through quickly turning halls. I came to a small room with an oddly curved curb snaking across the ground. It ran perpendicular toward the threshold to this room.

Maybe I wasn't supposed to win. Maybe I was supposed to die by the knight's sword. At the very least, I wasn't going to be rescued by anything. This was my fight alone.

Anger, the little bit of it left in me, was sapped immediately. I was instead filled with grim determination. I'd fight. I wouldn't run. If I was going to die either way, I'd rather do it looking death in the face than having my back to it. That would be my victory.

I'd come to the end of my journey, milked it for all it was worth. I may not have done a perfect job but I got what I could from it. There was nothing else to do but accept it and find comfort in my thoughts.

I wasn't scared any longer. I was ready. Hope peeled away, and something else replaced it. I'd before hoped to discover and overcome my ailment, recall my past, and survive. Now, I knew that wasn't an option. The hope left, but not to make room for despair. Instead, I was determined to make my final stand a meaningful one.

The sound of metal pounding on stone grew until I knew that I only had a few seconds. I waved the sword before me and my broken arm shifted, needles of intense pain exploding outward from within. I shook the shield from my arm, let it clatter to the floor then put the sword in my offhand. It would be awkward, but it was the best I could do.

I leapt up onto the tall curb, perhaps it was a bench of some kind. I waited.

Visions of all the shit I had seen since waking in the forest fled past my mind's eyes. But so did the good stuff. I relived it all in a moment, offered thanks to those that deserved it, and damned those that were worthy of punishment.

What would come after I died? I didn't really care. All that mattered was these last few moments in life. I'd relish what I could.

Orange light flickered to life in the hallway. The knight would turn the corner and be just a step from entering the room. He wouldn't see me until it was too late. My timing would be perfect.

And it was.

I took off at a sprint, three quick steps, then I leapt into the air and soared. I cocked back my arm, anticipating the strike. The knight turned the corner. I touched down.

My sword pierced black steel and sank to the hilt. I felt the knight stop suddenly and satisfaction bloomed in my heart. That was all I needed.

He was ready for me though. I pulled my sword and found that metal had a way of gripping together. I wasn't quick enough. The knight slammed the hilt of his blade into my chin, knocking me backward after losing my grip on my sword.

Teeth tumbled down my throat. Blood followed. My jaw was broken as well. It all registered in one terribly numb sensation. I knew my body was breaking in the same way one would watch their house slowly crumble under the onslaught of an earthquake. It hurt emotionally, felt like a piece of myself was being taken away. Only, all of me was about be stolen.

I was on my back, my vision swimming, seeing double. It cleared just in time as I sat up. I said that I would face my death, and I fucking meant it. I wanted to scream, but I was choking on teeth and blood, gagging. I looked the knight dead in the face and told myself that he wouldn't take all of me. I'd still have my soul. That was mine. It would always be mine.

Roiling flames and black steel came down. I put my chin up in defiance. Fire filled my vision. Steel sliced into my forehead.

Chapter 19

Soft light fell on everything, coming through the canopy created by the tall palms all around. Bushes, flowers and long grass sprouted from the earth, covering it all in green and other vibrant shades of colors. I felt grass brush across my shins, scratching against my pants. The light from the day was not overpowering like I was used to. It was comforting and the atmosphere cool.

I hadn't even thought of running from the vegetation or looking for fire. Only now did I realize that nothing came to kill me. Animals scurried here and there. I saw monkeys, deer, tigers, hawks, and more, all existing together in peace. A small stream trickled down into a pond off to my right. I barely made out the small fall between the greenery.

"It's nice, isn't it?" came a soft voice from right in front of me.

Awe struck through me. There was no way not to know who was standing before me. Just laying eyes on this man was enough to let any person know who he was. I locked eyes with God, the Creator.

"This place. It is nice, is it not? Much better than the forest you're used to."

His light smile calmed me, spreading warmth through me, allowing me to breathe finally. My mind reeled with the knowledge that I was in the presence of God. I was having a conversation with God. Well, one sided so far. The awe that had locked up my body had suddenly left.

I sighed, a loud noise to convey my disbelief. Then, I found my voice. "It is. You. You're... God."

He smiled again and nodded his head once.

"I've been looking for you. It's really you? God? You're really him. Of course it is. I feel it."

"Most people do."

A light wind blew through the trees, shaking the large palm leaves, pushing several yellow, soft flowers toward me until they caressed my hand. I looked down and let my fingers dance with them slowly. I found that my arm was no longer broken. In fact, I didn't feel a single ounce of pain. I just felt liberated, as if I had spent a lifetime in a dark hole to finally emerge into paradise.

Tears swam to my eyes as I thought of my journey.

God's voice pulled my gaze back to him, "This story you told, your journey, it's been such an interesting tale. You've been telling it since you woke up. And even before then." He paused for a moment. I was speechless. "You've been through so much. I'm proud of the man you became."

For the first time that I could remember, pride swelled in me. I had done well. If I couldn't take God's word for it as He stood before me, then I'd be inhuman.

"Thank you, God." Addressing someone as God in a serious tone was unusual. The word left an odd taste in my mouth, asking me to keep speaking.

But God said, "You have questions. Ask them, my son."

There were so many. Far too many to start. How did I settle on one? Couldn't God just delve into my mind and start by giving me the answers? But he waited patiently. "How did I get here?"

"You died. That is the only way one can get to this place."

The fire. The black steel.

"So this is heaven?"

"Not quite. It is a place before that. You are a rare case."

"What does that mean? Was anything I remember real?"

"You remember it all, don't you? You bled, and cried, and loved, and felt, didn't you? It is real to you. That is what matters. You'll carry those memories with you always."

"What about everything before? What happened to me?"

God seemed sad all of sudden. How could that be? This was a glorious thing. Heaven waited for me. A bark stopped him before he could make a sound, his mouth open slightly.

I knew that voice instantly. "Neo!" I called. And there he was. He bounded over a group of flowers on long stalks, moving them out of his way. He sprinted to me and we reunited like we had done in the kingdom the first time.

I wanted my answers though. It was my time for that. I looked back up and God knew what I wanted.

"You didn't die in the kingdom. Not really. Everything you experienced is a part of you, your soul. It was your soul's journey here. You died somewhere else. On Earth.

"When you died on Earth, your body was ready to go. It couldn't hang on any longer. But your soul wasn't. This has happened before, but only on a few occasions. When you died, your soul didn't depart to heaven like it was supposed to. It went somewhere else to live. It needed to understand that it was time to go."

"So the place I was, with Jacquelyn, the cub, Morrissett, none of it was real?"

"It isn't physical. It was something you created. Your soul is special. It was the most creative soul journey I've ever witnessed. It created a place that it found familiar in some way. Your will affected it in more ways than I've ever seen, keeping you there even when your soul was ready to go. The dreams you had were that of your soul's readiness to go. But your will stopped it. Your soul created a place that would push you through a journey similar to the one you were forced to undergo on Earth. Everything you did, and encountered was a metaphor for the thing that took you and the experiences you met with along the way."

"Then what happened before? On Earth."

"Once I tell you, you'll remember it all. Another one of those pieces will find its way into the puzzle, only it'll be the entire thing all at once. Just know that I love you."

My heart had begun to take up a quick rhythm, pounding a light drum in my head. This was the whole reason I had fought so hard. God said it was real, but I could have skipped it all. Why had I been one of the people whose soul went elsewhere when they died?

"You died of cancer, Ricky. You were only twenty-three."

The chemo. My parents. My sister. My uncles, aunts, cousins, god-family, friends, everyone. Neo and Apollo. I remembered it all. I saw them all through my eyes. Through Ricky's eyes...

Weakness. I fell. He caught me. Why? He should have let me fall. I didn't want Him to touch me. I wanted it all back. "Send me back," I said breathlessly, a wheeze of hopelessness.

"I can't, Ricky. My son. I can't."

He let me down to my knees. Not even Neo bothered me. He sensed it.

My journey through the other world flashed before my eyes, a parallel to what I'd experienced in life for the two years I fought against my cancer. I understood the things that had been trying to murder me the entire time as being my sickness, the complications, my fading hope and faith. Stardust and the path itself had been my medicine, the things that kept me partially safeguarded from the clutches of death as I struggled on. Those who I had come to love had been at my side, had helped keep the sickness at bay and made me feel valuable, even in my dysfunctional state. They'd set my heart in flight again when the abyss of hopelessness was moments from devouring it. I'd fought my way from the clutches of death as I'd done before, each time knowing in my soul that I wasn't ready. Until finally, when I realized I couldn't fight any longer, I accepted my mortality and faced it bravely.

These two stories, sitting side by side, brought understanding. I still struggled to accept my fate though. This could have happened to anyone else; why had it happened to me?

Tears were streaming from my face when I said, "You could have done something. You could have saved me. I believed in you."

"And that is why you're here."

I shook God's hands off of me and stared with hatred at Him. "Why didn't you? Why!?" I screamed, my face twitching in fury.

Then, I saw something that I didn't think was possible. God's perfect eyes turned red and wet. Tears carved a path down his cheeks. "I cannot. Intervening directly is not something I can do. If I could have reached down and washed the cancer from your body I would have, Ricky." He shook his head slowly, his eyes twinkling on the brink of spilling more tears.

My anger left. "How can you be crying? You're God."

"I still feel. Just as you do. Ricky, I'm so sorry. I've always loved you."

"I believe you." And I truly did. I may just be a soul, but I still felt human.

"You still feel that because you are. And this is the last few moments you will be. Take from it what you will. Use it how you want."

I thought about what I had always wanted to do while I was stuck in those hospital beds, barely conscious at times. There were so many things. I accepted it all, because I knew it to be real and that there was nothing to be gained from denying it.

"Could I just ask questions?"

God smiled. His eyes had become perfect again, although tears were still on his face. "You'll know everything you want to know when you enter heaven. You'll be with Neo and Apollo too." I briefly recalled Apollo, my furry companion who had come before Neo. "You will be bound to the same rules as me though. You will not be able to affect the world in a physical way."

"Can I now?"

He nodded. "Something small."

I thought of the people who had been close to me in life. I loved so many of them with all of my heart. If only there was a way for them to know that.

"That is perfect. Think of them, then cup your hands before your mouth and gently exhale."

I thought of them, and something amazing happened. I saw them after I had passed. I saw their love for me tearing them apart in the days and months after my death. I heard the prayers of safe passage and longing sent up to God for me. I felt the love my family and friends had for me flourishing, even now. I knew that they had taken inspiration from me to do things they had never done before.

For a brief moment, I thought about why my death was needed to spur some of them into action. I realized that none of them would have been inspired had I not lived a life that influenced them from the beginning. They were all good people, keeping me in their hearts and minds.

My birthday had passed shortly after my death. I tasted the beer my friends and family had set out for me to celebrate. I felt the essence of my prize, my height of life; my career as an actor and where it had taken me in life. My family had spent my birthday there, walking with me along the busy streets of New York.

I smiled, through the maelstrom of emotion swirling in me, I found happiness and clung to it.

Softly, I blew into my hands.

Fluttering wings beat at my fingers, asking to be free. I opened my hands and found a hundred butterflies flitting through the sky before my face. I looked up at them and saw the face of each person they were meant for. It was all so beautiful. It was perfect.

A shaft of dreamy sunlight coming from between the palms lit the butterflies. They began to depart. I wanted to watch them go.

As they flew up to leave the canopy, I followed them on foot. I pushed past the thick foliage and came out beneath a tree that didn't belong. I was standing on a concrete sidewalk, my forest was gone. Trees lined the path to my right, a street bothered by only a rare car was to my left. A man walked before me and I knew him. He was my god brother.

Then, I saw his butterfly. It arced through the air gracefully until it passed his shoulder and his gaze followed it. As it circled around his head, he didn't keep his eyes on it. He stopped beneath the tree too, an arm's length ahead of me.

His eyes locked onto mine as if he saw me, but I knew that he didn't. I knew that he couldn't. His butterfly danced through the air above his head, calming his hurt spirit. He smiled at me, and I smiled back. He knew I was with him, and always would be. Then, he turned back forward and continued on his path.

I love you, brother. I love everyone. You keep reaching for your stars, just like I did.

It was time to leave. I turned around and God was next to me. Neo was on my other side.

"You know, Neo waited for you to come home. Now that you're here, he can go with you."

"Thank you."

"No. Thank you, Ricky. You had every right to give up on your faith. But you didn't. You are a true child of mine. You are everything I want in a son."

I felt God's fingers leave my shoulder and I continued forward. The forest grew bright until I was immersed in golden light. I kept on into it, embracing it.

I felt warmth fill me.

I was at peace.

I was love.

I became the brightness.

About the Author

Keith lives in Stockton, CA with his wonderful fiancé and two kids. He's a black belt in Krav Maga, teaching children and adults in the art, and utilizes his bachelor's degree in business administration preparing financials and taxes for all manner of business owners. When he isn't getting his head banged around or crunching numbers, he enjoys head banging to metal, most craft beers, gardening, drawing, and most of all, spending time with his loved ones, especially outdoors.

Ricky (left) and Keith (right) on the pier in San Francisco

Connect with Keith:

Facebook - https://www.facebook.com/keith.english.359

Author website - www.keithedwardenglishauthor.com

Instagram- https://www.instagram.com/kedwardenglish

Twitter - https://twitter.com/kedwardenglish

www.ingramcontent.com/pod-product-compliance
Lightning Source LLC
Chambersburg PA
CBHW030304180626
46810CB00003B/909